Cassie would never settle for him. Reid would never let her.

But it didn't hurt to wonder, did it? It didn't hurt to indulge in a fantasy or two. He'd been doing it all his life, wanting and never having. Wanting a mother like he'd seen on TV. Wanting a father of any sort. Wanting to be a normal kid in a normal family living a normal life.

But wanting what you couldn't have *could* hurt. Every time he looked at Cassie, it hurt way deep down inside. Knowing that he had no one to blame but himself made it worse. Maybe the odds *had* been against him. But people beat the odds all the time. He'd had a chance, and he'd blown it. He'd made so many bad decisions, and now he was paying for them.

He was afraid he would be paying for them for the rest of his life.

Dear Reader,

Merry Christmas, Happy Holidays of all sorts and welcome to another fabulous month's worth of books here at Intimate Moments. And here's a wonderful holiday gift for you: *Captive Star,* the newest book from bestselling, award-winning and just plain incredibly talented author Nora Roberts. The next of THE STARS OF MITHRA miniseries, this book has Nora's signature sizzle and spark, all wrapped up in a compellingly suspenseful plot about a couple on the run—handcuffed together!

We've got another miniseries "jewel" for you, too: *The Taming of Reid Donovan,* the latest in Marilyn Pappano's SOUTHERN KNIGHTS series. There's a twist in this one that I think will really catch you by surprise. Susan Sizemore debuts at Silhouette with *Stranger by Her Side,* a book as hot and steamy as its setting.

And then there are our Christmas books, three tantalizing tales of holiday romance. *One Christmas Knight,* by Kathleen Creighton, features one of the most memorable casts of characters I've ever met. Take one gentlemanly Southern trucker, one about-to-deliver single mom, the biggest snowstorm in a generation, put them together and what do you get? How about a book you won't be able to put down? Rebecca Daniels is back with *Yuletide Bride,* a secret child story line with a Christmas motif. And finally, welcome brand-new author Rina Naiman, whose *A Family for Christmas* is a warm and wonderful holiday debut.

Enjoy—and the very happiest of holidays to you and yours.

Leslie J. Wainger
Senior Editor and Editorial Coordinator

Please address questions and book requests to:
Silhouette Reader Service
U.S.: 3010 Walden Ave., P.O. Box 1325, Buffalo, NY 14269
Canadian: P.O. Box 609, Fort Erie, Ont. L2A 5X3

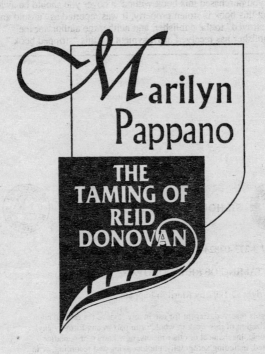

Marilyn Pappano

THE TAMING OF REID DONOVAN

Published by Silhouette Books

America's Publisher of Contemporary Romance

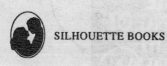

SILHOUETTE BOOKS

ISBN 0-373-07824-2

THE TAMING OF REID DONOVAN

This edition published by arrangement with Harlequin Books S.A.

® and TM are trademarks of Harlequin Books S.A., used under license. Trademarks indicated with ® are registered in the United States Patent and Trademark Office, the Canadian Trade Marks Office and in other countries.

Printed in U.S.A.

MARILYN PAPPANO

After following her career navy husband around the country for sixteen years, Marilyn Pappano now makes her home high on a hill overlooking her hometown. With acreage, an orchard and the best view in the state, she's not planning on pulling out the moving boxes ever again. When not writing, she makes apple butter from their own apples—when the thieves don't get to them first—putts around the pond in the boat and tends a yard that she thinks would look better as a wildflower field, if the darn things would just grow there.

You can write to Marilyn via snail mail at P.O. Box 643, Sapulpa, OK 74067-0643.

Chapter 1

Cassie Wade walked into the freshly painted classroom and gave a great sigh of relief. Everything was finished. The walls had been painted, the windows washed, the blackboards hung. Low tables in geometric shapes were scattered around the room, with child-size plastic chairs drawn up close. A sunny yellow bulletin board was hung near one corner, opposite a bright red one, and held a gaily decorated banner welcoming the kids to school. Whimsical animals spelled out the alphabet on the walls, and painted numbers danced across the tile floor. Against all odds, the work was done right on schedule.

The school's remodeling budget hadn't allowed for hiring professionals, not that any carpenter, painter or plumber she knew of would have been willing to come to Serenity Street for a job. It was all strictly amateur work, shared by Cassie, her boss, Karen, and husband, Jamey, his son, Reid, and the female staff and clients of Kathy's House, the neighborhood women's center. Cassie hadn't been convinced that they could pull it off in time for Monday's opening, but Karen had insisted they could. Once again, her boss's cockeyed optimism had paid off. The grant had come through, the two classrooms were ready, the teachers had been hired and the schoolbooks had arrived. In two more days at eight o'clock, the Serenity Street Alternative School would open right on schedule.

And Cassie was one of the lucky teachers.

The school had room for only fifty students, which was fine since not even half that number had registered. Besides, there weren't fifty school-age kids on Serenity or the two sister streets, Divinity and Trinity, that made up its neighborhood. Most of the families who could afford to move away—like her own—had done so long ago, taking their children to safer neighborhoods. The only ones left behind were those too poor, too defeated or too stubborn to leave their homes. The stubborn ones had been the first to sign up their kids. They understood the importance of education. Most of the poor ones had come with their children once they'd heard about the tuition plan. Hours of volunteer work translated into tuition waivers, work they were eager to do if it meant a better life for their kids. As for the defeated ones who'd given up under the weight of their burdens... Well, Karen believed that someday they would come around, and she was usually right.

Wandering over to the windows that lined one wall, Cassie looked out on what remained of the old crushed-shell drive. The school's small size was ideal for its location: a detached garage that had long ago housed horses and buggies, followed by more-modern means of transportation. It filled one corner of the yard behind the three-story Victorian that accommodated Kathy's House on the first floor and the O'Sheas on the second. Someday Karen had plans for the third floor...but someday would have to wait for time and money, something always in short supply at the center.

Cassie was willing to wait for someday, willing to work for it. After all, starting Monday, her career would be tied up with Serenity Street, and soon after, so would the rest of her life. Like Karen before her, she had decided that the neighborhood would be more than just a job. She was making a commitment to the school and the center, to the kids, their families and their neighborhood, by moving to Serenity Street.

She hadn't told anyone yet. To say her family would be dismayed was like saying that traditional Cajun cooking was a tad flavorful. After all, her parents had worked hard for years, raising thirteen kids on practically nothing, so that they could move away from Serenity. They had wanted to raise their children someplace safer, someplace not so defeating. They had wanted better for them than poverty, gangs and street crime. They wouldn't understand how any one of them could even consider visiting Serenity, much less working or living there. They would be bewildered and confused by her decision.

Her eldest sister, Jolie, would be most vocal. Jolie had spent seventeen hard years on Serenity, until a scholarship to the University of Mississippi had provided her with a way out. Her husband would be outspoken, too. Smith Kendricks knew little enough firsthand about Serenity, but what he knew came from his job. As an assistant U.S. Attorney for eastern Louisiana, many of the cases he'd prosecuted in the past few years somehow had ties to Serenity Street. As the recently appointed U.S. Attorney, he wasn't likely to support this decision.

Even Karen, who had faced the same opposition from her friends and family, was likely to protest. It had been one thing for her to leave her home four hours away, buy that great big dilapidated old house, sink everything she had in the world into it and make a new life for herself. She would still advise Cassie to stay right where she was, eighteen stories above the crime and the grime of the city, and commute each day, traveling with locked doors and rolled-up windows, coming after the sun rose and scurrying away like a frightened rabbit before it set again.

But that wasn't how Cassie wanted to live. She couldn't spend her days teaching the kids that they could succeed, that they didn't have to let the despair and depression of their neighborhood hold them back, and then return to her safe, luxurious home every night. She wanted to be a part of this community. She wanted to show them by example.

So she didn't intend to tell anyone until it was a done deal. Once she'd moved out of the high-rise condo Smith had made available to her rent-free upon graduation, once she'd gotten settled in her new place and made a home for herself, then she would come clean. Until then, she wouldn't exactly lie to anyone. She would merely avoid being truthful.

Circling the tables and pint-size chairs, she stopped in front of a cinder-block wall. It had been painted bright blue, with a remarkable rendition of the tiny park down the street in the center. Bright flowers bloomed along the iron fence, and happy kids played in the grass and on the swings. Along the outer border, in bright yellow paint, were the signatures of everyone who had worked on the school project. Cassie's own name was in the lower right corner. Karen and Jamey shared the lower left corner. There were Susannah and Elly, their nurses; Viola, the dietician; Dr. Pat, the psychologist; and Shawntae, Marina, Becca, Nicole, Irene, Mandy, Opal, Ruth and Berta.

The artist's name was missing.

She wasn't surprised. Once Reid had decided to cross over to the law-abiding side of the street, he'd done little to draw attention to himself. In the beginning, she supposed, it had been safer that way. Some of his former partners in crime hadn't wanted to let him go. Along with everyone else, they had been convinced that his attempt at walking the straight and narrow was just a temporary aberration, that sooner or later he would find honesty and respectability too impossible a goal and would return to his old pursuits with his old gang. It had been more than six months, though, and while Karen had faith in him, not many others did. Everyone was waiting for him to slip up, fall down and give in.

But not Cassie. She admired the changes he'd made. It couldn't be easy to turn your back on the only life-style you'd ever known, especially when the people who should be encouraging and supporting you were simply standing back and waiting for you to fail. She was surprised that he hadn't said to hell with them all and gone back to his old life. When he'd been running the streets with Ryan Morgan, people had feared him. People had respected him—for all the wrong reasons, admittedly, but wasn't that better than no respect at all? Wasn't that better than the wariness and suspicion he got now?

Obviously *he* didn't think so. He was still making the effort. He was working mornings at Scott's Garage just outside the neighborhood and evenings at O'Shea's Bar across the street. In the past month and a half, he'd spent every weekend over here, helping Jamey build partitions to divide the garage into the needed spaces, sanding and painting, repairing the roof, building cabinets, tiling floors. Everyone else had volunteered their time for various reasons—the staff because they were do-gooders, the residents because the quality of their children's lives was important to them. Reid's reasons for volunteering had had little to do with the school, she suspected, and everything to do with Jamey. He hardly knew his father, and their relationship, at best, was strained. There was so much bitterness and guilt between them that at times they could barely carry on a conversation.

None of which stopped either of them from wanting more. Reid wanted to be a good son, and Jamey wanted to be the father he'd never been, but neither of them knew how. So Reid tried to earn his father's respect, and Jamey tried to forget his son's past, and neither was succeeding very well.

Sometimes she found herself foolishly wishing that someday Reid would want *her* respect. She would give it, along with just about anything else he wanted to accept.

The acknowledgment made her laugh out loud. She sounded just like a schoolgirl with a crush. That would explain why, after a long week at her old job, along with hours of volunteer work at the center, she had always looked forward to the weekend work in here. It would explain why she, with her fear of heights, had volunteered to help repair the roof, why she had spent hours on aching knees helping Reid lay tile, why, after hearing that he liked blueberry muffins, she'd gotten up at four in the morning three Saturdays running to bake a double batch of them to bring to the work site with her.

A crush. It would be embarrassing if it were true, but, of course, it wasn't. She had outgrown crushes before she'd ever been old enough to have one. They were childish, and she had never indulged in things childish.

Sometimes she wished she had. Then maybe she wouldn't feel so grown-up now.

"I thought I would find you in here."

Cassie turned from the mural to face Karen. "Everything looks great."

"Are you excited?"

"Of course," she replied, well aware that her voice gave no hint of it. She had no problem expressing emotion. She was the youngest of thirteen children born to parents blessed with wild Irish passion. She simply expressed everything in the same even tones. Serene, people called her. She would rather be fiery like her sister Meg, passionate like Jolie or vibrant like Allison.

"Have you looked over the textbooks yet?"

"I have the first two weeks' lesson plans all ready. You've accomplished a lot, Karen. You should be proud of yourself."

The older woman smiled modestly. "I haven't done anything on my own. I've had tons of help along the way—from you and Jamey, the staff, the people who live here...."

"Reid," Cassie supplied when her list trailed off. At Karen's curious look, she gestured toward the mural. "I just noticed that he didn't sign the mural with the rest of us."

"Sure, he did. He just wasn't as obvious about it as we were." Karen moved around to the wall, studying the scene intently before finding what she was looking for. "There. R.D. Reid Donovan."

Cassie bent to look closely just above Karen's pointing finger. It was a tree inside the park, and carved into its trunk, visible only if you knew to look, were indeed his initials. They were unobtrusive, barely noticeable—exactly the way *he* tried to be. As if the best-looking six-foot-tall blue-eyed blonde this side of the Mississippi could ever go unnoticed.

"I see you brought a few things."

Turning, she saw that her boss's attention was on the boxes sitting on one of the tables. "Just a few odds and ends."

"Paid for with your own money?" Karen's tone was chiding, and it made Cassie laugh.

"Don't worry. This is the last time it'll happen. I'm going to work Monday for poverty-level wages. I'll need every penny I earn to keep myself going."

"Maybe someday the school will actually show a profit and you'll get a raise."

"Maybe." But showing a profit wasn't what the Serenity Street Alternative School was about, and they both knew it. Giving intensive one-on-one instruction to kids who badly needed it was their goal. Helping kids succeed when they started kindergarten with two strikes against them. Undoing the negative messages they were bombarded with from society, the media and their own neighbors. If the school ever began to show a profit, the money would be diverted from raises into hiring more teachers and providing more services, as it should be.

"I'm going to track down my husband before he goes to work. If you need anything, I'll be around the house or at O'Shea's."

"I'll find you." She had always managed before. Last August, when she'd barely known the woman, she had come looking down here and had found Karen, something to believe in and a prospective job. Now the job was reality, she believed in what they were doing more strongly than ever and Karen was still—always—there for her.

With a wave, her boss left, leaving the big door open so the warm March air, fragrant with honeysuckle, could drift in. Cassie breathed deeply, dispelling the lingering, faint odor of paint, then picked up the first box and carried it to the front. Rolling the creaky wooden chair away from the teacher's desk—from *her* desk, she thought with delight—she sat down on the floor, opened the deep bottom drawers on either side and began unpacking lesson plans, grade books, textbooks and other teacher's supplies.

When she'd gotten her teaching degree, she had known that jobs could be scarce, and she hadn't been convinced that it was even what she wanted to do. She had considered applying to graduate school and earning her master's degree. She had thought about studying abroad, preferably in Paris, since she spoke the language fluently and loved all things French. She had even contemplated joining the Peace Corps and traveling to some exotic corner of the world, helping others, broadening her horizons, learning new things.

But she had been tired of school and had already used up enough of her parents' and Jolie's money, in addition to her scholarships. As for living abroad—even in Paris—the inevitability of homesickness had stopped her. She had always been extraordinarily close to her family and couldn't imagine being more than a few miles away from them. With an entire ocean separating them, she would be too lonely to find pleasure in whatever she was doing.

That was how she'd wound up working in an office in the city's Central Business District. The pay had been sufficient, particularly since Jolie and Smith had offered her use of the riverside condo where he'd lived before their marriage. But the work hadn't been very fulfilling, and she had found herself all too soon dreading going to the office, daydreaming about other, better jobs. More satisfying jobs.

Now she had one of those better jobs. Granted, the pay was significantly less, and the hours promised to be significantly longer, but it was going to be a great job. She believed it in her heart.

And she *always* trusted her heart.

She was back.

From his vantage point at the living-room window above O'Shea's, Reid Donovan could see a fair portion of Serenity Street in either direction and the buildings across the street.

He had a good view of Kathy's House and the old garage set off to one side behind it and an especially good view of the woman standing outside the garage.

Cassie Wade had been coming down here since last August, when she'd shown up at Karen's first neighborhood cookout and volunteered her services. She was the only member of the Kathy's House staff who had ventured onto Serenity before the women's center opened, the only one besides Karen who had spent all her free time working on the house. She was one of only two staff members who were paid a salary—or would be as of Monday. And she was the only one of them all who got under his skin.

It wasn't just that she was a pretty woman. He'd known plenty of pretty women, some beautiful enough to make Cassie look plain, but none of them had ever bothered him the way she did. Maybe it was because she was different. All the women he'd known had come from Serenity or someplace just like it. Most of them were bold and brash. Some were trashy. All of them were hard around the edges. Coming from a neighborhood like this, they had to be. Weak people didn't survive on Serenity.

Cassie came from Serenity, too, but her family had been one of the lucky ones. They'd gotten out when she was just a kid. She probably remembered little about the place, and her few years in the neighborhood certainly hadn't left their mark on her. No one could ever look at her today and guess that she came from here. She was too self-assured. Too well ed-ucated. Too elegant. Too optimistic by a mile. Too foolish.

His scowl deepened. Last summer another do-gooder who was self-assured, well educated, overly optimistic and foolish had come to Serenity and knocked Jamey right off his feet. Reid didn't intend to let that happen to him. He wasn't going to be a case of like-father-like-son.

With an uneasy feeling tickling down his spine, he turned away from the window. There wasn't much chance of him following Jamey's lead in anything. They were father and son only through the mistake of birth. Jamey had been an absent father, and Reid had been a lousy son. After more than twenty-five years of anger and resentment, hostility and contempt, they were trying to build some sort of relationship, something they could both live with, but it wasn't coming easy. Sometimes he thought they were making progress. After all, hadn't Jamey given him this apartment and a part-time job in the bar downstairs? Didn't they have dinner together every Sunday? Weren't they able to keep a halfway civil tone to their conversations?

Other times he knew it was a lost cause. They'd been enemies too long. Some sins were too hard to forgive. Some things were never meant to be. Maybe Jamey and Reid as father and son was one of them.

Maybe an honest and trustworthy Reid was another.

Still scowling at the thought—at the possibility—he gazed around the living room for something to do, but there was nothing to occupy his mind. With a mother who had never quite grasped the concept of picking up after herself, he had learned at an early age that he would have to do whatever cleaning would be done. It was second nature to throw away the newspaper when he finished reading it, to make his bed as soon as he got out of it, to sweep the floor whenever it showed dirt. Sometimes he wished he were more of a slob. At least then he would have something to do. He wouldn't have an entire weekend stretching ahead of him with nothing to fill the hours. He wouldn't have time to brood over the sorry state of his life. He wouldn't have time to brood over Cassie Wade.

He usually spent his weekends away from here, doing nothing special in no place special. He wandered around the Quarter, watched the tourists and the street performers and listened to the music. He ate in some of the city's lesser-known restaurants, spent hours in darkened movie theaters and occasionally bought a few drinks in someone else's bar. His wanderings were aimless, his hours wasted. But what were the alternatives? Stay here with no television, no radio and nothing to read? Go downstairs and watch the TV mounted on the wall while Jamey tended bar? Hang out on the street and risk running into his old friends and former partners? See if there was any work to do at Kathy's House and risk running into Cassie?

A day alone and away from Serenity sounded better with each suggestion.

Even if he was damn tired of spending his life alone.

He went into the bedroom, pulled on a shirt, then laced on his sneakers. Yesterday had been payday at the garage, giving him another hundred dollars in his savings account and a hundred in his pocket. With no one to spend it on but himself, the hundred bucks would buy two weeks' worth of groceries and cover his out-of-pocket expenses until next payday. He didn't make much working the two part-time jobs, but with his lack of education and his reputation, he wasn't complaining. He was lucky to have either job. Most people around here would hear his name, lock up anything that wasn't nailed down and throw him out the door. Most people wouldn't trust him to do anything but rob them blind.

And he had no one to blame but himself. He had spent the better part of his life building a reputation as a punk, a thief and a thug, one of Ryan Morgan's boys—which meant he was also one of Jimmy Falcone's boys. Intelligent people were afraid of Jimmy Falcone. Honest people were scornful of him. Everyone was suspicious of him and the losers who worked for him. Reid had earned every bit of the fear, scorn, suspicion and distrust directed his way.

Sliding the money into his pocket, he left the apartment and locked the door behind him. There were two identical units on the second floor of the building, each with a living room and bedroom and sharing the bathroom in back and the kitchen downstairs. After their friendship had been shot to hell last summer and Reid had no longer been welcome at the apartment he'd shared with Ryan Morgan, Jamey had offered him this place. Reid had moved in soon after Jamey had moved out of the second apartment and into Karen's house across the street.

The building was old and wore an air of neglect. The fur-

nishings were shabby and sparse—a sofa, chair and a couple
of tables in the living room, a bed, night table and bureau in
the other room. Still, it was the nicest place he'd ever lived.
Tattered and worn though it was, it was comfortable, and it
was private. He had no roommates to contend with, no neighbors to disturb him. For the first time in his life, he had a place
that was his alone, off-limits to anyone he didn't invite in.

In the six months he'd lived there, he hadn't invited anyone
in. Turning his back on the Morgans had meant turning his
back on his only friends. As for girlfriends, the kind of women
he knew how to be with weren't the kind of women he wanted
to be with. They were the easy kind, the kind who didn't mind
getting intimate with someone like him, the kind who reminded him too strongly of the life he'd lived for so long,
who might tempt him to return to that life.

They weren't like Cassie.

Scowling again, he took the narrow stairs two at a time.
He'd spent enough time in the past six months obsessing over
Karen's pretty young friend. Now that the school was about
to open, now that Cassie would be here every day, five days
a week, it was time to get that obsession under control. They
lived in different worlds. She was everything he wasn't. She
wasn't like any woman he'd ever known, and it was damn
certain that he wasn't like any man she'd ever known. He
wasn't respectable. Educated. Trustworthy. Dependable. His
own father had probably already warned her away from him,
the way he'd warned Karen last summer to keep her distance,
the way he would soon warn off Reid himself. *Punk.* That had
long been Jamey's favorite way of describing him. *Punk*, with
special emphasis, with particular derision.

Punk. Reid hated the word. He hated that he'd earned such
a description, hated that he would probably never live it down,
no matter what he did, no matter how hard he tried.

The stairs ended in a short hall. Straight ahead was the bar.
On the left a swinging door led into the kitchen, easily twice
the size of his apartment and fully equipped for the restaurant
O'Shea's had once been. The equipment was ancient, older

than Jamey, though the six-burner stove, one oven and the industrial-size refrigerator were all in working order. Reid didn't use any part of it but the refrigerator and the microwave, the only addition in recent memory. Cooking had never been one of Meghan Donovan's strongsuits. He'd grown up on sandwiches, soup from a can and fast food, and that was how he still ate—quick, easy and for one.

Bypassing the kitchen, he went into the bar. Though it was twenty minutes till ten, the ceiling fans were already turned on, the doors were already open and Jamey was already moving the upturned chairs from the tabletops to their proper positions on the floor. He glanced Reid's way but didn't stop working. "Morning."

"Yeah." Though he wanted nothing more than to walk straight through the room and out the French doors without exchanging another word, Reid stopped near the bar. "You're in early."

"Karen's working on a new grant proposal. I decided to get out before she roped me into helping."

His stepmother had requested Reid's help on a number of projects in her quest to save Serenity. He had scraped the boards that sided the three-story house and painted them pale blue, planted grass and watered it, dug holes for new trees, rehung doors and gates and painted a graffiti-proof mural on the brick wall that enclosed Serenity's only park. Any job that required brute strength, patience for tedious tasks or attention to detail was deemed appropriate for him. Anything requiring brains Karen handled herself or delegated to Jamey.

He didn't blame her. Life with Meghan hadn't been compatible with regular schooling. Back in Atlanta, where she'd taken him when he was a baby, stability had been sorely missing from their lives. They had moved often, usually only a step or two ahead of the landlord demanding the unpaid rent and threatening eviction. By the time he'd come to Serenity, he had been enrolled in twenty-one schools, and he'd missed two days for every one he'd attended. He had come to hate always being the new kid in class and always being so far behind the others. On Serenity, he had written off school for good. He had given no thought at all to finishing high school, hadn't even considered the remote possibility of ever attending college. All his energies had gone toward survival and antagonizing his father.

And he had succeeded. After eleven years on Serenity, he was still alive—more than he could say for Ryan Morgan or any number of others—and Jamey had been antagonized to the point that there might be little salvageable between them.

"What are you going to do today?"

Reid shrugged. "Probably see a movie."

"By yourself?" Without waiting for an answer, Jamey offered a suggestion. "Why don't you ask Karen to go? Remind her that weekends are for relaxing."

"Maybe." Reid liked his stepmother. From the day she'd moved into that big old house across the street last August, he'd known there was something different about her—something special. She'd never seen a place like Serenity before, but she hadn't let it beat her down. She had come in full of hope, optimism and big plans, and not even the vandalism against her house or the beating she'd received from Ryan Morgan had dampened it. Her dream of a center to help the women of Serenity was now a reality. Kathy's House had opened its doors to steady business last October. Her biggest threat—Morgan—was dead, and the punks who had once done his bidding now followed Jimmy Falcone's orders and pretty much left Karen and the women's center alone. The people in the neighborhood had forgotten that she was an outsider and accepted her as one of their own. She was friendly, resourceful, not arrogant, never holier-than-thou and was convinced that there was good in everyone, even Reid. She loved her work, her neighbors, her home and Jamey, and everyone adored her, including Reid.

But he didn't want to ask her to spend the afternoon with him. She had better things to do, and frankly he wasn't up to sunshine, happiness and isn't-life-wonderful today.

Pushing away from the bar, he started for the front door,

taking a moment to set the chairs he passed on the floor. With a muttered goodbye, he stepped out onto the uneven sidewalk and, with his first glance across the street, locked gazes with the one person he had seriously hoped to not see again this morning.

Cassie was removing a sign from the open trunk of her car—or, at least, she had been. Now she was standing motionless, her long brown hair falling straight down her back to her waist, her fingers clasped tightly to the corners of the sign, and she was watching him. She did that sometimes, as if she didn't trust him enough to ignore him or as if he were some specimen requiring further study, some form of alien life deserving of curiosity, suspicion, wariness and distrust. He *was* alien to her. Guys like him didn't make it into nice, middle-class neighborhoods like hers, not unless they'd gone there to burglarize and terrorize. Guys like him usually never met women like her.

His mind was giving the command to turn and walk toward Decatur, toward the street that would take him away from Serenity and Cassie Wade, but his body wasn't yet obeying when she spoke. "Good morning." Her voice was sweet, pitched low, full of rounded tones that, by rights, should soothe. It was always even, always warm, had once been easy on the spirit.

He couldn't remember exactly when he'd stopped finding it soothing or easy. Maybe it had been last month, when she'd offered him hot coffee and a warm blueberry muffin on an unusually chilly Saturday morning. Maybe it had been the neighborhood Christmas party, when she'd arrived bearing gifts for the kids on Serenity and looking like a gift herself, all wrapped up in green velvet and satin ribbons. Hell, maybe it had been the first time he'd ever seen her, at Karen's first cookout last summer. His old gang had shown up to cause trouble, and Karen had accommodated them. In the few minutes they'd been there, Reid had spent most of his time restraining Ryan, holding him back from a physical confrontation, but he'd still managed to notice the stranger at the

party. Pretty, elegant, self-possessed women in a place where
shabbiness, poverty and squalor were the norm were difficult
to overlook.

With a sigh, he slowly stepped out into the street. "Hey."

Breaking eye contact with him, she began tugging the sign.
Unlike the thin metal rectangle that hung near the middle gate
and identified Kathy's House, this sign was large and heavy,
protected by Plexiglas and encased in a metal frame. Unlike
the Kathy's House sign, it wasn't meant to be easily replaced
after random vandalism but rather was intended to survive
such acts intact. He wondered if she realized that the kids
prone to painting, trashing, torching and destroying other people's property would take such solid construction not as a reason to leave it alone but as a challenge to be defeated. He
should know. He'd done enough damage on these blocks himself in times past, back when he was younger, wilder and much
stupider.

She didn't ask for help. He would be perfectly within his
rights to walk away and leave her to deal with her sign all
alone. She might think less of him for it, but what she thought
wasn't important. He didn't know her. He didn't want to know
her.

He just wanted to get *real* close to her. Intimately, inde-
cently close.

Still, he crossed the street to her car, parked where eighty
years ago the shell drive had made its exit back onto the street
after circling behind the house. Silently accepting his help, she
released the sign and moved to stand on the curb.

"Where does it go?" he asked as he lifted it from the trunk.

"Over there." She reached inside to pull out a handful of
tools and bolts, then gestured toward the single section of iron-
rail fence between the gate and the brick wall next door. He
positioned the sign from the sidewalk while she went inside
to the grass and secured it to the rails in a half dozen places
with heavy-duty bolts. When the last bolt had been tightened
in place, she came to stand beside him and look.

The sign was white with the name of the school painted in

building-block letters in bright primary colors. In the center was an old-fashioned little red schoolhouse surrounded by green grass and flowers, and around the edges blue and yellow numbers formed a border. There was a childlike look to the sign, perfectly appropriate to its purpose.

"My nieces and nephews did the original. I used their work as a pattern for this. How long do you think it'll last?" she asked, matter-of-factly acknowledging that nothing had much chance of staying new, bright and shiny for long down here.

"Until someone gets smart enough to realize that they might not be able to damage it but they can get rid of it entirely by removing the bolts." He thought of the kids responsible for most of the vandalism on Serenity these days—teenagers mostly, dropouts like him, with nothing to fill their hours but trouble and no one to care about the trouble—and added, "Maybe a while."

She smiled.

He hadn't meant the words to be amusing. There was a serious shortage of smart kids on Serenity. Smart kids either went on to someplace better or pickled their brains in booze, dulled them on drugs or got themselves killed. They didn't roam the streets or gather in the park at night with the punks. They didn't spray-paint graffiti, break windows, scatter garbage, trample newly planted flowers or vandalize signs.

"If they figure out how to take it off, I'll weld the next one in place." She brushed a carpet fiber from the thick plastic, then looked at him. "You don't work weekends."

Though it wasn't a question, he shook his head in answer anyway.

"What do you do? Hang out with friends?"

The question made him stiffen. It was one thing to be friendless by choice, another altogether to be alone because it was everyone else's choice. There was something shameful in no one wanting to know you, in having your every move scrutinized, in seeing suspicion, wariness and distrust in every face you looked into. It was even more shameful when you'd earned those responses. When you knew you were every bit as worthless as everyone believed. When you couldn't even say for sure yourself that you deserved trust. Wasn't that a hell of a situation? *He* didn't know himself whether he was trustworthy.

"No," he said, his voice as cold as hers had been friendly. "Not with friends."

"Then..." She looked away, then back, and smiled awkwardly. "Want to go to lunch with me?"

He gave her a long, hard look. "Hasn't O'Shea given you the standard stay-away-from-Reid-he's-a-punk speech yet?"

Her smile turned gentle. "I don't think he gives that speech anymore. I'm just asking you to lunch in a restaurant with other people. No one could find anything wrong in that."

She was wrong. Jamey could. No doubt the Wades could. Even Karen, the only person in the world who had any faith in Reid at all, would object to his spending time with her young assistant. Hell, even he knew it was a bad idea.

So why the hell was he about to agree?

The restaurant was a hole-in-the-wall downtown, a place open only for lunch and only six days a week. Cassie had eaten there at least three times a week until she'd quit her downtown job. Lunches from now on were likely to be brought from home and eaten at school with the kids, and she could hardly wait.

Folding her hands together in her lap, she watched as Reid studied the menu. Jamey had stopped giving the warning speeches, she had told him, but it wasn't true. One day she'd gotten too obvious in her scrutiny of Reid, and his father had informed her that Reid's reputation was well deserved. She hadn't asked for further information, and Jamey hadn't offered it. She'd heard enough gossip from neighbors to understand what he was talking about. Reid had grown up with no father at all and not much of a mother. He had run wild and had been in trouble with the police since he was a kid. His best friend had been a major felon by the time he was twenty and had died at the age of twenty-five.

So Reid had run with the wrong crowd. That didn't mean he was like them. He'd never killed anyone. He'd never hurt anyone, had never taken part in any crime against a person. Yes, he'd broken plenty of laws, but that was what kids with no parental guidance did in places like Serenity. Maybe he had been a punk, but there was plenty of blame to go around for it—to Reid himself, to Jamey and Meghan Donovan, to society in general.

And he was trying to change, even though it meant giving up his friends. Even though it meant still living with suspicion and contempt. Even though no one but Karen had any faith at all that he was making a serious effort. Didn't that count for something?

"The menu is limited, but the food is good," she said at last.

He closed the menu and laid it aside. "You come here often?"

Delia, the waitress, had greeted her by name and hadn't bothered handing her a menu. She ordered the same thing every time she came through the door: a chef's salad, minus the ham and turkey and with dressing on the side. "I used to. I used to work a block and a half that way." She waved toward the wall hung with photos of the downtown district as it looked seventy-five years ago, then smiled. "Starting Monday, my income's going to drop so drastically that I probably won't see the inside of a restaurant again unless I take a part-time job washing dishes in one."

"So why did you take Karen's job?"

"I want to teach."

"Teach in some exclusive private school."

"I want to teach on Serenity."

The look he gave her was flat and blank. "Why?"

"Because I can make a difference."

"Anyone who can teach can make a difference, whether it's in a public school, private or some dump like Serenity. Why waste your time in a school with no budget with a bunch of hopeless kids in the neighborhood from hell when you can get better results elsewhere with better conditions and better pay?''

"I like a challenge. Besides, I don't believe the kids on Serenity are hopeless. They've just never had much of a chance. With such small classes, we'll be able to give them the attention they need to catch up to and even surpass their grade level. When they've gone as far as they can and have to leave us to transfer to public school, at least they won't be behind the other students. They will have learned everything those kids have learned and more.''

He shook his head, his disagreement faintly derisive. "You're talking about kids with every disadvantage in the world against them. Teaching them to read and write isn't going to magically improve their lives. It's not going to change the fact that they're poor. It's not going to bring an end to the violence they live with. It's not going to change who they are or where they come from.''

"We don't want to change who they are or where they come from. There's no shame in being from Serenity. My parents lived more than half their lives there. My brothers and sisters grew up there. I lived there myself.''

"For how long? A couple of years?''

She answered evenly, unapologetically. "I was four when we moved away.''

"Four.'' He looked and sounded as if he didn't know whether to be scornful or amused. She decided to give him a nudge toward the latter.

"I was a very mature four-year-old,'' she announced in all seriousness.

One corner of his mouth almost lifted into the beginning of a smile, but it was such an unaccustomed expression for him that he couldn't quite manage it. In all the times they'd been together, at the neighborhood parties and working at the school, she had never seen him smile. Not when everyone else was laughing and talking and he was standing just far enough back to be apart. Not when he was putting his considerable

talent to work on his murals. Not when he was carrying on
the simplest of conversations with his father or stepmother.

"What do you remember from those four years on Serenity?"

"Nothing. I grew up hearing about it, though."

"Hearing about it isn't the same as living it."

"If you dislike it, why do you stay? Is it because Jamey's
there?"

His harsh, mocking look returned. "That would make
everyone happy, wouldn't it, if I packed up and left."

"Karen would be sorry to see you go. Jamey would be
sorry." And *she* would be sorry. She would regret that she
hadn't had enough time to get to know him. She would regret
what might have been. "Why do you stay?"

"Where would I go?"

"Someplace where they don't know you. Where they don't
expect the worst of you. Someplace where you could start over
again, where your reputation didn't precede you. Someplace
where you could be just Reid Donovan. Not Jamey O'Shea's
son. Not Ryan Morgan's friend. Not Jimmy Falcone's boy.
Just Reid."

He didn't answer. Maybe he didn't want to appear senti-
mental—or worse, foolish—by admitting that his father was
the reason he stayed in a place where acceptance was so hard
to come by. Or maybe he didn't want to acknowledge that the
idea of going someplace new, where he would have no ties,
where he would be a stranger to everyone, was too daunting
to contemplate. Maybe he found Serenity, for all its despair,
hopelessness and lack of welcome, an easier place to be. At
least it was familiar. At least there people knew him. Maybe
they didn't trust him, but they shared a history with him.

Instead, he watched silently as Delia served their food. His
hamburger, greasy and seasoned heavily with black pepper,
smelled good enough to make Cassie's mouth water, tempting
enough to remind her that she hadn't had a burger in years.
She wasn't a strict vegetarian. She indulged an occasional
craving for chicken, and it was practically impossible to be

New Orleans born and bred and not nurture a fondness for seafood. She tried to avoid red meat, though at the moment she couldn't help but think that one burger every year or so couldn't hurt.

Almost as if he'd read her mind—or maybe the hunger in her stare—Reid asked, "Why don't you eat meat?"

Swallowing, she turned her attention to her salad, drizzling dressing over it. "What makes you think I don't?"

"You've never had a hamburger at one of Karen's cookouts. You always bring salads and eat those."

He was right. Salads of all varieties were her specialty, fixed whenever she needed a dish for family meals, office parties or neighborhood cookouts. Everyone liked them, and she ensured that there was always something she could eat on the menu. She was surprised, however, that he'd noticed. No one else had. "I quit eating meat when I was fifteen."

"Why?"

"I wish I could say it was out of respect for the animals with whom we share the planet, that I was acknowledging their equality with us, that I no longer wished to take part in a carnivorous ritual based on our arrogant and inaccurate presumption of superiority." She shrugged. "Truth is, I was fifteen, and I did a lot of weird things then. I made a serious effort to be different from all the other kids my age. I dressed all in black. I listened to Celtic music, read the great Russian novels for pleasure and went only to foreign films. Life was one great drama. Eventually, to my family's tremendous relief, I grew up and started behaving more normally. I just never got back into the habit of eating meat."

A moment's silence descended over the table as they focused on their food. After a time, though, Reid spoke. Reluctance colored his voice, as if he didn't want to be making conversation. She wondered why he did. "I did a lot of stupid things when I was fifteen. I hitchhiked from here to Atlanta, then back again, without telling anyone I was going. I quit school, got arrested a half-dozen times, hooked up with the

Morgans, did my first job for Falcone and punched out Jamey."

Cassie's expression remained unchanged, although inside she was wide-eyed and openmouthed. She couldn't imagine any circumstance in the world where she would even talk back to her father, much less physically strike him. A child, no matter how old, no matter what the provocation, simply didn't do that to a parent. But Jamey O'Shea—now a devoted husband, good friend and protector of Serenity Street's vulnerable—hadn't been one-tenth the father Patrick Wade was. No doubt he had been as much to blame for the incident as Reid. "Why did you go to Atlanta?"

"I was looking for Meghan."

Meghan Donovan, Cassie knew from gossip, had been a Serenity Street girl. She and Jamey had married young and divorced a few months later, soon after Reid's birth. She had taken their son out of state—explaining in part, at least, Jamey's failure as a father—and then had brought him back to live with her mother. Other than a derisive comment from Karen that Meghan's mothering had been worse than Jamey's fathering, Cassie knew nothing else about Reid's life before he'd come to Serenity. "This was after she'd brought you here to live?"

His mouth curved into a thin, bitter smile. "She brought me here to meet my grandmother and my father. When she didn't come back in ten days the way she'd promised, I thought maybe she had forgotten, so I hitched a ride back home."

She needed a moment to consider that: a mother who could *forget* to reclaim her child after a visit to another state. With thirteen kids, it would have been perfectly understandable if Rosemary Wade had occasionally left one behind somewhere, but it had never happened, not even for an instant. She had always known where each of them was at any given time. She had always looked out for them, had always loved them. Even now, with all of them grown, their mother still worried over them, still kept tabs on them. Cassie simply couldn't imagine any mother as thoughtless and unconcerned as Reid was so casually describing. "Did you find her?"

He shook his head. "A neighbor told me all I needed to know. There was this man...." The bitter smile reappeared. "Meghan always did love men—any man who would support her for a while, buy her booze or feed her drug habit. I'm sure whatever he offered was too good to turn down just because her kid was expecting her to come back for him."

Cassie pushed away her salad so she could rest her arms on the edge of the table. "I'm sorry."

"It doesn't matter." He said it carelessly, as if the fact that his own mother had abandoned him with strangers in favor of an affair with yet another temporary man meant nothing to him. Surely it was just an act. Surely it must have hurt tremendously to be callously rejected by the one person required by the laws of nature to love him.

"So you came back to Serenity and stayed."

"I was fifteen. What else could I do?"

He'd come back, dropped out of school and started getting into trouble—classic signs of teenage rebellion. Too bad someone—his father, his grandmother or social services—hadn't intervened and given him the guidance needed to turn his life around. Too bad the only people interested in him had been the wrong ones. Of course, people like Ryan Morgan and Jimmy Falcone preyed on kids like Reid—the abandoned, the rejected, the disillusioned, the hurting. They became family to kids whose own families didn't want them. They gave them a place to belong and a group—a gang—to belong to.

One of Karen's goals, both with Kathy's House and the alternative school, was to give those kids a choice, to show them that they had options. They could get an education and improve the quality of their lives. They could have family and friends. They could belong somewhere without taking their lives into their hands, without turning their backs on society, without stooping to the level of the Ryan Morgans and the Jimmy Falcones.

It was too late to save the fifteen-year-old boy whose mother had abandoned him with strangers who wouldn't or couldn't fulfill their obligations to him. But it wasn't too late to help the man he'd become. It wasn't too late to be the friend he needed.

She wondered if there was even the slightest chance of ever being the woman he needed.

Forcing the question away, she smiled. "So you came back to Serenity. You ran wild for a while—" most of his life, she thought to herself "—then straightened up. You don't associate with your old friends. You work. You support yourself in a law-abiding manner. Have you ever considered doing volunteer work for Karen?"

The look he gave her was blank. He was probably thinking about all the hundreds of hours he'd spent painting, scraping, repairing, tearing down and building back up, all for no pay, for nothing more than Karen's gratitude and his father's grudging respect. What more, he probably wondered, could she expect him to do?

"I know you've done a lot of work at the house. I was thinking about with the kids. The young boys. Most of them don't have fathers living in the area. If they have older brothers, they're usually in trouble, in gangs or in jail. They could use a role model."

For a moment, he simply stared at her. Abruptly he got to his feet, pulled some money from his pocket and picked up the bill, then settled his gaze on her again. "We used to call Karen the crazy lady when she first came to Serenity." His voice was cold and derisive as he shook his head. "Darlin', she ain't got nothin' on you."

Chapter 2

A role model.

A day later, Cassie's suggestion still held the power to amuse Reid. It still held the power to rankle. Nobody in his right mind could ever consider him a role model for anything, other than budding juvenile delinquents. Hell, he'd never even managed to be very good at that. He had lacked Ryan's aggressive instincts, Vinnie's viciousness, Trevor's utter lack of conscience. He hadn't gotten a kick out of taking someone else's property, had always been uncomfortable with the idea of profiting from illegal activity. He had never enjoyed threatening, intimidating or the possibility of assaulting anyone.

He had only wanted to belong, and Serenity Street was the only place he'd ever managed that. The punks everyone was so scornful—and so afraid—of were the only people he'd ever fit in with.

And this idiot teacher thought he would make a good role model for young boys at risk. Hell, the kids with a parent or guardian who gave a damn had been warned away from him since they were babies. Half of them were afraid of him. None of them trusted him. As for the kids with no one who cared enough to protect them, they weren't interested in learning from his mistakes. Any lessons they might care to learn from him would involve hot-wiring a car, the quickest way to pop a stereo out of a dash, the best place to fence stolen electronics or which local drug dealer paid the highest salary to his juvenile lookouts.

A role model. Only if he was the ''don't'' in a pair of ''do's'' and ''don'ts.'' That was the only advice he could give anyone. *Don't do what I've done. Don't screw up your life.* And the biggest don't of all. *Don't be like me.*

As the digital display on the clock advanced to 11:59, he left the apartment. One of the first things Karen had done after her September marriage to Jamey was institute a regular Sunday dinner. It was the way families did things, she had insisted, and even though Reid had never been a part of any family, he had accepted her decree. He showed up every Sunday. Karen cooked, and they ate in the dining room or, on a hot day, outside in the shade of a tall live oak. His stepmother was responsible for most of the conversation because, all too often, he and his father had little to say to each other. Once dinner was over, he helped with the dishes, then left. It was an uncomfortable few hours, stilted and often sinking into hostility. It made a mockery of the Sunday dinners Karen was trying to recreate from her own family traditions, but she kept trying. She kept hoping.

Though it pained him to admit it, *he* kept hoping. Maybe this would be the week that things would go smoothly. Maybe this meal would be less strained. Maybe this time nothing would bring that look into Jamey's eyes.

Sometimes he thought his father wasn't even aware of the emotions that came into his gaze—the disappointment, the distrust, the disapproval. Sometimes he thought it was simply habit. They had shared so much anger and resentment for so long that disappointment in Reid came as naturally to Jamey as love for Karen. After all, for so many years, that was all his father had ever felt—that and scorn. Contempt. Shame.

And a little regret, honesty forced him to admit. In his first months on Serenity, Reid had received any number of apologies from his father. Jamey had been sorry for the divorce, sorry Meghan had taken Reid away, sorry he had never bothered to find out where they'd gone. He'd been sorry he had never been a father, sorry Reid's life with Meghan hadn't been easy and sorry she had abandoned him here. After the incident Reid had mentioned to Cassie, though, there hadn't been any more apologies.

He had been in trouble again—arrested again—and Jamey had been concerned enough to try to talk to him. The idea of this man who had ignored him for his entire life suddenly deciding to play father had made Reid's anger explode. He had landed only one blow, a solid jab that had connected with Jamey's jaw, and he had waited for some response, half hoping that his old man would hit him back. Fists were something he understood. Meghan had taught him that.

It had been a test, he knew with the clarity of hindsight. If Jamey had overlooked the punch and still tried in his awkward way to exert some influence, then Reid would have known that his father really did give a damn about him. If Jamey had hit him, that would have meant something, too. Physical blows had been the closest Meghan had ever come to expressing affection.

But Jamey had walked away. He had given Reid a look that made him feel like the lowest, most contemptible bastard on the face of the earth, and he had walked away. He had never intervened again, had never offered advice or warnings or anything kinder than utter indifference. He had never again, in all the years since, made the mistake of trying to act like a father.

That was when Reid had gone to work for Jimmy Falcone.

Downstairs the bar was quiet and shadowy. Sunday was the only day of the week the doors remained closed. It had been that way from the beginning, back when Kevin O'Shea had first opened the place in the early part of the century. Sunday had always been a day of rest, a day for spending in church and with family.

The closest thing Reid had to family was waiting for him across the street.

He let himself out, then locked up again before crossing the street and passing through the center gate into Karen's yard. Fixing the rusted, broken gate had been his first job, one that he had tried to accomplish before dawn one morning. It hadn't been early enough to avoid her, though. He had lingered to pet the scroungy mutt she'd adopted for her own, and she'd caught him. She had thanked him politely and asked him about the puppy. She had been the first person in longer than he could remember who hadn't subjected him to some variation of Jamey's distrusting looks. She had been open, warm and friendly, as if he were deserving of such treatment, and he had been well and truly caught. He had fallen half in love with her right then and there.

He climbed the steps to the veranda. Although the door was open and the latch on the screen door wasn't secured, he knocked a couple of times, then waited. Clients walked right in during the hours the women's center was open, but there was an unwritten code allowing some measure of privacy the rest of the time. Besides, it wasn't as if he was family in the real sense of the word.

His back was to the door, his gaze on the yard, when footsteps approached in the foyer. Before he could turn, a familiar, soft voice spoke. "Good afternoon."

His gaze skimmed Cassie's face before darting toward the street where she usually parked her car. It wasn't there. If it had been, even at the risk of disappointing Karen, he wouldn't have come.

"I parked around back. I had a few more things to unload." She pushed the screen door open, but he didn't move. After a moment, she politely asked, "Aren't you coming in?"

He didn't ask if Karen had invited her for dinner. Of course she had. Just as Kathy's House had an open-door policy, so did Karen. Anyone who walked past was asked in for a visit. Anyone who came to visit was invited to share a meal. So today he got to have dinner with both Jamey and Cassie.

He'd rather be home alone.

Finally he reached for the screen door, pulling it from her hand, waiting until she backed away a few feet before he stepped inside. He took care to close the door without banging it and to slide the hook into the eye bolted into the doorjamb—dawdling, he suspected, in the hope that she would return to the kitchen or wherever she'd come from. She didn't.

"Karen and Jamey are out back."

Of course. It was a pretty day, warm and not too humid, perfect for eating at the picnic table he and Karen had built last fall.

Cassie folded her arms across her chest. "Are you not speaking to anyone at all today, or is it just me?"

Just you, he wanted to reply. She had caught him off guard. He had come prepared to deal with Jamey, but dealing with both of them was more than he could handle. "You haven't said anything yet that requires an answer." He heard the stiffness in his voice and felt it spread to his neck and shoulders.

"It's customary when someone greets you to return the greeting."

"Yeah, well, it's too late now."

She studied him for a moment with a cool, penetrating gaze that saw too much. "I don't suppose you gave any thought to my suggestion yesterday."

Although he knew exactly what she was referring to, he preferred to pretend ignorance. "What? That I leave Serenity?"

"I never suggested that. I'd like you to come by and spend some time with the boys in my class."

"Yeah, right." He walked past her and headed for the kitchen and the door that led into the backyard. Bordered on all three sides by the brick walls of the neighboring houses, the yard had never been particularly large, and it was smaller than ever now that most of it had been turned into a parking lot for the Kathy's House staff. A small patch of grass remained, though, right at the foot of the steps leading from the house, shaded part of the day by the live oak nearby and just big enough for a charcoal grill, the picnic table and benches.

The grill was smoking now, the coals almost ready for the thick hamburger patties stacked on a plate on the table. The buns had been toasted and were wrapped in a cloth napkin inside a basket, next to a platter of onions, tomatoes and pickles. There was a bag of potato chips, a casserole of baked beans and— Cassie's contribution, no doubt—matching bowls of tabbouleh and salad.

"Hey, Reid." The greeting came from Karen, comfortably stretched out in the sole chair, a weathered, peeling Adirondack. Jethro, the puppy he had fed until she'd taken him in, was scooted as far under the chair as his bulk would allow, snoring with his eyes closed.

"Hey."

From his position next to the ice chest sitting on the end of one bench, Jamey asked, "You want Coke or tea?"

"Coke." What he really wanted was a stiff drink or two, something that might ease the tension in his muscles, but the only place to get a drink was across the street at O'Shea's. Neither Karen nor Jamey drank, and Reid doubted that he should, either. Jamey's old man had drunk himself into an early grave, and Meghan also had a drinking problem. She had never understood the word *moderation*, whether in reference to her men, her partying or her drinking. Every time she'd started drinking, she had gotten drunk. Usually the booze had made her morose, but sometimes it had made her mean. He still had a scar or two to prove it.

He accepted the soda and sat down at the opposite end of the bench. Cassie got her own soda, then glanced around as if deciding where to sit. Not across from him, he silently hoped. He didn't want to see her face every time he looked up. He didn't want to notice for the hundredth time how pretty she was, what a deep brown her eyes were, how appealing her smile was. He didn't want to watch her, so cool and composed, and wonder what it would take to shatter that composure. He didn't want to waste his time, because whatever it might take, *he* didn't have.

When she moved away from the bench across from him, he said a silent thanks. When she came around and sat down between him and the ice chest, he mouthed an equally silent but savage curse.

Her cologne, subtle and exotically different, perfumed the air around her. It clung to her skin, her clothing and her hair and made him wonder how it would smell on him, transferred in the most intimate way possible, from her skin to his, from her body to his. Would it still be sweet and clean, or would it turn sour, as so many things had in his life?

He wasn't ever going to find out. Karen wouldn't approve. Jamey *really* wouldn't approve. Cassie would never settle for him. He would never let her.

But it didn't hurt to wonder, did it? It didn't hurt to indulge in a fantasy or two. He'd been doing it all his life, wanting and never having. Wanting a mother like the ones he'd seen on TV—pretty, affectionate, motherly, sober. Wanting a father of any sort. Wanting a place that would be home not just today but next week, next month and next year. Wanting to settle long enough to make friends, long enough to finish just one year in the same school where he'd started. Wanting to be a normal kid in a normal family living a normal life.

But wondering *could* hurt. Wanting what you couldn't have could hurt. Every run-in he had with Jamey left him feeling raw. Every time his simplest gesture was met with hostility or suspicion, every time he saw how different his life was from those of other men his age, every time he looked at Cassie, it hurt way down deep inside. Knowing that he had no one to blame but himself made it even worse. Maybe he'd had a lousy home life and lousier parents. Maybe the odds had been against him. But people beat the odds all the time. He'd had a chance, back when he was fifteen, and he'd blown it. He'd made so many bad decisions, and now he was paying for them.

He was afraid he would pay for them for the rest of his life.

* * *

Once they'd finished eating, Cassie reached across for Reid's empty plate and fork and watched him shrink away from the possibility of even the most casual touch. With a sigh, she stacked his dishes with hers, then handed them to Karen.

She knew he liked women. Just last fall he'd ended a long-term relationship with a woman who lived down the street, and according to Shawntae Williams, one of the mothers who devoted much of her free time to the center, there had been plenty of others before her. Maybe it was just casual physical contact that he tried to avoid.

Or maybe it was physical contact with *her*. Cassie had seen him with his girlfriend a time or two last fall. A person would have been hard put to squeeze anything more than a breath of air between them, even though they'd been on the street, in full view of anyone around. Of course, it had been Tanya doing all the clinging, but he hadn't complained, pushed her away or done anything to suggest that he was uncomfortable with such a public display.

One night Cassie had gone home and compared her reflection in the bathroom mirror to Reid's girlfriend. Her long, straight brown hair with Tanya's dramatically short and spiky black 'do.' Her everyday-average voice with Tanya's bedroom-husky purr that promised heat, satisfaction and all sorts of wicked things. Her outfit of denim shorts, plain cotton top and sandals with Tanya's high-on-the-thigh black leather micromini, daring red halter that left most of her bare and four-inch heels that made her legs look a mile long. Miss Prim-proper-and-damn-it-all-serene against Miss I-can-make-your-wildest-dreams-come-true. No man with a single functioning hormone would even notice that she existed as long as Tanya was in the same universe.

Reid certainly hadn't.

"Karen tells me that ten of your thirteen students are boys," Jamey remarked. "Are you sure you're up for that?"

"No problem. I have a million nieces and nephews." Cassie smiled immodestly. "Little boys like me."

Karen polished off the last pickle on the platter before stacking the dishes on it. "I bet big boys do, too."

The only big boy Cassie was interested in was sitting right beside her, pretending he was someplace else. He'd been that way ever since she'd sat down. Feeling perverse, she decided to make him stop ignoring her. "I asked Reid over lunch yesterday if he would come by in the afternoons when he's not working and spend some time with my class. I think it would be good for the boys to have regular contact with a man who isn't on welfare, doesn't steal from others, doesn't use or sell drugs and works to support himself. Unfortunately he doesn't agree with me."

He still didn't look at her, but if his scowl was any indication, at least he was no longer ignoring her. "I didn't say I disagreed," he muttered.

"No, you didn't." She allowed a small smile. "You said I was crazier than Karen."

A flush warmed his face even as his stepmother laughed. "It's all right, Reid. You've called me that to my face before. It's okay to say behind my back." Then she sobered. "It is a good idea, Cassie."

"But?" She knew there was a *but*. She could hear it in her boss's voice. She could see it in the look Karen exchanged with Jamey. She could actually feel it in the air.

Now it was Karen's face that was flushed. "Maybe you should wait awhile. Give the kids a chance to settle in. Some of them haven't been to school for a long time. All of them will be behind. You'll have your hands full just trying to get them caught up."

"I realize that. But it was my understanding that the emphasis isn't supposed to be strictly academics, that we're supposed to deal with *all* the problems the kids face. That includes the pressure they're up against to join a gang, to take the easy way out."

"That's true, but..." Karen looked at Jamey again, then shrugged awkwardly.

"But what?"

When neither Karen nor Jamey spoke, Reid did. He got up, tossed his empty soda cans into the garbage can, then faced her. "I thought I made it clear yesterday that I'm not interested in being your classroom example of everything a kid shouldn't do. It's a stupid idea. I'm the last person in the world those people want their kids learning from. People don't trust me. They don't want me around. They sure as hell don't want me influencing their children."

Cassie turned on the bench to face him. "But don't you see? That's exactly why you *should* talk to them. You faced the same choices they do, and you made the wrong ones. You've lived the life they have to turn away from, and you got out of it alive. *You* telling them not to go that route would be a hundred times more effective than us saying it."

He drew a short, deep breath before flatly refusing. "No." Without another word, he turned and walked away, disappearing around the corner of the house.

When she started to stand up, Karen reached across the table to touch her hand. "Let him go, Cassie."

"People have been letting him go all his life." But, with a sigh, she sank back down. "Is he right? Would the parents refuse?"

"They wouldn't like it," Jamey admitted. "Didn't you notice the way the mothers who helped at the school treated him?"

With a faint smile, Karen answered for her. "Of course not." She wasn't around the mothers that much because she was always volunteering to work with Reid.

Cassie thought back to those weekends. Reid had always been distant. When the others had gathered first thing each morning for coffee, pastries and small talk, he had gone straight to work. When they had taken a break to eat lunch together on the side veranda, he had remained apart from them, eating some distance away or taking the meal back to the carriage house. No one had ever suggested that he should stay away, but no one had invited him to join them, either.

She had never witnessed any blatant hostility toward him, but she'd never seen any overt friendliness, except from Karen.

"J.T. hung around him, and Shawntae didn't seem to mind," Cassie said. Reid had let Shawntae's young son help on several of the easier tasks. They had talked and worked with comfortable familiarity, and the boy had bragged about the drawings Reid had done for him that hung on his bedroom walls.

"Last summer Shawntae had four rules for J.T. to follow." Karen ticked them off on her fingers. "Don't open the window. Don't go outside. Don't talk to strangers. And don't talk to Reid. I think she's given up on them now. She and J.T. spend a lot of time over here, and so does Reid. But I wouldn't say they're friends."

"But she's willing to give him the benefit of the doubt." That was all he needed: people willing to give him a chance. Willing to reserve judgment until he'd done something deserving of it. Willing maybe not to trust him but at least to not *distrust* him until he gave them reason.

"And she's the only one, Cassie, of all the people in the neighborhood," Jamey said. "She looks at him and sees J.T.'s friend and Karen's stepson. Everyone else looks at him and sees the punk who used to run around with Ryan Morgan, who used to work for Jimmy Falcone, who used to make their lives hell. He and his buddies have stolen from these people. They've harassed and intimidated them. They've terrorized the entire neighborhood. No, the neighborhood isn't going to turn around now and give him the benefit of the doubt. They're not going to offer him friendship. They're not going to trust him until he's proven he can be trusted."

And his own father was part of the neighborhood, Cassie acknowledged. Maybe he didn't want to be. Maybe he wished he could offer Reid the same sort of trust, faith and affection that Karen did, but he couldn't. He knew too much about Reid. He'd lived through too many long years with the old Reid to have faith after only six months that the new Reid was here to stay. Unfortunately, without his father's faith, the new Reid might get tired of trying. He might figure that if his father couldn't trust him, no one else ever would. He might say the hell with them all. Then everyone would lose.

Shaking off the melancholy that accompanied her thoughts, she offered to help Karen clean up. When her boss refused, she thanked her for the meal, then went to her car and, with Jamey's help, unloaded the boxes she'd brought. At her request, her sisters and sisters-in-law had donated their kids' toys that had fallen out of favor and books that had been outgrown, all well used but in good shape.

When she had placed the last book on the shelf, she locked up. She was turning away from the door when she saw Reid across the street, sitting on the porch of the house next to O'Shea's. He was so still that she wouldn't have noticed him if some sort of internal radar hadn't alerted her to his presence. His back was against the wall, and a sketch pad was braced on his knees. She hadn't seen any of his work besides the two murals. She doubted that if she strolled over and asked, he would feel kindly about showing her anything else.

But she headed that way anyway.

She entered the yard through the broad opening in the fence. Once a gate had hung there, wrought iron like the fence, with curlicues surrounding a fancy *D*. Now it lay off to one side on a pile of rubbish, the hinges twisted and broken, the black paint flaking off, the bare iron rusted.

Reid glanced up, then back down. His scowl deepened, and he concentrated harder on his sketch, but he didn't speak. She sat down on the top step, tucked her long skirt around her legs and rested her arms on her knees. "I owe you an apology."

"For what?"

"Trying to use Karen and Jamey to get what I wanted."

"You didn't expect them to take my side, did you?"

"No. But I still think you're wrong."

"We're all wrong and you're right?" He glanced at her again, shaking his head. "We know Serenity, and you don't."

"I know. I have a lot to learn." Twisting around, she studied the front of the house. Because she was curious, she told herself without believing it. Because it gave her a chance to study him, too. "Is this house empty?"

"Yeah, for as long as I've lived here."

"Who owns it?"

"Someone desperate enough to walk away from it." Then he relented. "Probably the city. People who abandon their houses tend to quit paying the property taxes."

"So if a person wanted to buy it—"

He laughed, for just a moment not scowling, not hostile or sullen but simply, purely amused. The moment passed, though, and scorn colored his words. "Any person who wanted to buy it should have her head examined."

Cassie gave him a long, level look. She wasn't suggesting that she might like to buy the place. She had just quit a decent-paying job to start one that would place her somewhere around the poverty level. There was no way she could afford a house, not even one that could be had for no more than back taxes. "I'm looking for a place to live."

"Well, this house isn't it." Then, as if her statement had been slow to register, he looked sharply at her. "Down here?"

She nodded.

"So it's not enough that you'll be spending your days down here. You want to spend the nights, too." His words were flat, his tone critical. "Have you told anyone?"

"Just you."

Finally he laid the pad down and dropped the colored pencils on top of it. She automatically glanced at the sketch. It was O'Shea's, maybe as it was ninety years ago, maybe as it had never been. The lines were clean, the colors soft. There wasn't a hint of shabbiness or decay, no crumbling brick, no torn window screens, no faded sign. Long, low boxes were bracketed underneath each upstairs window and were filled with blooms that spilled profusely over the edges. Their soft, creamy hue was the perfect complement to the faded red brick and the stark black shutters that flanked each of the four French doors.

"Even Karen will think that's a bad idea."

"Maybe she will. Frankly, though, I'm not asking for permission or approval. I'm simply stating my intent."

He looked as if her words amused him. They *had* sounded snooty, she admitted on reflection. "You're not telling anyone, because you know they'll try to talk you out of it, and you won't even be able to argue with them because they'll be right."

"I don't argue."

"Uh-huh."

She ignored his skepticism and gestured toward the pad. "That's nice. Is that how O'Shea's used to look?"

"It's the way Karen would like it to look. She's got this idea that she can fix up the entire neighborhood."

"Since she married an O'Shea, she *can* fix up the bar."

"So we'd have two pretty places on a street full of dumps." He closed the pad, then nodded toward the street. "Which of these dumps were you thinking about renting in?"

"I don't know. Any recommendations?"

"Yeah. Stay in your condo. Get your old job back. Forget this place exists."

"I'll make you a deal. The day you move away from Serenity, so will I." She extended her hand. He looked at it as if it were a foreign object, too risky to touch. She could do the awkwardly polite thing and withdraw her hand. Instead, she waited. After one long moment dragged into another, she injected a note of chiding into her voice. "Come on, Reid. You used to run with Ryan Morgan and Vinnie Marino. You worked for a man who would just as soon kill you as look at you. You grew up on the mean streets of Atlanta and moved here to the meanest street of them all. Surely you're not afraid to shake hands with me on a bet."

He gave a slow shake of his head. "I don't like your deal. I don't plan to leave Serenity."

She leaned closer to him. If the wall hadn't been at his back, he would have moved away. "Neither do I," she murmured, her voice cozily soft. "I guess you're stuck with me."

* * *

In the cavernous kitchen that filled more than two-thirds of the bar's ground floor, Reid was making a sandwich and zapping a bowl of canned soup in the microwave when he heard the front door open. For just an instant, he became still, then forced himself to return to his task. Occasionally Karen borrowed Jamey's key and came over to ask one favor or another, but usually any off-hours visits were from his old man himself. He always had an excuse—working on the books, checking inventory or some other legitimate business—but Reid half suspected Jamey of checking up on him. Though the suspicion rankled, it made good sense. It hadn't been easy for his father to turn his business over to someone else, especially someone he didn't trust. Maybe someday that would change—like in thirty or forty years—but, in the meantime, it was only natural that Jamey would want to keep tabs on him.

The microwave dinged as footsteps entered the hall from behind the bar. Reid removed the soup and set it on the stainless counter as Jamey came through the swinging door. "Hey, Reid. Is this a good time?"

"For what?"

"To talk."

With a shrug, Reid took a bite from the sandwich. Things did change. It wasn't so long ago that, if Jamey had wanted to lecture him, he would have done so at his convenience, and, by God, Reid would have stood quietly—and damned resentfully—and listened. Now he got asked if it was convenient before he got chewed out. Progress.

Jamey leaned against the next counter over and went straight to the point. "Cassie's a nice kid."

Four lousy words, and the flavor disappeared from Reid's supper, right along with his appetite. He had known from the minute she opened her mouth about having lunch together yesterday that this conversation would come, that Jamey would make time to point out to him that he should stay away from her, that he wasn't good enough for her, that she deserved better. Well, he didn't need the reminders. He knew. Damn it all, he *knew*.

"Cassie's sister Jolie and I go way back. She and Nicky were my best friends all through school."

Reid had his own vague connection to Jolie Wade, not that he was about to mention it. It wouldn't amuse anyone to know that Nick Carlucci had once offered him twenty bucks to break into Jolie's car late one night a few years ago. It certainly wouldn't amuse them to know that he'd done it for free.

Ignoring the soda beside him, he removed a beer from the cooler and took a long, bitter drink before facing his father again. "Don't waste your time or mine," he said stiffly. "Cassie's a nice kid. You and Karen worry about her, and you don't want her around me. Fine. I don't want her around, either, but she keeps coming around anyway. You need to have another talk with her. You need to make clear to her just what a worthless bastard I am, because I don't think the first time sunk in."

For a moment, Jamey simply stared at him. Then he muttered a curse, swung around and walked away. He didn't deny that he had warned Cassie to stay away or that he'd come here tonight to make the same warning to Reid. He *couldn't* deny that he was a hundred times more concerned with the well-being of a woman he'd met only six months ago than with the son he'd fathered more than twenty-six years ago.

The swinging door banged the outer wall as Jamey shoved it open, then banged the counter as it swung back in. He didn't walk through it, though. Swearing again, he came back. "Do you remember when I called you that?" he demanded, his temper barely in check.

"Yes." Reid had a lifetime full of little moments like that. The first time Meghan had rejected him in favor of a new boyfriend. The time she had explained to him in a drunken rage just how little she wanted a brat like him in her life. The first time Jamey had looked at him with such scorn. Every time Jamey had walked away from him.

Oh, yeah, he remembered the day his father had told him what a worthless bastard he was. He remembered that he'd had a few things to say, too, sorry attempts to inflict the same sort of pain, unforgivable insults. He remembered the shame, the hurt and the bleak certainty that Jamey was right, that he *was* worthless.

"It was the day of your grandmother's funeral—the funeral you couldn't bother with because you had to party with your friends." Jamey's voice was harsh with anger and accusation. "She was your *family*. She took you in when your mother ran out on you. She gave you food, clothes and a place to live. She took care of you for *two years*. She was family. You owed her."

The bitterness in Reid's smile went all the way through his soul. "She kicked me out less than six months after I came here. She said I was old enough to take care of myself. I slept in the park most nights. When Ryan's old man was gone, they let me sleep on the floor in their living room. Finally his mother died and his father took off for good, and they let me move in with them."

Once again Jamey simply stared. His mouth opened, then closed. He didn't want to believe Reid—that went without saying—but he did. Reid wasn't sure why. Maybe something he'd said rang true. Maybe it was just gut instinct. Whatever the reason, for the first time in his entire life, his father believed him.

When the silence in the room had almost reached the unbearable stage, Jamey broke it. His voice was low, heavy. "Why didn't you come to me?"

"You'd already made clear what you thought of me." Relenting, Reid shrugged. "I'd spent my whole life with people who didn't want me."

"I'm sorry."

"Yeah." Everyone was sorry. *He* was the sorriest of them all.

Jamey rubbed his eyes hard with both hands, then sighed. "I really am sorry, Reid. You would have been better off with any other parents in the world. Meghan and I were too stupid and selfish to ever have responsibility for a child."

"I know. You never wanted a kid. She told me often enough."

"That's not..." Apparently seeing the argument as futile, he shook his head and shut up. When he spoke again, it was on a different subject. "I came here to talk to you about Cassie."

Irritation streaked up Reid's spine, making his voice sharp. "I'm not going to get involved with her, okay?"

"I just wanted to remind you that she's not like Tanya or the others. She seems very mature, and she's very responsible, but she's also—"

Speaking very clearly, Reid finished for him. "Not my type."

Jamey gave him a wry look. "Be careful what you say. The last woman I thought wasn't my type? I ended up married to her."

Marriage wasn't something that figured into Reid's plans. Karen seemed to think it was only natural that someday he would meet a woman, fall in love, get married and have kids, but Karen came from a different world. Her parents had been married a respectable time before she and her twin sister, Kathy, were born, and they were still married nearly forty years later. Her own solid marriage to her first husband had ended only with his death, and all her friends were happily married.

Well, things weren't like that in his experience. Meghan's parents had been separated for as long as she could remember. Jamey's parents, by all accounts, had been miserable right up to their deaths. Few of his old friends had come from two-parent families. Some had been illegitimate and hadn't known who their fathers were. Ryan's parents had lived together without benefit of marriage for twenty years in a relationship marked by spectacular fights, infidelity, two kids as unwanted as Reid himself and no affection to speak of. Ryan's girlfriend Alicia had been raised by her grandmother. J.T.'s father had run out on Shawntae as soon as he'd heard the news of her pregnancy, and her own father had abandoned the family a year or two earlier.

Then, of course, there were his own parents. They had both been seventeen when they'd married, and Meghan had been nearly six months' pregnant. Reid wasn't sure why they had bothered to marry at all. It certainly hadn't been with the intention of making it last. If Jamey's plan had been to give his kid his name, it hadn't worked. By the time Meghan had left him, only days after Reid had been born, she'd hated Jamey so much that she'd wanted nothing from him, not even his name. The birth certificate might list his name as Reid O'Shea, but he'd been a Donovan for as long as he could remember.

No, marriage wasn't something he saw in his own future.

"Just be careful with Cassie, would you?" Jamey continued. "For all her intelligence and maturity, she's naive, a little vulnerable. Don't hurt her."

"I'm not getting involved with her," Reid repeated, but his voice was lower, less hostile, less sure. He was too preoccupied with what Jamey *wasn't* saying: *Stay away from her. You're no good for her. Leave her alone. She's not your type.* In fact, it almost sounded as if Jamey wouldn't object to a relationship between him and Cassie, as long as he didn't hurt her.

As long as *he* didn't hurt *her.* That was a joke. Cassie wasn't the one at risk. All he could offer was entertainment, a diversion, while she had the power to destroy him.

"I'll let you get back to your supper." Pushing away from the counter, Jamey started toward the door. He was almost there when Reid finally spoke.

"She's planning to move down here."

His father looked back at him.

"Cassie. She wants to follow in Karen's footsteps, move in here and become part of the community. She asked which building I would recommend for a rental."

"What did you tell her?"

"To stay in her condo. To have her head examined."

"She didn't agree with you, did she?"

Reid shook his head.

"Stubbornness runs in the Wade family. Jolie's as hard-headed as they come, and apparently Cassie takes after her." Jamey gave a rueful shake of his head. "We'd better come up with some suggestions before she moves into an apartment with Vinnie Marino on one side and Satan on the other. Think about it, will you?" With a nod of farewell, he left the kitchen, setting the door to swinging. A moment later it stopped. Another moment later came the click of the French door closing.

Reid poured the beer down the sink, picked up his soda, soup and sandwich and headed into the bar. He didn't bother with any lights but turned on the television mounted on the wall, sat down at a table against the far wall and ate his dinner to the accompaniment of a Sunday-night sitcom. He didn't laugh at any of the jokes, didn't notice any of the commercials, didn't even take note of the drop-dead-gorgeous actress in the leading role. His thoughts were a few miles distant in a riverside condo.

He had been to Cassie's place only once. On a hot August night last summer, Karen's friendship with Alicia Gutierrez had finally pushed Ryan Morgan over the edge. Karen had wound up receiving treatment at the emergency room, and Alicia had gone home with Cassie for a few days. Reid had gone to see her while Cassie was at work. He had never felt so out of his element in his entire life. The condo belonged to Cassie's rich brother-in-law, Alicia had informed him, but the knowledge hadn't made a difference. It was an impressive place, with a cool absence of color, highly polished and rough-textured surfaces, undoubtedly expensive furnishings and a quiet, calm, serene feeling. Whether she owned the place or not, whether she had that kind of money, whether she'd been born, like him and Alicia, in poverty on Serenity Street, Cassie belonged there.

There. Not here. Sure as hell not with him.

Not even if Jamey did seem to think it would be all right.

On the television, the comedy gave way to an issue-of-the-week movie. Leaving the table, Reid wandered over to the

French doors. Two buildings stood directly across the street—one an abandoned storefront with a floor of empty apartments above, and Kathy's House. Karen's house. It looked out of place, a lovingly-cared-for Victorian set down in the midst of disrepair, neglect and deterioration. In Karen's perfect world, all the buildings on Serenity would be brought back to their original state—the Victorians, the Creole cottages, the brick apartment buildings, the shotgun houses and every one of the abandoned businesses.

Of course, in Karen's perfect world, every woman who wanted to be a mother would be one, and every mother would love her children. Every marriage would be happy, not one family would be poor, and violence, despair and hopelessness would be things of the past. In Karen's world, parents wouldn't hurt children, men wouldn't hurt women and everyone would have value.

In Karen's mythical, magical world, even he would have value. Maybe even enough to deserve a woman like Cassie Wade.

Movement on the street distracted him from his thoughts, drawing his attention to the car moving slowly down the street. Six months ago, it had been an Impala, beat-up, impossible for Reid, whose mechanical abilities were the only talent he possessed, to keep in good condition. The Impala had been stolen from a neighborhood not much more prosperous than Serenity, and it was hard to say whether the owner had ever missed it. The Morgans had driven it, often through that same neighborhood, for more than two years before Trevor totaled it in a crash with a police car on the same day Ryan had died.

This car was a Ford, no doubt also stolen, a slight improvement over the last. Its dented and crumpled body was the color of flat gray primer, but it ran a little smoother. As always, Trevor was behind the wheel. Vinnie had taken Ryan's place in the front seat, and Elpidio Rodriguez was in Reid's place in the back. Tanya was still in the same place, though, pressed up close to Rodriguez, making out as if she didn't notice they weren't alone. She noticed, of course. She just didn't care.

Reid sighed and stepped farther into the shadows as the car crept past. Six months ago, it had never occurred to him that he might actually miss Tanya. He'd had little patience for her then, little use for her, he was ashamed to admit, outside of bed. Everything about her was loud and vulgar, which hadn't bothered him at all in the beginning. Toward the end, though, he'd wondered why she had to be so flashy and bold. Why had she craved everyone's attention? Why had she been so blatantly sexual? Why hadn't she shown just a hint of class like Alicia, Karen or Cas—

With a scowl, he forced his thoughts back to Tanya. The surprise was that he did miss her. She was easy to be with. She was generous in bed. So what if she had embarrassed him from time to time with her clinginess and her absolute lack of inhibitions? What did it matter if she didn't know the meaning of fidelity? Who cared if she wasn't too bright, if her only goal in life was to have a good time, if she was very much like Meghan had been twenty years ago? He missed her.

What he really missed was the sex. The intimacy. The companionship. The warm body in his bed. The affection. He missed the connection with another human being. He missed the feeling—however temporary, for fifteen minutes or all night long—that he mattered. When he was with Tanya, he'd been important to her. What she'd wanted couldn't be done without a man, and when he was the man, she'd needed, wanted and appreciated him.

He missed being wanted.

After shutting off the television, he carried his dishes to the kitchen, then went upstairs. The second floor was quiet. His apartment was the closest thing to a real home he'd ever had, but he felt like a guest. This was Jamey's apartment, Jamey's building. His father had never wanted him here before. Now that he did, Reid couldn't quite seem to fit in. He couldn't trust that he was welcome here now and that he would continue to be welcome next month, next year and the year after that.

Kind of like his life. The only place he'd ever fit in was

with the Morgans and Vinnie, but he didn't belong there now. He didn't belong anywhere. He had to find a new place for himself, a new life for himself, or give up trying.

But he couldn't quit trying. No matter what happened, he couldn't quit. And who knew? Maybe someday everything he did would add up to enough. Enough to make things right with his father. Enough to deserve everything his stepmother had already given him. Enough, maybe, to someday earn a place of his own. A place to belong.

And someone to belong to.

Chapter 3

By four o'clock Monday afternoon, Cassie was pooped. The last of the students had been escorted home, a responsibility she shared with Jaye Stephens, the other teacher. The classroom had been swept, the chairs put back in some order and tomorrow's lesson plans reviewed. It was time to go home, put her feet up and go over the work the kids had done in class today.

She would use these first few weeks to determine each student's level and to design a personal learning plan for each one. Some of them had never been to school before. The others had gone, but only sporadically. J.T. was the only one of her thirteen kids who had attended regularly and practically the only one who received support at home. Shawntae read to him daily, checked his homework and discussed the school day with him. Just as important, she didn't discount his dreams or rein in his imagination. She never hinted that he couldn't be a doctor, an astronaut or a superhero because he was black and poor or because the odds were against him.

Serenity could use a lot more mothers like Shawntae.

A rap at the door caught her attention. Jaye, her arms full of papers and books, was standing in the doorway. "You've got a message here to see Jamey over at O'Shea's when you're done," she said with a nod toward the yellow sticky note on the door. "I'm outta here. See you tomorrow."

"Be careful." As Jaye left, Cassie repeated the words softly. How many thousands of times had she given the admonition or been on the receiving end of it? So many that it had lost its meaning. It had become synonymous with farewells of lesser importance: *Goodbye, See you later, Take care.*

But not on Serenity. Down here when a person said *Be careful,* it was important. It could be the difference between living and dying.

Gathering her own armload of work, Cassie shut off the lights and securely locked the door behind her. She left the work in her car, then crossed the lawn, waving to Elly through her office window. The nurse made an exaggerated face, and a shriek from behind the woman reminded Cassie that today was immunization day. Once a month, the three rooms shared by Elly and Susannah Sinclair were home to screaming babies and teary toddlers unable to find any good at all in getting stuck with a needle. Cassie didn't envy them the job.

As soon as she stepped through the gate and onto the sidewalk, Cassie's thoughts narrowed in on the apartment above O'Shea's. The windows were open, the curtains fluttering in the light breeze. There was no sign of its occupant, though. Maybe he'd worked late at the garage. Maybe he was running errands. Maybe he was with a woman. Maybe, if she was very, very lucky, he was downstairs in the bar.

The interior of O'Shea's was dimly lit, requiring a moment's adjustment before she could see clearly. There was an elderly gentleman seated at one table, a glass of whiskey and the remains of a sandwich in front of him. Though Jamey had initially been against Karen's plans for the women's center, it was no surprise that he'd eventually come around. What she wanted to do for the entire neighborhood, he had long been doing for his customers— looking out for them, making life easier for them. If anyone ever used his own favorite description of the volunteers at the center on him—do-gooder—he would adamantly deny it, but he was.

Cassie greeted the old man, then slid onto a stool at the bar. Jamey was standing behind it, but Reid wasn't around. "Hi. I got your message."

He removed the toothpick from between his teeth and leaned forward, resting his arms on the bar. "How was your first day of school?"

"Tiring. I'd forgotten how wild thirteen little kids can get."

"I thought you'd be an old hand with kids, what with a million nieces and nephews who adore you."

"They do adore me. But I don't keep thirteen of them for seven and a half hours straight." She shrugged. "It was fine. Fun. I'm looking forward to tomorrow."

He reached into the cooler behind the bar to pull out a cold soda. She accepted it with thanks and was taking a deep drink when he spoke again. "I understand you're looking for an apartment down here."

She almost choked on the drink. Managing to swallow without spilling any, she set the can down and fixed her reproachful gaze on him. "Why am I surprised he told you?"

"When Karen told me that her friends didn't know she had moved to Serenity, the first thing I did was call Jolie and break the news. She and Smith were over here in less than three hours to try to change her mind."

"So tattling runs in the family."

His faint smile was regretful. Karen insisted on calling their little group a family, but to Cassie's knowledge, Jamey didn't. Reid didn't, either. She had little doubt, though, that they would *like* to be a family, if they could ever figure out how.

"Please don't try to talk me out of it. I'm a grown woman. I have a college degree, a job and everything. I've been spending most of my free time down here for the past six months, and now I'm going to be spending all of my work time down here. Living here is the right thing to do."

"I wasn't planning to try to change your mind. You're a

bright kid. You're also stubborn—I believe even more so than Karen, and you see what success I had in changing *her* mind.'' He straightened, glanced down the hall behind the bar, then back at her. ''Actually I wanted to make you an offer. You probably know that there are two apartments upstairs. Reid lives in one. I used to live in the other. It's nothing fancy, but it's as good as any place you're likely to find on Serenity and better than most, and the rent is within your budget. You can have it for free.''

She tried to contain her excitement. ''I can afford to pay.''

''Yeah, right. Don't forget—I know how much you make.'' Then he shook his head. ''I don't want your money, Cassie. I've got the place, it's empty and someone might as well make use of it. Besides, when you tell Jolie and your folks that you're moving down here, maybe it will help appease them if you're moving into my place. So...'' He grinned. ''Want to see it?''

''Sure.'' She slid to the floor as he called to the old man to watch the bar. He led the way down the hall and up a narrow flight of stairs that opened into a hall that ran front to back down the center of the building. Three doors opened off the hall, one on the right, one on the left and one at the back.

''That's the bathroom,'' Jamey said, gesturing toward the end of the hall. ''There's only one on the floor, so both apartments share. Are you comfortable with that?''

''I come from a family of fifteen. We had one bathroom on Serenity. When we moved to Oak Street to a house with two bathrooms, Daddy thought he was in heaven. He actually had an occasional chance at getting an uninterrupted moment to shave every morning.''

He turned to the door on the right, which meant that the door on the left led to Reid's apartment. Was he in there? Did he know his father had planned to make this offer? Would he mind having a neighbor?

The door wasn't locked. Jamey opened it, then stepped back for her to enter first. Nothing fancy, he'd said, and she agreed. Better than most down here, he'd added, and she agreed with that, too. The living room was a nice size and practically empty, with a sofa that sagged in the middle and a scarred coffee table. The only furniture in the bedroom, through a double-wide door, was a full-size bed.

"When I moved out, I moved the rest of the furniture into Reid's apartment," Jamey said. "You can use this or get rid of it. I don't care."

"What about a kitchen?"

"It's downstairs."

She walked into the bedroom and took a look around at its high ceiling, bare floor and closet in one corner, then slowly smiled. "Can I paint it?"

"Doesn't matter to me. Ask Karen before you buy anything. She's got gallons of paint, brushes, rollers, the works, out in the workshop. You want it?"

She turned in a slow circle, imagining different colors on the walls. Yellow, she decided. The rich, buttery yellow that Karen had used in the tower room that served as a nursery for the center's clients. A few rugs on the floor, bright white paint on the woodwork, the old wicker dresser her mother had been storing for her for years and soft white bedding... She gave him her biggest smile. "Yes. Absolutely. Thank you."

With a nod, he turned to leave. She followed as far as the bedroom door. "Jamey? Does Reid know?"

He shook his head.

"Will he mind?"

"I don't know why he would," he said with just a touch too much innocence. "You're not going to have wild parties or play loud music in the middle of the night and disturb his sleep, are you?"

She could think of better ways to disturb Reid's nights. She just wasn't sure she was capable. After all, compared to Tanya the sex goddess, she was pretty plain and tame. She'd never been wicked a day in her life. She was totally lacking in experience...but not in imagination. Not in curiosity. Certainly not in desire.

She cleared her throat to chase away the unaccustomed huskiness that had settled there. "Maybe you'd better talk to him first."

"It's my place, Cassie."

"Yes, but he lives here. He may be perfectly comfortable alone."

"He spends too much time alone."

She couldn't argue with that. Unfortunately she was pretty sure he would prefer solitude to her company. "I really don't want to disturb him."

Jamey grinned again. "Darlin', everyone needs to be disturbed from time to time. Look, if it makes you happy, I'll talk to Reid. Unless he objects—"

"To what?"

Jamey turned, and Cassie gazed past him to the door. Reid was standing there, a take-out bag from a French Quarter restaurant in one hand and a soda in the other. "Unless Reid objects to what?" he asked again.

His father looked at Cassie and shrugged. "I've got to get back downstairs. Why don't *you* talk to him?"

"Coward," she mumbled under her breath as he left. Forced to move from the doorway to let him pass, Reid came a few steps farther into the room. "Hey, Reid."

His gaze settled on her, shifted away for a look around the mostly empty place, then came back again. There was suspicion in his blue eyes and an all too familiar scowl tightening his mouth. "No." He drew the word out, part question, part distaste, part plea.

She said nothing and tried to look innocent.

"You're not moving in here."

"Your father offered me the place, as long as you don't mind."

"I mind. There are a hundred empty apartments on Serenity. Why this one? Hell, why not stay in your million-dollar condo?"

"We've already been over my reasons for wanting to move here. If you don't want me in this building, that's fine. Jamey was just trying to do me a favor. He knows I don't make much money, and he thought maybe my family wouldn't mind so much if they knew I was close to him and Karen. But it's okay. I'll look elsewhere.'' She started to walk past him, but he stopped her with a grudging question.

"Where?"

"I don't know. Maybe the house where my family used to live. The gray one on the other side of the street.''

"Vinnie Marino lives in that building.''

She knew that. Tanya lived there, too. Cassie had occasionally caught herself wondering which apartment Tanya lived in and whether Reid had ever spent much time there with her. Wouldn't it be a hoot if she lived in the old Wade apartment, if she slept in the bedroom Cassie had shared with too many sisters, if Tanya and Reid had shared their wicked fun in Cassie's very own room?

She hated the thought. She hated the jealousy. She particularly hated the other woman.

"I imagine at least one disreputable person lives in every building in the neighborhood,'' she said softly. "I can't pass up a place to live for that reason.''

"Some of those 'disreputable persons' would kill you if they had the chance.''

"So I won't give them the chance. I'll tell Jamey thanks but no thanks. I'll find some other place.'' This time she made it as far as the door before he stopped her again.

"Damn it, you can't make things easy, can you?''

For a moment, she kept her gaze on the hall. It was lit by a single overhead bulb and clearly considered the least important part of the living quarters. The walls hadn't been painted in so long that, in the dim light, it was impossible to tell exactly what color they had once been. The floor was wood planks painted dark brown to match the doors and the casing that bordered them. There were no rugs, nothing hanging on the walls, no furnishings at all. Given free rein, she would paint it some bright and airy color. The wood would be white from one end to the other and all the way down the stairs. Thick, nubby rugs would cover much of the floor, and she would add a small half-round table to one side and a bench with clean, uncluttered lines to the other. She would turn the walls into a miniature gallery to display Reid's work, and she would add lights overhead and on the walls, plus maybe a funky, one-of-a-kind floor lamp next to the bench.

Finally she turned back to face him. Other than the blond hair and blue eyes, there wasn't a particularly strong resemblance between him and his father. Jamey was handsome enough, but Reid was gorgeous. Of course, her perception could be skewed by the fact that Jamey was old enough to be her father and was head over heels in love with his wife. Jamey didn't make her nerves flutter, cause her restless nights or tantalize her with wicked desires.

"What would constitute making things easy? Going away? Disappearing from Serenity forever?" She smiled coolly. "That's not going to happen. If you mean finding someplace else to live, I just told you that I would."

"In Vinnie Marino's building? If you move in there—or anywhere else—and something happens, you know who'll get the blame—me."

And that worried him. It would be one more obstacle between him and his father. "Then you have to decide which you would prefer—having a guilty conscience for sending me away or having me for a neighbor." Again she smiled and this time allowed a little teasing into her voice. "I wouldn't be a bad neighbor. I don't watch much television. I don't listen to loud music. I don't have parties. I never get drunk or noisy. I don't take long showers, I wouldn't use up all the hot water and I don't waste time primping in front of the mirror. I keep to myself, I read a lot and I'm usually in bed by eleven. You wouldn't even know I'm here."

"Oh, I'd know."

She found the taut, muttered words interesting. She would know he was next door, too, even if he never made a sound, if she never saw him. She would *feel* him. That odd awareness that always alerted her to his presence would keep her informed. Did he feel it, too? And if he did, did it mean that he was the slightest bit interested in her?

Yeah, right. Interested in keeping her away.

She waited for some further response, some definitive yes-you-can-stay or no-I-don't-want-you-here. With one last, long, reluctant look around the place, he gave it with a grimace of a smile and a faintly cynical inflection.

"Welcome to O'Shea's."

Cassie certainly didn't waste any time, Reid thought sourly as he tended bar on a slow evening. As soon as he had agreed to her moving in this afternoon, she'd smiled one of those rare, bright smiles of hers and left, only to return in less than an hour in paint-spattered shorts and a T-shirt, with her long hair caught back in a braid. She'd stopped over at Karen's, then had begun carrying painting supplies upstairs. She was still up there.

He must have been out of his mind to agree to this. She'd made it clear that, regardless of what Jamey said, the final decision was *his*. He could have said no, and she would have gone someplace else. Why the hell hadn't he?

Because he hadn't wanted to cross his father. Because she was, as Jamey had pointed out, naive, vulnerable and a whole lot stubborn. Because she would think moving into Vinnie Marino's building—or Elpidio's or Tommy Murphy's—a perfectly reasonable solution. Because any of those bastards or their buddies would find her too easy a target to resist. Because if she was going to insist on living in the neighborhood, this was the safest place. Jamey wanted her here. *He* wanted her here.

Even if she would drive him crazy.

Realizing that he'd been staring at the front of the *Times-Picayune* long enough to have read every word twice, he turned the page, but he didn't look at the photographs or try to focus on the stories. All his attention was upstairs. As carefully as he listened, he couldn't hear any sounds at all, not even footsteps on the wooden floors. He could smell paint, though, just a faint whiff that drifted down the stairs. As Karen had done before her, in no time at all she would turn shabby, dreary and bleak into cozy, welcoming and pretty without frills. Cassie wasn't a frilly sort of person. Everything would be neat, tailored and subdued, not ruffly or lacy, neither blatantly feminine nor tastelessly loud. She would create for herself a haven of comfortable elegance, while across the hall he would continue to live in shabby, dreary and bleak.

She hadn't even moved in yet and was already undertaking a major redecorating. He'd been living there more than six months, and he hadn't hung so much as one picture on the walls for fear that he would soon be asked to move on.

At last he heard footsteps on the stairs. He tried to actually read one of the headlines on the newspaper page, but it was hard when he could see her peripherally coming down the hall, looking as relaxed as he was tense, moving more gracefully than he ever had. With a smile, she came around the end of the bar and climbed onto a stool. "Can I have a soda?"

He removed one from the cooler and set it down without looking at her. He studied the paper until his eyes damn near crossed, but all he was aware of was her. She smelled of paint and mineral spirits, of sweat and dust and, under all the layers, a subtle, spicy fragrance. It was an intriguing combination.

Finally admitting defeat, he closed the paper and set it aside. "Get much done?"

"Some. I'd like to be able to move in this weekend."

"Do you need any help with that?"

His grudging question surprised her as much as him. After a moment, she responded with a smile that was enough to take any red-blooded man's breath away. It wasn't particularly big or intense. It didn't spread into a grin the way her smiles occasionally did. It was really just a slight upturn of the corners of her mouth, small, private, intimate. As if it were for him alone and no one else. "Yes, I do. I thought I would borrow Smith's Blazer. I can fit more stuff in it than in my little car."

"Are you going to tell him why you're moving 'stuff'?"

The smile turned rueful. "Not until I'm completely moved in. He would tell Jolie, and they would only try to change my mind. Frankly I'm tired of people trying."

"People worry about you. It's only natural, being so young."

"So young? I believe I'm only a few years younger than you, and I've always been mature for my age." She used a paper napkin to wipe the sweat that dotted her forehead and made the wisps of hair that framed her face cling to her skin. "Are you an only child?"

He nodded. After a couple of unfortunate mistakes when he was a kid, Meghan had taken steps to ensure there wouldn't be any more, not from her, at least. Jamey hadn't had any other children, either, and Karen couldn't have any, so it looked as if he would always be an only.

"I love my family dearly, but I used to have these fantasies when I was much younger about being an only child. About not having to share my parents' attention with twelve others. About having quiet family dinners instead of chaotic free-for-alls. About being able to fit the entire family into one car, one church pew, one dining room." She smiled again. "About having one mother instead of one mother and eight sisters who thought they were my mother."

"It beats my family. No one wanted to be the mother *or* the father." He made the statement matter-of-factly. There were no secrets on Serenity. It was common knowledge that his family was as dysfunctional as they came, that Jamey had married Meghan only because he had felt forced, that she had taken Reid away only to spite Jamey, that his parents had hated each other and hadn't felt much more kindly toward him. Common knowledge and, around here, common circumstances. There were more failed relationships in this small area than in a place ten times the size. Family, obligations and responsibility were concepts with little meaning here. Most relationships went sour. Most kids were unwanted by one parent or the other, and all too often by both. Most people down here didn't give his upbringing a second thought because they were used to such stories.

But Cassie did. She looked pained. Dismayed. Sympathetic.

Damn it, he didn't want her sympathy. He didn't want anything from her...except her body. Her time. The sweet, soothing sound of her voice. Maybe another of those intimate little smiles.

Hell, he didn't want anything at all except her. All of her.

His expression hardening, he didn't wait for her to make some apologetic comment and changed the subject instead. "You're going to need some furniture for that place."

"I know. Once I get settled, I'll have to start hitting the garage sales. Until then, I thought I'd go for the minimalist look. It's easier on the budget. All I really need is a bed, and the one up there is in decent shape. I'll give it a coat of paint, some new sheets and a comforter, and it'll be perfect."

Now, there was an image he didn't need: Jamey's old iron bedstead, freshly painted and made up to look new, and Cassie, her body long and slim under the comforter, her deep brown hair spread like silk over pillows and bare skin. Every time he walked into his bedroom, he would imagine her that way. Every night when he crawled into his own bed to sleep, he would want her that way, long, slim, naked and under him.

Oh, hell, he was in trouble.

"How about another round, Reid?"

Gratefully he tore his gaze from her and nodded to Virgil, seated at a table with old Thomas. There had been a time, when he'd first taken over the bar, when the two elderly men had shown up every night and most of the days and drunk steadily from the time they came in the door until, following Jamey's orders, Reid had cut them off and sent them home. Lately they came as often, but they didn't drink as much. Some evenings they didn't indulge in more than a couple of drinks, spending their time instead talking. The past few weeks, they'd begun to bring a checkerboard with them and nursed one drink through four or five games. Their slacking off on the booze didn't help business any, but it pleased Jamey.

He filled two glasses and carried them to the table by the door, then, with a look at Cassie, stepped out onto the sidewalk. It was a cool evening. The breeze carried the faintly sour scent of the river, a fitting accompaniment to the long, low whistle of a ship headed into or out of port.

"It's a sad sound, isn't it?"

He glanced at Cassie, who had come to stand on the opposite side of the double doors, then shook his head. "Right after I came here, I used to sit by the river and watch the ships. For a while, I thought that was what I wanted to do—go to sea. See other places."

"Why didn't you?"

Why hadn't he signed up on some cargo ship heading out to sea? It would have taken him away from Serenity, away from the father who didn't want him and the friends who wanted only to corrupt him. It would have taken him someplace new, someplace where he wouldn't have to be Reid Donovan, troublemaker, thief, troubled kid, punk. It would have taught him job skills that could have kept him off the streets, out of jail and on the right side of the law. It would have given him a whole new life.

But his life had been *here*. The mother who hadn't wanted him had dumped him here. If she had ever changed her mind and gone looking, here was where she would have looked. The father who hadn't wanted him was here, too, and if he had ever changed his mind and decided he wanted a son after all, then here was where the son needed to be. His friends were here, the only friends he'd ever had, the only people who had ever accepted him. As for going someplace new and becoming a new and improved Reid Donovan, hell, even at fifteen he'd understood that he would always be exactly what he'd always been: unwanted, neglected, a punk. Nothing could change that. Not a fresh start in a new place. Not a law-abiding job. Not new friends. Not a woman. Not even *this* woman.

She was waiting patiently for an answer. Leaning back

against the brick wall, he gazed into the sky. Though darkness had long since fallen, the city lights obscured all but the biggest and brightest of the stars. "For a long time, I thought maybe Meghan would come back," he admitted at last. "That maybe the guy she'd taken off with would dump her, like they always did. She would need someone to take care of her, and since I had done it practically all my life…"

He shrugged. Some dreams died hard. In his head, he had known the minute he'd let himself into their Atlanta apartment—through the window, since there was a new lock on the door—that she was gone for good. It was almost as if he'd been expecting it, as if he had known that one day she would reach the limits of her tolerance for him and she would leave. Still, for a long time he had hoped. He had awakened more mornings than he could count, wondering if this might be the day she would return. Her birthday, his birthday, Christmas Day and Mother's Day had all been cause for hope. All had been marred with disappointment.

"Did she ever come?"

He shook his head. "For all I know, she could be dead. She had a drinking problem. She liked to experiment with drugs. She loved men." Any one of her vices could have killed her, and no one would have known that she had a son to notify. She hadn't cared much for him when she was around. It was a sure bet she hadn't bragged on him once she'd gotten rid of him.

Cassie sighed heavily, but she didn't offer a useless apology, didn't sympathize or commiserate with him, for which he was grateful. Instead, she pulled her keys from the pocket of her shorts, then laid her hand for one moment on his arm. "I've got to get home. Thanks for letting me have the apartment."

Once more he shook his head. "It wasn't my decision."

"Yes, it was. I'll make sure you don't regret it." After giving his arm a squeeze, she released him, then crossed the street to her car.

"Too late," he murmured as she climbed inside, then

slammed the door. Like so many other things in his life, he already regretted it. And like all those other regrets, he would have to learn to live with it.

Saturday was warm, bright and sunny, a perfect day for a drive in the country or one of those lazy two-hour riverboat cruises to nowhere that Jolie and Smith indulged in every year. It was a perfect day, too, Cassie thought as she backed out of the rear seat of the Blazer, for moving into her very own apartment.

She had offered to treat Reid to breakfast before they started moving this morning, but he had turned her down. She had suggested that she pick him up in her car and take him along while she picked up the Blazer, but he'd vetoed that idea, too. He hadn't even wanted her swinging by after she'd picked up the Blazer. He would meet her at the condo, he had announced, and she hadn't argued. Since they were going to be neighbors, she planned to pick her fights with care.

She was approaching the elevator that would take her to the eighteenth floor when she saw him, leaning against the smooth concrete wall and watching her. Like his father, he dressed casually, always in jeans and T-shirts or an occasional button-down shirt. This morning the jeans were faded and snug, and the T-shirt was navy and equally snug. He looked good enough to make any self-respecting woman swoon. Though she'd never indulged in anything so frivolously feminine in her life, she was sure she could do a decent job. After all, with just one look at him, her breath was coming faster and she was already weak in the knees. It took every ounce of self-possession she had to hide it when she came close. "Good morning."

He nodded as he pushed the elevator call button.

"Been waiting long?"

"I came in right behind you. You took your time parking."

"I was putting the back seat down. We'll need the room." When the elevator door opened, she stepped inside, then pressed the button for her floor. "I really appreciate your help. I know you're not thrilled about this."

"You guessed that, huh?"

She couldn't help but smile at his dry tone. "Well, the fact that you've pretty much ignored me the last four days is something of a giveaway."

"That's nothing new. I've always tried to ignore you."

"Why? Do you dislike me that much?"

His startled gaze met hers. "I don't dislike you."

She waited for something more, something along the lines of *I don't have any feelings at all for you. I've hardly even noticed you because you're quiet and plain. You're nothing like Tanya—you're a serene little mouse.* He didn't offer more, though. He left it at that, a simple statement. It wasn't much. It wasn't *I like you fine, but I'd like to know you better.* Or *I like you fine, but I'd like you better in my bed.* But it could have been worse.

"It's not a bad start for neighbors," she remarked evenly as she watched the numbers light up, then blink off. "I'll like you, and you can not dislike me. Maybe sometime down the line, you'll get past not disliking me and learn to actually like me." And where would she be by then? What seriously intense emotions would she be suffering by the time he eventually got over this antagonism toward her? *If* he got over this antagonism?

He didn't take kindly to the faint teasing in her voice. It made him scowl and look away. He had the best scowl—all dark and sullen. It reminded Cassie of the young, pouty, pretty-boy models she came across in magazine ads, except Reid's scowl had real substance to it. Where those oh-so-handsome models were only posturing, with Reid it was real. They pretended to be sullen, tough and bad, while *he* was— or, at least, he could be.

"All right. So if you don't dislike me, then why do you try to ignore me?" She didn't expect a straight answer. To her great surprise, she got one.

"You make me uncomfortable."

"Why?"

He shrugged impatiently. "You don't belong on Serenity."

"But I'm *from* Serenity." The elevator came to a stop, the doors sliding back. For a moment, she stood motionless, but when he stepped off, she quickly followed. Sorting through her keys, she found the one to the front door and opened the lock.

"No," he said flatly as she pushed the door open. "You were born on Serenity. But you belong *here*." He gestured inside the apartment.

She stared inside, trying to see what he saw. The condo was huge and expensive. It was the sort of picture-perfect place that appeared on the pages of upscale magazines and architectural digests. It was beautiful in a cold, sterile sort of way. And he thought it was *her*.

Thanks for the compliment, she thought dryly.

Back when she was fifteen and trying to turn her life into a great melodrama, the place would have suited her. Her constant black attire would have blended well into this many-shades-of-gray decor. The sleek lines and the spare furnishings would have suited her, too, along with all the hardness—the marble, the granite, the metal. But not anymore. Now she liked softness and color—the warm, buttery yellow of her bedroom and the deeper salmon in the living room. The snuggly weight of the woven throw she had tucked over Jamey's old couch. The downy thickness of the comforter waiting to go on her new bed. There would be no stark lines, no monochromatic schemes, no sleek modern furnishings in her new place.

Sliding her keys into her pocket, she gestured toward the boxes neatly stacked in the foyer. "There's most of my stuff. There's a chair in the office and a couple more boxes in the bedroom. I thought I'd leave my hanging clothes hanging since it's such a short move."

"Why don't you get the chair? We'll work around it."

With a nod, she headed down the hall. When Smith had moved out of the condo and into Jolie's little yellow house, he hadn't taken a thing with him beyond the personal stuff.

He had paid a fortune for the place and another fortune to have it decorated, and he'd walked away from it all without a single regret. It had been his home for years, but other than his clothing, his papers and a painting by Michael Bennett, it might as well have been a very expensive hotel. She felt the same way. Beyond the spectacular views, there wasn't a thing about the condo that she would miss.

Living across the hall from Reid, she imagined she would have some pretty spectacular views of her own.

In the office, she pulled back her desk chair, a mix of teak and walnut more than seventy-five years old, and slid into its place Smith's own chair, an incredibly ugly combination of highly polished steel and black leather. She rolled her chair down the hall, stacked a couple of boxes on the seat and, with Reid carrying his own stack of boxes, headed for the elevator.

It took four trips to fill the back of the Blazer but only two, with Jamey's help, to unload everything into her apartment. As they moved slowly through traffic back toward the condo—the French Quarter was having yet another of its thousand and one festivals—she glanced at Reid. "Alicia brought Sean by the center yesterday."

Alicia Gutierrez had been Ryan Morgan's girlfriend. After he'd hit her the same night he'd beaten Karen, Alicia had taken refuge in the condo with Cassie for a few days. She had started the visit angry and frightened, had made excited plans to remove Morgan from her life, leave Serenity and make a loving, safe home for the baby she was expecting at any moment. Soon, though, anger had given way to apology and regret. Maybe she *had* provoked him. Maybe she had deserved what he'd done.

Cassie had tried to argue with her, but Alicia had turned stubborn and refused to listen. Cassie didn't know, the other woman had pointed out, what it was like to be poor and pregnant, to have so few options. She didn't know what it was like to be *in love*. Alicia had been right. Cassie hadn't known about any of that. But she knew that any man who would hit a nine-months'-pregnant woman whom he claimed to love was no man at all. She knew that Alicia would never be truly happy, and neither would her child, as long as Ryan Morgan was in their lives.

Now he wasn't. Fate, and the bad decision he'd made in choosing to work for Jimmy Falcone, had done what Alicia couldn't. On the day she had given birth to a sweet, adorable little baby boy, Ryan Morgan had been found by the river with a bullet in his brain.

"How is she?"

Reid's question drew her out of her grim thoughts. "A little hopeless."

He shrugged as if not surprised. "Maybe she really did love him."

"Not that he ever did a thing in the world to deserve it."

"And what would you know about that?"

She felt his gaze on her. Slowing to a stop inches off the bumper of the car in front of her, she turned to look directly at him. "What would I know?" she asked with a hint of sarcasm. "He hit her when she was carrying his baby. He beat Karen because he didn't like her presence on *his* street. He never did an honest day's work in his life. He supported himself by working for the biggest criminal in the state. He was a thief, a liar, a punk, a murderer, a crook—"

"He was the best friend I had."

She gave him a long, steady look before turning back to the street ahead. "Then you're badly in need of a better class of friends."

They traveled a block or two in silence before he surprised her with more. "Ryan did what he knew how to do. His father beat him. He learned young that that was how you deal with conflict. Might makes right, that sort of thing. His old man was a drunk who never did an honest day's work in his life, either. His mother was a drunk, too. Sometimes she worked as a waitress or a housekeeper in one of the hotels, but usually she collected welfare checks or worked the streets." His expression turned cynical. "We're not talking Ozzie and Harriet

here. Ryan and Trevor didn't stand much of a chance from
the start.''

"Neither did you, but you were never like them."

"I was more like them than you want to know."

Cassie shook her head. He had run with them, yes. There
was no denying that. But according to Jamey and Karen, when
his buddies' activities had turned to crime, as often as not,
Reid had managed to be someplace else. He had never gotten
involved in the big stuff—the assaults and death threats. He
had never hurt anyone, and he had certainly never killed anyone.

"I could have been a hundred times worse than any of
them."

Any other young man on Serenity who made that statement
would be boasting. Reid's voice was flat, a grim acknowledgment of what he believed to be fact. She didn't believe it. To be as bad as the Morgans, Marino and the others
required some inherent and very basic character flaw, and Reid
didn't have it. If he did, he wouldn't have spent the past six
months making an effort to turn his life around. He wouldn't
have traded his only friends for a world that didn't trust him.
He wouldn't have imposed such isolation on himself, wouldn't
have persevered in the face of such suspicion and doubt. He
wouldn't still be trying, no matter how lonely the battle, no
matter how uncertain the outcome. He could spend fifty years
doing everything right and never make everyone forget the
first twenty-six, when he'd done everything wrong.

But he was trying. Ryan Morgan had never tried. He had
enjoyed his life. He had liked the power, the reputation and
the intimidation. He had fed on the fear he'd created in everyone around him. He had liked being the biggest, the baddest,
the meanest son of a bitch to whom Jimmy Falcone entrusted
his business. It was ironic that what had given Ryan such pride
had taken his life. It was Jimmy Falcone who'd ordered his
death. There was no proof, of course. There rarely was when
Falcone was involved. But it was no secret. Everyone knew.

"If you were so much like Morgan, why aren't you still part of that gang? When he died, why didn't you take over?"

"I lost interest, I guess. I didn't want to take over. I just wanted to get out."

Drawing to a stop at a red light, she looked his way once again. This time she smiled. "And maybe, Reid," she said softly, "you never were quite so much like him after all."

Chapter 4

It was their final trip into the condo. Reid stood at the expanse
of glass that made up the outer wall of the bedroom and gazed
down while Cassie gathered the last of her belongings from
the closet. From up here, the city was both familiar and foreign. There were places so well known that they couldn't be
mistaken even from a distance, but at the same time there was
an alien feel to them. There was no shabbiness, no dirt, no
poverty or decay. From eighteen stories up, New Orleans was
no less than a lovely city cradled in the river's bend. From
eighteen stories up, there were no problems.

Too bad he lived eighteen stories down.

"Great view, huh?" Cassie laid the clothing on the bed,
then came to lean against the glass.

He glanced at her just long enough to get a glimpse of silky
brown hair, smooth skin, long lashes and lightly colored lips.
"Yeah," he agreed, with no thought at all to the city below.

"When I first moved in, all I did was look out. I couldn't
believe I had the good luck to have the place for my own—
temporarily, of course. After a while, though, I got kind of

restless. I mean, you can't live your life looking out. The apartment is too big for me. I felt lost half the time. It's too cold, too. I swear, I don't ever want to see gray again until my hair starts to turn.'' She smiled, and he saw it reflected in the glass. ''And then there are the neighbors.''

''What's wrong with the neighbors?''

''They're rich.''

''So's your brother-in-law.''

Another faint smile. ''Smith has money. These people are rich. There's a difference.''

''Not where I come from,'' he said dryly. ''On Serenity anyone with money is rich.''

''Smith is smart, talented and works hard. The fact that he has family money is immaterial. It doesn't affect how he does things.''

''So your sister is married to a man rich enough to not care about how rich he is. It must be nice.''

''I guess. Frankly I never wanted to be rich, although I do sometimes think about all the good the right person—like Karen—could do with a few million bucks,'' she said. ''But I try to live by my friend Judith's philosophy. She says she'll never have a lot, but she'll always have enough. I would be satisfied with that.''

Lately he'd had more than enough, money-wise, but money wasn't all a person needed in his life for satisfaction. Friends would be nice. Family. The promise of a better future. A woman, he added, giving Cassie a sidelong glance. A woman—the right woman—could make up for not having anything else.

With a sudden, loud sigh, she turned away from the window. ''I guess I'm ready to go. After we drop this stuff off, I need to pick up something from my parents' house. If you'll go with me, I'll treat you to lunch afterwards.''

He almost answered without thinking. Sure, he would go. He would help with the rest of the stuff. He would sit down to eat across from her. He would deliberately prolong this time with her. In time, though, he stopped himself and gave her invitation careful consideration. *I need to pick up something from my parents' house.* He knew little about the Wades, but it was enough to know that they weren't like any parents he'd ever met. They were married, for one thing, and apparently happily so. They'd raised thirteen kids to be good, productive adults and hadn't abandoned a single one. They'd worked hard to escape Serenity, they went to church and had probably never broken a law in their lives, neither God's nor man's, and they were still protective of their youngest daughter. How thrilled would they be to see her with *him?*

"I'd love to tell you that we could slip in, get the dresser and slip out again in under ten minutes, but it wouldn't be true," she admitted as she began gathering the hangers. "No one gets in and out with *my* mother in twice that time. She'll be full of curiosity because it's been a long time since I've taken anyone male to the house, and she'll want to know all about you."

He waited until she moved toward the door before he approached the bed and scooped up the last thick pile of clothes, dividing the hangers evenly between both hands. "And what would you have me tell her? That I grew up on Serenity? That I have an arrest record a couple of miles long? That I used to work for Jimmy Falcone? That I finally gave up that life when my best friend got shot in the head? That now I work in a seedy bar and a two-bit garage and live in a shabby apartment above the bar? Right across the hall from you?"

From the door, she gave him one of those unnervingly cool looks that she was so good at. "I would expect you to say, 'It's nice to meet you, Mrs. Wade,' and leave the rest to me."

The rest. Answering the questions, fending off the curiosity, brushing off the concern. There *would* be concern. No self-respecting mother in the city would want him hanging around her daughter. Even Tanya's mother, who lived over in Gretna with her fourth or fifth husband and saw her daughter only once in a blue moon, hadn't approved of their relationship.

With a stubborn set to her jaw, Cassie left the bedroom. After a moment, he followed, waiting by the door while she made a quick trip around the apartment, checking to make sure she had everything. The place was spotless, not a thing out of place anywhere. She could walk out one minute, and the pickiest tenants in the world could come in the next and find nothing to complain about.

Once she finished her inspection, they left. He waited until they were in the garage and had hung all the clothes on the bar that stretched across the back seat before he rather grudgingly accepted her invitation. "Would you also expect me to say, 'It's a pleasure meeting you, *Mr.* Wade'?"

Her expression was guarded. "My father always takes an assortment of grandchildren out on Saturdays. He won't be there." Then she gave in and almost smiled. He discovered he wanted her to smile, wanted it too damn much. "I don't expect any male acquaintance to meet my father right up front."

Acquaintance. It was a perfectly acceptable term to describe their relationship. After all, they weren't friends, and they certainly weren't anything more intimate, even if he did lie awake nights thinking about it. They were acquaintances. Still, he thought as he slid into the seat and fastened the seat belt, the word rankled. "What was wrong with the last acquaintance you took home?"

She grinned as she backed out of the parking space. "Trevor? My parents couldn't stand him. He was a rebellious sort—or, at least, he thought he was. He dressed in black leather and behaved sullenly most of the time. He reminded Mama and Daddy too much of this guy that my sister Jolie used to date on Serenity. His name was Nicky Carlucci. I think he was a friend of Jamey's."

"I know Carlucci."

"I guess that's logical, considering that you both worked for Falcone. It's hard to imagine Jolie's old boyfriend and Jamey's best friend turning out the way he did."

Reid's only response was a shrug. He wasn't sure Carlucci was so bad. In his few dealings with him, the man had been fair. He'd been a good lawyer who had gotten Reid out of jail

a few times. More in his favor, Jamey had remained friends
with him right up until he went to prison. Whatever Nick
Carlucci had done hadn't been enough to undo their lifelong
friendship.

Occasionally Reid found himself wishing that Jamey could
be so forgiving of the things *he* had done. He was willing to
bet his crimes weren't as serious as Carlucci's. But then, he
and his father had never had a relationship to survive.

Forcing his attention back to the original conversation, he
asked, not completely free of jealousy, "Whatever happened
to Trevor?"

"He got accepted at Princeton. He cut his hair, ditched the
leather, straightened up his act, kissed me goodbye and headed
back east. The last I heard, he was in graduate school working
on an MBA." She sighed dramatically. "He was just a
pseudorebel."

As opposed to the real thing sitting beside her. Was that it?
She was interested in him because she had a thing for rebels,
for guys who didn't conform to her parents' standards of the
proper man for her? Wouldn't that be a joke if it was true? If
he was trying to mend his ways so he could have a decent
relationship or two, and she wanted a relationship only because of his old ways? Quite a joke, but he didn't find it the
least bit amusing.

"So you like guys who are a little crooked."

"No. I like guys who are decent, responsible and mature.
Who understand loyalty and commitment. Who can make a
few mistakes without letting them ruin their lives. Who can
accept a woman as an equal. Who can be kind to fatherless
kids and homeless puppies."

Feeling the beginnings of a flush, he turned to stare out the
side window. She was aware of his friendship with J.T., only
grudgingly permitted by Shawntae out of respect for Karen
and Jamey, and that mutt... So he'd fed a scrawny puppy
enough to keep it alive until it found an owner. It was no big
deal. Jethro didn't even remember. He treated Reid to the same

mildly ferocious stance that any other man who went close to Karen got, including Jamey.

She parked the truck in front of O'Shea's and climbed out to unload. The street had never been intended to provide two lanes of travel and parking, so the Blazer blocked half the street. It was all right, though. Other than Karen and Trevor Morgan, only a couple other people in the neighborhood had cars. Most of them had all they could do to cover the necessary expenses of rent and food. Like him, they walked wherever they needed to go or at least as far as the nearest bus stop on Decatur.

Jamey was busy behind the bar when they went inside, their arms full of clothes. It was probably a payday weekend for most of the customers. That was the only way to get so many of them into O'Shea's by noon on a Saturday. With no more than a slight nod of greeting to his father, Reid followed Cassie up the stairs, into her unlocked apartment and straight back to the bedroom.

There was something personal about being in this bedroom. The one in the condo was so big, so formal and unwelcoming. It was the sort of place he couldn't imagine himself ever setting foot in, the sort of place where he couldn't in a million years imagine himself sleeping or doing anything else. But this room was smaller, warmer, cozier. In size and shape, it was exactly the same as his room next door. It was familiar, a place where he not only could imagine himself sleeping but virtually the same as the place where he did sleep.

It was more intimate.

He stood near the open closet door, his gaze focused on the room while Cassie hung the clothes. She had mixed a little of the same yellow from the walls into the ceiling paint, giving it a faint warm glow. She'd done a nice job of painting, sanding and cleaning. Even the old bed looked new with its fresh paint. Once she'd made it with the sheets and the thick comforter, still in their packages on the bare mattress, it would be transformed from a ratty old piece of junk into something worth having. When she was finished with the apartment, she would have created another oddity like Karen's house—a neat, nicely done place that could belong in practically any other neighborhood in the city instead of the shabbiest and dreariest. If she was like Karen, though— and she was—she wouldn't be satisfied with this small success. Next she would probably want to fix up the hall, the bathroom, his apartment and the kitchen, then the bar. And if she got away with that, she would want to turn her attention to the exterior of the building.

Maybe that was the way Serenity would be saved. One apartment, one house, one building at a time.

Cassie took the last of the hangers from him, sending into the air a faint whiff of her fragrance, and sorted them onto the closet rod, shirts on one side, skirts opposite and dresses in the middle. Though she was wearing jeans today, she didn't often. He'd noticed only one pair in the pile of clothing. Mostly there were long skirts, some loose enough to wrap around her slender waist three times, others fitted to the curve of her hips and her legs. The dresses were loose and long, perfectly suitable for sitting in a kid-size chair or for getting down on the floor with thirteen rambunctious students.

His hands empty, he turned away from the closet and went into the living room to wait. Again the size and shape were identical to his own, but the similarities ended there. His walls were faded institutional green, his curtains some sort of patterned gold. He remembered seeing them in the front windows on his very first day on Serenity, when Meghan had walked him down the street on their way to her mother's building and she had pointed out the place. ''O'Shea's. That's your father,'' she had said matter-of-factly, and he had looked to see a dilapidated building and ugly gold curtains at every window. He hadn't looked in the open doors below those windows, hadn't made any effort at all to see inside to the man who he'd been taught since infancy was responsible for all their troubles.

His smile was faintly bitter. After a while, blaming Jamey must have lost its appeal for Meghan. By the time he'd turned ten, it had shifted to him. *He* was at fault for everything that had gone wrong in Meghan's life. If she'd never gotten pregnant, if she'd never married Jamey, if she'd never had a baby, if she'd never been saddled with such responsibility... She had managed to look past her own role in all her complaints and lay the blame squarely on him.

"I'll be ready in just a minute," Cassie called from the bedroom. Her words were followed by the tearing of plastic, then the sharp flap of sheets being shaken out. She was making the bed, and damned if he didn't want to offer to help. He didn't, though. No way was he going to touch her sheets and comforter. No way was he going to stand across from her with only the bed between them and help spread the sheets that she would be sleeping on tonight or stuff into cases the pillows where she would lay her head or smooth out the comforter that would cover her. No way in hell was he going to learn the feel and smell of her bed and linens.

"I'll wait downstairs," he said abruptly, hearing the tension that made his voice edgy. If she noticed or thought his abrupt departure odd, she didn't comment.

Leaving the door open, he took the stairs two at a time. Jamey was talking to old Thomas, but Reid felt his gaze as he passed between tables and went through the nearest set of doors. He hadn't escaped, though. In fact, he just might have been better off if he had stayed upstairs getting hard and hot for Cassie.

"Hey, sugar. Haven't seen you in a long time." The words were greeting, admonishment and pout all wrapped up together as Tanya strolled across the uneven sidewalk and right up to him, so close that he could feel her breath on his chin. "You've been keeping busy."

"Tanya." With his hands on her shoulders, he tried to back her up. When she didn't budge, he tried to back away, but the wall was at his back.

"I've missed you, darlin'," she murmured, wriggling even closer, raising her hands to his chest. "Have you missed me?"

He gazed down at her as if for the first time. There was a brittle air about her that he'd never noticed before, as if the toughness she wore was pretense that could be easily shattered.

She had flaws, but all in all, she was pretty. Her black hair was overstyled and heavily sprayed, and her makeup could use a lighter touch. The hazel eyes were nice, though, and her mouth was made for smiling—as well as other, less innocent activities. She wore a tight skirt only inches long from waist to hem and a sheer shirt with the skimpiest of bras underneath, chosen to play up her sexuality. She considered herself a very sexual being, not because she enjoyed the act so much but because she thought that was all she had to offer. Smart women had brains, rich women had money, nice women had personality and Tanya had sex. It was the only thing, in her opinion, that she did well, the only reason any man might want her.

"Yeah," he answered at last. "I've missed you." But he lied. He missed having sex with her. He missed her talented mouth, her soft, willing body and her eagerness to please, but he didn't miss *her*. That fact saddened him.

"We can do something about that, darlin'. I'm not busy right now. Why don't we go upstairs to your new place and...?" Taking the final step that brought her body into contact with his, she rose onto her toes to whisper in his ear, tantalizing words of sweet pleasure and satisfaction to die for, promising him everything when he could offer her nothing. She wanted some sort of connection, an hour or two when she didn't have to be alone, when she could forget all the problems in her life and be touched, held, kissed, but all he could give was sex. Meaningless, sordid, the purely physical release of desire created by someone else. He was one of those men who wanted her only for sex, and he felt like a bastard for it.

But when she traded words for kisses and rubbed seductively against him, all that self-disgust did nothing to suppress his body's response. For one guilty moment, he let himself enjoy the sensations before, with unsteady hands, he gently, firmly, pushed her away. She smiled, her eyes hazy. "Yeah," she agreed in a breathy voice to what she perceived as an unspoken invitation. "Let's go upstairs and I'll—"

He caught her hand as she reached for the waistband of his jeans. "Listen, Tanya, I—"

"Oh, come on, Reid," she coaxed, and another voice from a dozen feet away echoed the sentiment.

"Yeah, go on, Reid."

He moved away from Tanya with such haste that he almost tripped over his own feet. His lack of grace amused one woman. It didn't have any effect at all on the stony expression of the other. His face burned as hot as if he'd been caught in some illicit behavior—or, worse, some sort of betrayal. But that was impossible. There was no relationship between him and Cassie to betray. Hadn't he acknowledged just this morning that they weren't even friends?

But that knowledge did nothing to ease his embarrassment.

Before he could think of anything to say, Tanya fixed her attention on Cassie. On ridiculously high heels, she crossed the sidewalk to where Cassie waited beside the Blazer and gave the other woman a long, measuring look. "You must be the new schoolteacher, Miss Cassie. My niece Starr is in your class. She talks about you all the time."

Cassie's expression lost its tight-lipped mockery. "She's a bright girl."

"Yes, she is. I've got bigger plans for her than Serenity. She's gonna be the first Stanford to make something of herself."

"I'll do my best to help with that."

"I'm sure you will." After a moment, Tanya returned to Reid, stopped close again and used one red-tipped thumb to wipe away traces of lipstick from his jaw. "All you had to say was no," she said in a quietly chiding voice. "My feelings wouldn't have been hurt." She offered him a smile as proof, then turned and strolled away. Before she'd gone far, though, she looked back over her shoulder. "I'll be seeing you around, darlin'. You, too, Miss Cassie."

There was a phrase years ago used to describe particularly sexy young women like Tanya, but standing there on the sidewalk and watching her go, Cassie felt relatively sure that it needed updating in this case. *Sex kitten* just sounded entirely too harmless, and Tanya Stanford was anything but harmless. *Sex tigress* was much more appropriate.

And if she was a tigress, what did that make Cassie? A timid little mouse?

Pulling her keys from her pocket, she scowled at Reid. "Sorry. I didn't realize I'd interrupted mating time."

The snide edge to her voice brought back the heat that had started to recede from his face. He *should* be embarrassed, she thought with petty satisfaction as she circled the truck and climbed in behind the wheel. It was the middle of the day and there were people in the bar right behind where they'd stood, and his little girlfriend had been about to climb right on top of him right there on the sidewalk. She didn't know why it had surprised her. She'd seen him and Tanya in heat before, getting up close and personal in public. He hadn't complained then, and he certainly hadn't been complaining just now.

She had been surprised, she admitted as she started the engine, because she'd thought he was no longer seeing the other woman. She'd been under the mistaken assumption that he'd broken his ties with all the people he had once run wild with. She had thought... The strength of her ego brought a blush to her own cheeks. She had thought that he was interested in *her*. She had thought that the attraction she felt was too powerful to be one-sided, that no matter how well he hid it, he felt it, too.

But it seemed she'd been wrong.

Down the block, Tanya crossed the street to the house where Cassie had once lived. Even from this distance, it was easy to see that she moved with such grace, as if she was thoroughly comfortable with her body, her sexuality and her effect on men. If she'd lived anywhere else, Cassie would have thought such poise came from breeding or, more mundanely, from years of dance. But Tanya didn't live anywhere else. She lived on Serenity, and the grace came from confidence.

One day Cassie would like to have such sexually charged confidence.

With a sigh, she pressed the button to roll down the opposite window and ducked her head so she could see Reid. "The dresser I have to get from my mother's is relatively light. She and I can handle it on our own if you don't want to go."

His gaze narrowed into a look of pure annoyance. "If you don't want me to go, at least be honest enough to say so."

Her temper straining to break free, she leaned closer to the window. "Honest?" she repeated, hearing the shrill undertone to the word. "You want me to be *honest?* All right. Why do you act like being with me is some punishment you have to tolerate, but *her*... Hell, you can't even wait long enough to find a bed with *her*. Every time I've seen you two together, it's like...like..." she sputtered, unable to find the right words.

He supplied them with sarcasm. "Mating time?" Finally moving, he came to stand next to the truck, leaning down to rest his arms on the open window. "I'm not interested in Tanya."

"Well, pardon me for not noticing that. It was hard to tell when you were holding on to her for dear life and she had her tongue down your throat."

"She didn't..." He didn't finish that denial. "I wasn't holding on to her. I was trying to push her back. I was trying to tell her that I wasn't interested."

"Oh, so that was it. It's not so hard, you know. You just say, 'Sorry, Tanya, I'm not interested.' You'd be surprised how well it works."

"All right. Sorry, Cassie. I'm not interested." His voice was soft, adding impact to his statement, making her breath catch in a hard knot in the center of her chest. For a moment, she was numb, then a curious ache started building. Hurt, surprise, disappointment, regret, shame. She felt them all.

"Doesn't feel so great, does it?" he asked with an odd gentleness as he reached inside to unlock the door, then opened it. "You owe me lunch."

Bewildered, she stared at him. Feeling flustered and unbalanced, she grudgingly said, "You can stay here if you want," but she accompanied the words with a gesture toward a house. Tanya's house.

"I don't." He climbed in, closed the door and fastened his seat belt.

For a time, she simply sat there. Once she did finally pull away from the curb and head for the corner where she could make a U-turn, she stiffly said, "I'm sorry. I had no right to be jealous."

She wished he would tell her that she had no *reason* to be jealous, but he didn't. He didn't say anything at all until they were winding through the narrow streets of the Quarter. There, as they waited for a group of camera-laden tourists to cross the street, he finally spoke with the same honesty he had demanded of her. "Tanya was just looking for someone to be with, and I...I was just looking to be distracted from you."

"Why?" Her voice was soft but even. It didn't hint at her confusion.

The last tourist stepped onto the curb, but still Cassie didn't move, not until the driver behind her blared his horn. With a glance in the rearview mirror, she eased forward and into an empty parking space, then faced Reid, waiting for his answer.

"Look at yourself and look at me, then ask that question again. Your family may have come from Serenity, but no one would ever guess. They're respectable. Your sister's a hotshot reporter. Your brother-in-law's a hotshot prosecutor who's richer than sin. You graduated from college. You've been to England and France. Your friends are people just like you—educated, responsible, different."

"And you were once the bad boy of Serenity. I don't see your point."

His expression turned frustrated. "I quit school when I was fifteen. Before that, I went so rarely that I *might* have completed four or five years. I'm not educated. I'm not respected. I'm never going to be a hotshot anything."

She allowed a small smile. "I don't know about that. Tanya seems to think you're good enough at *something* to deserve another chance."

"Tanya's lonely."

Cassie's smile faded. If she'd been asked to give a one-word description of the other woman, it would have been vastly more cruel. *Slut.* Wasn't it a worthy description, along with *idiot,* of anyone who lived a promiscuous life-style these days? But wasn't the reason behind the life-style more important than the derogatory insults attached to it?

"She has family," she argued.

"Yeah. A sister with an illegitimate daughter whose father died in prison last year. She's got a mother across the river who believes wholeheartedly that every man she marries is Mr. Right, that every new marriage is going to last forever. She's so busy trying to please all those men that she doesn't have time for the kids. Tanya's desperate for affection, and having sex is the only way she knows to get it."

"There must be some other…"

The look he gave her made the words trail away. "Did your mother ever hug you? Kiss you? Hold you in her lap? Did your father ever pat you on the arm or hold your hand when you were scared?"

"Of course they did."

"Well, not all parents are like that. The only time Meghan ever touched me was to hit me. Tanya's mother wasn't much better. Sometimes you find yourself needing to be touched, even if it means having sex with someone to get it."

The only time Meghan ever touched me was to hit me. Cassie stared sightlessly at the street, the nerves in her stomach tied in knots. She couldn't begin to imagine that kind of relationship. Little kids were so sweet, so innocent. How could a mother feel anything besides love, awe and tenderness for them? How could any woman show so little affection for her child that all he could remember years later was the physical abuse?

She had so many precious memories of her mother from her childhood—sitting beside her in church, holding hands as they walked to the corner grocery, crawling onto her lap at story time, getting her scrapes bandaged and her bruises kissed, snuggling into bed together. Oh, there had been punishments, too, though not nearly as often or as strictly as the older kids and never when it wasn't well deserved. Even deserved, it had never been more than a swat or two, only enough to catch her attention. It had been so rare and so minor that she couldn't remember a specific incident.

For Reid it had been just the opposite. All he could recall was the discipline, never the love. No wonder he'd been reluctant to push Tanya away. He knew what it was like to be hungry for affection.

Would he ever be willing to accept hers?

She wouldn't hold her breath waiting.

"I'm sorry." She felt his glance but didn't meet it. She didn't know what might show in her eyes, didn't know if the sympathy or sorrow she was feeling might offend him.

"For what?"

"The way things are. I was blessed with a wonderful family, and I forget that not everyone was that fortunate."

"I would be willing to bet that more aren't than are."

Finally she gave him a faint smile. "I'd love to be able to argue that with you, but I can't. Since I can't, let's get going and I'll introduce you to one of the reasons my family is so wonderful." With a glance over her shoulder, she pulled into the street, then talked, practically without pause, about unimportant subjects until she turned into her parents' driveway.

The house was nothing fancy, but it was neat and lovingly cared for. After spending so much of their lives in crowded apartments, Patrick and Rosemary had taken to home ownership like fish to water. Not a chip of paint flaked from the wood siding before he had the paint and brushes out. Not one weed sprouted in the flower beds that edged every straight line on the lot before she was on her knees plucking. They scraped, painted and maintained, mowed, planted and fertilized, and they got results. They had the loveliest house in the neighborhood, with the prettiest lawn and the most-gorgeous flowers.

They climbed the broad steps to the porch, and Cassie used

her own key to open the door. "Mama," she called as soon as she stepped inside. The house was quiet. It smelled of furniture polish and spring flowers and didn't show a speck of dust anywhere. "Saturday is cleaning day," she remarked over her shoulder to Reid as she started toward the kitchen. "Of course, the house is spotless all the time, but you can't tell Mama that. She can spot microscopic flecks of dust from a hundred paces."

"You must take after her."

Momentarily puzzled, she burst out laughing. "You mean the condo? Heavens, no. Smith has a housekeeper come in three times a week. She was there yesterday afternoon. That's why it's so clean. My style is more...shall we say cluttered?"

The kitchen was empty but warmer than the rest of the house, thanks to the cookies baking in the oven. Another batch was cooling on a wire rack on the counter. She took one for herself and offered Reid one, then walked to the screen door. "Mama?"

From somewhere out of sight came the pleased sound of her mother's voice. "Why, darlin', I wasn't expecting you. Hold on. I'll be right in." A short moment later, Rosemary came in, carrying a basket full of fresh-cut flowers. She greeted Cassie with a hug and a kiss, then fixed her gaze on Reid.

Cassie leaned back against the counter. "Mama, this is Reid Donovan. Reid, my mother, Rosemary."

Clearly uncomfortable, he accepted the hand that her mother offered and murmured, just as she'd instructed, "It's nice to meet you, Mrs. Wade."

"A young man with manners," Rosemary said. "There's something we don't see every day—particularly with that one." She nodded toward Cassie, then, still holding his hand, she pursed her lips. "Donovan. We knew some Donovans in the old neighborhood. Bertrice and... What was her girl's name?"

"Meghan. She's my mother."

Cassie carefully watched her mother's expression. With all

she knew of Meghan Donovan, she would bet her mother hadn't been fond of her. She wouldn't have approved of her daughters running around with her, and she very well might not approve of Cassie running around with her son.

Rosemary's expression didn't change, though, as she released Reid's hand and set the basket of flowers on the counter, then removed the cookies from the oven and made room for them on the wire rack. "I remember reading in the paper quite a few years back that Bertrice had died. I was sorry. How is your mother?"

The faintest hint of defensiveness crept into his eyes. "I don't know. I haven't seen her in a while."

Cassie would bet that, if pressed, he knew to the day how long it had been. Maybe Meghan had been a lousy mother, maybe she had abused and neglected him before abandoning him, but he still felt something for her. Hadn't he admitted that he'd never gotten onto one of those ships and sailed off to a better life because he'd hoped that one day she might come back for him?

"I suppose you two met through her job," Rosemary went on as if there was nothing unusual about his answer.

"My boss is Reid's stepmother," Cassie volunteered. "You probably remember his father, Jamey O'Shea."

"Oh, yes, I remember Jamey. He was a good-looking boy, and he never held a grudge against anyone, not even those parents of his. I don't mean to be saying anything bad about your grandparents, Reid, but they left that boy to fend pretty much for himself from the time he was little. Of course, Serenity was different back then. There were problems, but most of the people looked out for each other. People looked out for Jamey." Removing a vase from under the sink, Rosemary filled it with water and began trimming stems, then arranging the flowers in the vase. "I don't mind telling you, this family isn't too pleased with Cassie's new job. We worked a long time to get our kids away from Serenity, and then she goes back there to work."

"You always taught us to be charitable and help those who are less fortunate," Cassie reminded her.

"Yes, but this wasn't what we had in mind." Pausing in her work, Rosemary looked up at Reid. "Do you think Serenity is a fit place for a young woman to be working?"

"No, ma'am." He looked past her toward Cassie. "It's certainly not a fit place to live."

Cassie made a face at him behind her mother's back while Rosemary talked on. "It certainly isn't. At least we don't have to worry about *that*. With the salary this alternative school is paying, she can't afford to move out of Smith's condo. If we thought she had even the vaguest notion of moving down there, her father would have to put his foot down. We simply wouldn't allow it." Drawing a breath, she stuck the last bloom in place, surveyed the arrangement with satisfaction, then turned to Cassie. "I never asked what brings you and your friend by here this morning."

"Furniture. Remember that wicker dresser I asked you to keep for me?"

Her mother's nod made her gray hair bounce. "It's in the garage. So you're moving that into the condo. It doesn't exactly go with all that awful gray, does it?"

"It'll go fine. I have the perfect place in mind for it."

"I can't imagine where it might be," Rosemary said skeptically even as she removed a heavy ring of keys from a drawer. "Here you go. Be sure to lock up when you're done. When you come back, I'll have some cookies for you to take."

Cassie accepted the keys on their way out. She was sorting through them, looking for a possible match, when Reid fell into step beside her. "What are all those keys for?"

She smiled. "Heaven only knows, because Mama sure doesn't."

"Why doesn't she throw them away?"

"A suggestion various family members make every time we have to get into the garage. She says she can't throw them out because then she might find out what they go to, but then it would be too late." She sorted out seven padlock keys as they reached the garage and started through them methodically. The sixth one opened the lock.

The garage was dusty and warm. Narrow aisles stretched from front to back and all the way around the perimeter. Poverty's lessons could be hard to overcome, and for her parents, getting the most out of everything was one. They never threw anything away if there was the slightest chance that it could be fixed up and used again. Some of the stuff in the garage was truly important, to them if no one else, but some was just junk. Cassie liked to think that her wicker dresser fell into the first category, but she couldn't blame anyone for thinking otherwise.

"This is it." She began moving the boxes stacked on top, then Reid helped her carry it out into the sun.

"What color are you planning to paint it?" He gave it a shake, checking just as she had the day she'd bought it for five bucks. It was solid, old and of better quality than she could afford to buy new.

"Pale green. Tomorrow morning I'll take it to the classroom, spread out some drop cloths and spray it." She would line the drawers with pretty scented papers and slide it against the wall in her new bedroom, where it would look beautiful.

"Your mother's right. It would never fit in the condo."

She wiped away a cobweb from the dresser top, then uncomfortably met his gaze with its vague disapproval. Who would have guessed that Reid tough-guy Donovan wouldn't approve of lying to one's mother, even if it was for the mother's own peace of mind? "I plan to tell them that I've moved," she said lamely.

"When?"

"Eventually."

"You know they'll be hurt."

She wandered back into the garage, heading down one aisle to the shadowy stacks in the back. "They'll be upset," she disagreed even while acknowledging to herself that he was right. Her parents *would* be hurt. They wouldn't understand that this was something she felt compelled to do. They wouldn't even try to understand the connection she felt to Kathy's House and the school, to Karen, the rest of the staff, the kids, their families, to Jamey and to Reid. But they would accept it. Eventually.

Moving a box to a higher stack, she rested her hand on an old table that had stood beside the front door in the Serenity apartment. It wasn't particularly pretty, a half round painted a deep, almost black shade, with scalloped edges and turned legs, but she liked it. It would be perfect, with an old-fashioned lamp, in the hallway. "What do you think of this?"

He gave it the briefest of glances. "This isn't a store, you know, where you can walk up and down the aisles and say, 'I'll take this, this and this.'"

"Of course it is. That's why Mama and Daddy keep all this, so that someday it can be used again." She pulled the table out and carried it along in front of her. In the opposite corner, she found a bookcase, only two feet high and painted the ugliest rusty orange she'd ever seen. With no more coaxing than her best smile, Reid unearthed it and carried it outside.

"So you found something else." Rosemary approached them, a bouquet of flowers in one hand and a plastic-covered platter of cookies in the other. "If there's anything else you'd like, by all means, take it. All this stuff is just gathering dust out here."

"Thanks, Mama, but this should do it for now. Are the cookies for me?"

"No, the flowers are. If you want cookies, you can come over here and get them, like a daughter should. These are for Reid. You can just give the plate to Cassie when you're done," she said, turning her attention to him, "or bring it by the next time you're over this way. I'm almost always home."

He looked for a moment as if he didn't want to accept the gift. Was he so unused to anyone giving him anything but grief? Hadn't he ever been on the receiving end of such a simple gesture? Finally, though, he did take the plate with a murmur of thanks and carried it to the truck along with the bookcase.

"He seems like a nice young man, considering."

Cassie looked at her mother, who was watching Reid. "Considering what?" That he was from Serenity? That he was Meghan Donovan's son?

"That he has this look of desperate fear in his eyes. Has the boy never gone to meet a girl's parents before?"

"I don't know." She didn't go further, didn't explain that on Serenity few parents—*if* they were around—were interested in meeting the guys their daughters were involved with. Rosemary knew that. She also didn't point out that today's visit had nothing to do with Reid meeting Rosemary, that they didn't have that kind of relationship.

Yet.

"What does he do?"

He returned to pick up the dresser, easily hefting what she would have scooted along by herself. Once he was out of earshot, she replied, "He's a mechanic, and he helps out at O'Shea's."

"I seem to remember Jamey marrying that Donovan girl. Lasted all of three months. Why doesn't he have his father's name?"

"I guess Meghan didn't want him to. When she left Jamey, she took Reid to Georgia, then brought him back here when he was fifteen. He never saw his father the entire time."

"She was a pretty girl, but, heavens, was she selfish. I don't envy him for having lived with her." Rosemary shook her head in dismay, then heaved a sigh and patted Cassie's arm. "At least he's an improvement over that last one you brought around—that Trevor."

Cassie couldn't resist teasing. "A mechanic from Serenity Street better than an Ivy League MBA?"

"A fancy degree doesn't make a person worth knowing. It certainly takes more than that to be good enough for this family." Her mother handed her the flowers, then closed and locked the garage door. "Don't just stand there like a helpless female. Take that table to the truck so Reid can load it. Come back and see us soon." She gave Cassie a kiss, then raised her voice. "Reid, it was nice meeting you. Come back with Cassie to see us."

His only response was a nod, which Rosemary took for agreement. As she carried the flowers and the table to the truck, Cassie knew it was only acknowledgment. Maybe he would come back. Maybe he would find a reason to want to like her family. Maybe someday he would be happy to make regular visits over here, the way Smith did, the way all the other husbands did. It was wishful thinking, sure.

But wasn't that part of being Irish?

For all but six months of his life, Reid had lived in apartments so poorly constructed that privacy was only an illusion. At the Morgans' place, they had routinely gotten an earsplitting blow-by-blow of the next-door neighbors' daily fights. At his grandmother's apartment, he'd known as much about the intimate side of that neighbor's life as *she* had. In all the countless places he and Meghan had lived in Atlanta, there had been no secrets.

For the first time, that wasn't the case. So far, true to her word, Cassie was quiet. In the past eighteen hours or so, he'd heard little from next door—the occasional creak of a floorboard, the sound of something tumbling to the floor, the shower running this morning—but he hadn't forgotten, not for one second, that she was there. During the shower, he'd found it impossible to forget.

It was nearly nine o'clock on a warm, sticky Sunday morning, long past time for him to be up, but he still lay in bed. Thanks to his new neighbor, he'd had a restless night, too preoccupied with what was going on in her bedroom to relax enough to sleep in his own, too distracted by what had happened yesterday to rest through the night.

Cassie had been jealous. *Jealous.* Over *him.* In a perfect world, she shouldn't even know him. She certainly wouldn't have any interest in him. But hadn't he known for the past twenty years that this world was far from perfect?

Any average living, breathing man would have been flattered by the knowledge that she was interested in him. The idea scared him. It was one thing to want her and know he couldn't have her. It was another entirely to want her and know that he could. That he shouldn't, that maybe he wouldn't, but he *could,* for a while at least, until the novelty wore off for her. Until she realized once and for all that the reality of an affair with a rebel wasn't as romantic and appealing as the fantasy. Until she got tired of trying to relate to a man with whom she had nothing in common besides geographical location. Until she began longing for the companionship of her intelligent, elegant and sophisticated friends, the ones who read the same heavy, literary novels that had filled several of her boxes, the ones who shared her esoteric tastes in music, the ones who had accompanied her on her trips abroad.

The friends who couldn't be more different from him than light from dark. Good from bad. Mr. Right from Mr. Wrong.

He was wrong. He knew it, even if she didn't.

But just for a moment, lying there in his too-long-empty bed, he allowed himself the fantasy of wondering. Could they have an affair without either of them suffering for it? Could they move successfully from friendship to dating to intimacy, making love, sex?

He'd never engaged in casual sex. Sometimes his feelings for the woman were casual, he was ashamed to admit, but never for the act. He'd learned a long time ago that sex was one time when it was all right to touch and be touched, one time when physical contact didn't involve pain.

He suspected that sex with Cassie would be a whole new experience, one that he just might not ever get over.

He was in the process of untangling the threadbare sheet from his legs when a knock sounded at the door. In all the months he'd lived here, the only person who had ever come knocking at his door was Jamey, but something told him this wasn't his father. Maybe it was the sudden tightening in his chest or the queasy, anxious sensation in his stomach, but he knew it was Cassie.

Rising from the bed, he took a pair of clean jeans from the closet and pulled them on, fastening the metal buttons as he went to the door. For his own protection, he didn't open it wide, and he braced it with one hand on the knob. After the thoughts he'd just been having, the last thing he needed was to get too uncomfortably close to the object of them.

She looked as cool as an early-spring morning, her hair pulled back in a heavy braid, her summery dress so long that it almost hid the clunky sandals she wore. She was lovely, so incredibly perfect and untouchable that he wanted nothing in the world more than to do just that—to touch her bare shoulders, covered with no more than the narrowest of straps, to glide his hands over the swell of her breasts, her waist, her hips, to pull her close and undress her slowly, to look at her, kiss her and bury himself inside her.

"What do you want?" he asked abruptly, his voice hoarse, thick and heavy with desire.

"And good morning to you, too. You look like you just got up."

"I did."

"I'm sorry. I didn't mean to wake you."

"You didn't." He watched her go still, not breathing, not blinking as her gaze shifted toward the bedroom. "No."

She glanced at him. "No?"

"No one's in there. I'm alone." He had never brought a woman here because... Well, hell, because he'd thought that the only woman he had wanted in the past six months was way off-limits. But yesterday she seemed to have been telling him that she didn't want to be, and he wanted to believe it. Damned if he could, though.

With a hint of relief, she got to the point of her visit. "I came to invite you to a picnic."

"A picnic. I haven't had breakfast yet, and you're talking about lunch."

"A breakfast picnic." She pointed to the basket on the floor at the top of the stairs. It was large, round and filled with all the necessary items. Now that his mind was on it and off

Cassie's body, he could smell muffins, biscuits and bacon. He was hungry, he realized, for more than his usual cold cereal. He wanted to share her food and the old comforter folded over the stair rail. He wanted to share her morning.

"Let me get dressed," he said, hearing the grudging acceptance in his voice, hoping she didn't. If she did, she gave no sign of it. As he turned away, she was smiling, a quiet, private smile of triumph. She was genuinely happy that he had accepted her invitation, he reflected as he returned to the bedroom. He hadn't ever had an easy time of pleasing people. Whatever he did had always been wrong in Meghan's eyes, and for eleven years Jamey hadn't been much different. He hadn't liked the way Reid had behaved, the way he'd talked, the things he'd done, the people he'd hung out with, not even the way he had looked.

But Cassie was pleased, and over something so simple.

He dressed quickly, then locked up the apartment on his way to the bathroom down the hall. She was sitting on the top step, the basket beside her, the blanket cushioning her elbows on her knees. She was the first thing he saw when he came out of the apartment and the last thing he saw before he closed the bathroom door. Of course, she and her basket of food were the only things in the hall, but he doubted it would have made a difference if a crowd had surrounded her. He still would have zeroed in on her.

The bathroom was long and narrow, with a tub on the side that adjoined his bedroom. It wasn't a great old claw-foot like the one in Karen's house, but it was comfortably oversize, freestanding, with a shower head extending from the wall and a long plastic curtain that completely encircled the tub. Years ago, probably at the same time two apartments had been created from the original one-family unit, someone had knocked together shelves that reached all the way to the ceiling. Last week he had cleared his stuff off the lower shelves, leaving them for Cassie, and she had filled them in one afternoon. There were towels in bright red and yellow, each about twice as thick as one of his own, washcloths to match, shampoos, conditioners, creams, lotions, makeup and every other item a woman could possibly need.

He wouldn't even know she was here, she had promised, and he'd known then that it was a lie. In this small, drab room, he could close his eyes, could block out the sight of all her bright feminine belongings, and he would still know. Instead of dust and dampness, the scent was clean. Instead of Ivory soap, cheap shampoo and shaving cream, there were exotic scents blending together. One came from the clear pink bar of soap on the sink's edge, another from the cobalt blue perfume bottle on a shelf. All her toiletries had their own rich fragrances, all sweet, all feminine, all Cassie. They were better than the most expensive potpourri.

Scowling at his fixation, he turned on the water in the sink, brushed his teeth, combed his hair and quickly shaved. With one last, deep breath, he left the bathroom and joined Cassie at the stairs, smelling the same scents all over again. "Where are we going?"

There weren't many places of picnic quality within walking distance of the bar—just the little park Karen had rescued for the kids, Jackson Square or the park fronting the river. None of those offered any privacy at all, but if she'd wanted privacy, he reminded himself, she would have invited him to breakfast in her apartment, not out in public. But would he have accepted?

"You'll see." She led the way downstairs and out of the bar, across the street and around Kathy's House to the carriage house. Reid was puzzled until she turned the far corner and headed toward the back. When they'd finished the major work on the school, he and Jamey had built a pergola between the carriage house and the brick wall next door. They'd painted it pale blue to match the buildings and planted flowering vines that crisscrossed the top and shrubs that provided privacy front and back. The arbor was intended for use as an outdoor classroom, a perfect, somewhat secluded place to conduct lessons on a warm spring day.

He would be willing to learn a few lessons inside its sweet-scented cover.

They spread out the comforter, old and lumpy in places, then she began unloading the food while he watched from the opposite side. She knew he was watching, but she didn't seem to mind at all. In fact, if pressed, he would say she rather enjoyed it.

Finally the food was ready. She handed him a plate, along with a small chilled bottle of orange juice, as she asked, "Did I remember to thank you for all your help yesterday?"

"Yeah." From her mother's house, they had gone to a Greek restaurant tucked between a Laundromat and an insurance office. The dining room was cramped, the food good, the prices low. After the meal, they had come back to Serenity, unloaded the furniture at her classroom, and then she had walked across the street and upstairs with him. At her door, she had given him one of those smiles that no woman should ever wear with anything else. Those intimate little smiles should be reserved for sex, for those first few minutes after she'd been well and truly satisfied, when she was naked and within reach and willing to be seduced again, pleading to be satisfied again.

She had thanked him for helping, though the smile had been thanks enough, and then she had gone into her apartment and closed the door, leaving him standing in the hall, so damn needy that he hurt. He would have sacrificed everything he had and everything he might ever have for just one touch of her hand, for just one brief brush against her body. He had gone to his apartment feeling utterly empty and hadn't come out again except for his shower—his decidedly cold shower, which hadn't helped a bit.

"I could have managed," she remarked as she broke a freshly peeled orange into halves and offered him one. "But I'm glad I didn't have to. I enjoyed your company."

Her last, simple words brought him such pleasure that he had to force his attention to his breakfast. The plates were pottery, heavy, bright orange and fuchsia. They must have been in one of her boxes, because they certainly hadn't come from O'Shea's kitchen. There were biscuits, some with butter, some with grape jelly. She had put all of the ones with bacon sandwiched between the layers on his plate. She had also baked blueberry muffins and peeled and sliced a sweet ripe cantaloupe to go with the oranges. It was a simple breakfast, but eating here in the arbor made it special.

Or was it Cassie who made it special?

"What are your plans for today?" After wiping her fingers on a cloth napkin, she pushed her plate aside and stretched out on her side, resting her head on one hand.

He simply shrugged. His only weekend plans usually involved staying away from Serenity, usually alone. He hadn't managed on either point yesterday. Every trip they had taken away from Serenity had brought them back again, and he hadn't been alone until the middle of the afternoon. Then he'd spent the rest of the day wishing he wasn't.

"You'll have dinner with your folks. By the way, I've been invited. Do you mind?"

A week ago, he had minded a hell of a lot. Now he shook his head.

"What else? What will you do this afternoon?"

"Not much."

"You work mornings at the garage and evenings at the bar. When do you see your friends?"

He met her gaze evenly, unflinchingly. "I don't have any friends," he said, his voice deliberately mild. "You know that."

She didn't flinch, either. "Tanya is willing to be your friend."

"Tanya likes sex."

"Liking one doesn't preclude the other. When the time comes, I'm sure I'll like sex, too, but it won't diminish my capacity to be a friend."

Reid stilled in the act of stacking his plate on top of hers. He would have sworn that he'd heard wrong, but the faint color creeping into her face confirmed that he hadn't. "You mean you've never—"

She shook her head.

"You're a—"

A nod this time.

A virgin. She was a virgin. God help him, he'd been having all sorts of lewd fantasies about a *virgin*. The very idea should appall him, and there was some tiny part of him that *was* shocked. By the age of fifteen, girls who didn't put out—who weren't looking for affection wherever they could find it— were a rarity on Serenity.

But there was another part that found the idea oddly, powerfully arousing. He had never been with a virgin before. From his own very first time on, the women in his life had been at least as experienced as he was, usually more. But Cassie wasn't. He could be her first. He could seduce her. He could teach her everything he'd learned, could make it an experience neither of them would ever forget. He could promise her a great deal of pleasure in exchange for her virginity, and he would do his damnedest to make sure she never regretted it.

Then a bitter ache settled over him. Sure, he could be her first, and it would be incredibly sweet. But how much sweeter it would be if he could also be her last.

If he could always be her only.

Chapter 5

At least he hadn't run the other way.

Cassie lay on her back, her eyes narrowed against the sun, her attention centered on the man a few feet away. She would have understood if Reid had greeted her announcement with a departure. There had been a time when an unmarried woman would have paid for the loss of her virginity with banishment, shame or even death, but these days it didn't seem to matter much. Most teenage girls were eager to be relieved of it, and although there were a few who considered it proof of their prowess, most boys and young men weren't thrilled by the burden of taking it. The last few men she'd dated had thought her odd for considering it something worth keeping. Her girlfriends thought she was strange, too. Saving oneself for marriage was an idea that had long ago fallen from favor.

Actually she wasn't waiting for marriage. That was something that might take years, if it ever happened at all. Marriage after thirty was becoming increasingly common—Jolie had been closer to forty when she and Smith got married—and while Cassie wanted to wait, she didn't want to wait forever.

No, she was simply waiting for the right man. When she knew in her heart that she'd found him, she would give up her virginity willingly, happily, even eagerly. But not until then. Not for a few hours of questionable pleasure. Not for physical satisfaction that didn't touch her heart.

Maybe that was why she had so casually and out of the blue announced her status to Reid. Because he *did* touch her heart. Because he had from the very first time she'd seen him. He hadn't even noticed her that evening; she was sure. There had been a lot of people at Karen's, and he had been preoccupied with keeping Ryan Morgan in line. But she had noticed him. After the party had broken up and everyone else had gone, she had stayed to help Karen clean up and tried to find out everything about him. Her boss hadn't been willing to offer much, but it had been enough to send Cassie home feeling as if something momentous had happened. It had been enough to fuel all her favorite fantasies for quite a long time.

Now the man himself was providing the fuel.

Across the blanket, he stretched out, resettled. Deliberately she focused her gaze on the vines overhead. She loved wisteria, with its clusters of cascading lilac blooms. When the family had moved to the Oak Street house, there had been a thick, ropy wisteria vine entwined around the live oak outside her bedroom window. In the brief time it bloomed each spring, the delicate flowers had been the first thing she'd seen every morning and, thanks to her mother's storytelling, the last thing on her mind at night.

Slowly she smiled. She hadn't thought of the tale in years, but she remembered it clearly. "Do you know why, in nature, the wisteria vine prefers to wrap itself around the oak?"

Reid's only answer was a shake of his head.

"Want me to tell you?" She'd always had a fondness for storytelling, one that all her young nieces and nephews and now her students appreciated, but she had never indulged herself with a mature audience, particularly one who'd never been indulged with many tales as a child.

Again his only response was movement, a shrug this time. She took it as a yes.

"There was once a man living in a lovely forest. He was strong and brown from working hard in the sun all day. He lived alone, and he was lonely until one day a woman came to live nearby. She was a kind woman with the longest, brownest hair he'd ever seen, and she always dressed in purple." Remembering that her dress today was the brightest, purest, fit-for-royalty purple, she grimaced. If Reid accused her of making up the story and tailoring it specifically to them, who could blame him? Still, this was the way she'd heard the story countless times, and so she went on.

"The handsome man and the pretty woman became friends. Soon their friendship turned to love, and their love grew and grew. One evening the man returned from a hard day's work, and the woman, wearing her purple dress, met him in the forest. As he held her, they knew that they had never been so happy, and they wished they could be together like that for all time. In the blink of an eye, their wish came true. He was transformed into the strongest, tallest oak in the whole forest, and she became the wisteria vine, clothed in delicate purple blossoms, entwined with her true love for all eternity."

From the other side of the blanket, there was momentary silence, then a sudden burst of laughter. "That's the sappiest story I've ever heard."

The sound of his amusement spread warmth through her and made her smile as she turned her head toward him to gently scold. "You're not a romantic."

"No," he agreed, sobering. "What I know about romance is probably far less than you know about sex."

"Hey, I go to movies and read books. I've got twelve brothers and sisters and a million nieces and nephews. I know plenty about sex. I just haven't experienced it yet." She looked up at the wisteria and the patches of blue sky that showed through. "My mother used to tell me that story at bedtime every spring when the wisteria was in bloom. It was better than any fairy tale. I wanted to be the wisteria lady."

"You're certainly dressed for it."

"Coincidence." She didn't point out that he was equally suited to the costarring role. He was handsome and strong, and his skin was the loveliest shade of golden brown. He was lonely and lived alone—sometimes so alone that her heart ached—and he had a nearby neighbor with long brown hair who wanted to be friends and so much more, who thought eternity with him sounded like a wonderful place to be.

Rolling onto his back, he pillowed his head on his arms. "Let me see if I can remember one of Meghan's bedtime stories." He was silent for a moment, then began. "'I'm going down to the bar on the corner. Don't answer the door, be asleep when I get back and if you hear anything from the bedroom, stay the hell out. I should be back in eight or ten hours. Be good and don't whine about dinner, and maybe for breakfast I'll take you to McDonald's.'" His smile was thin and bitter. "I like your mother's better."

Cassie swallowed over the lump in her throat. "Why would you whine about dinner? Was she a lousy cook?"

"When Meghan was ready to party, the last thing she wanted was to take care of a hungry kid, so she didn't."

So she put him to bed hungry, and *maybe* the next morning she fed him. What a lovely mother.

Cassie rolled onto her stomach, closer to his side of the blanket, supporting herself on her elbows, and studied him. His expression was open, no longer amused but not particularly bitter, either. "Do you hate her?"

"She's my mother."

"She's the woman who gave birth to you. She's not a mother, not in any real sense of the word. She should have given you up for adoption. The state should have taken you away from her."

His shrug was the mere lifting of one shoulder. "I was okay."

Okay. He had been neglected, abandoned, mistreated, abused and unloved, but he was *okay.* She wanted to rail at the unfairness of his life, to vent her anger and disgust. She wanted to weep. Mostly, though, she wanted to make everything all right. She wanted to somehow undo the damage Meghan had done, to give him all the things his mother had denied him—security. Affection. Maybe even love.

Gently backing away from that last thought, she studied her clasped hands. "You're a better person than me. I would want to punish her."

From the corner of her eye, she saw him look her way, but he didn't speak right away. He simply waited for her to meet his gaze, waited until she couldn't stop herself if she wanted. "You think her life isn't punishment enough?" he asked once he had her undivided attention. "She's been poor since she was born—not just Serenity Street poor, but going-hungry-living-on-the-streets-selling-her-body-to-survive poor. She's gotten drunk, gotten high, gotten laid and gotten beaten too many times to count. She's degraded herself just trying to live. She's got nothing to be proud of, no dignity, no self-respect and no one to give a damn about her when she dies. What more could you possibly do to her?"

Cassie bit her lower lip. He was right. When someone's life had already sunk as low as it was possible to go, there was little that could be done to punish them further. She wanted to anyway. She wanted Meghan Donovan to suffer for what she'd done to her son. But maybe she did. Maybe in all these years she'd lived without Reid, she had come to realize what a precious gift she had thrown away. Maybe she'd finally understood that her son had been her best chance to be loved and her best reason for living a better life. Maybe she was drowning in regret. But probably not.

"You're wrong, you know," she said quietly. "She does have something to be proud of. You."

He carried such burdens, both emotional and spiritual, that he usually gave the impression of age and soul-deep weariness, but the blush that colored his cheeks now made him look adorably younger. It didn't last long, though, only until he changed the subject without comment and asked, "Are you planning to work on the dresser today?"

"Yes. Since I provided breakfast in such a lovely setting, are you willing to offer your help?"

"So the food was a bribe."

"It was," she admitted without hesitation. "You got a free breakfast, and I got the pleasure of your company."

"Hardly a fair trade."

Feigning injured feelings, she let her lower lip jut out. "I think I'm a pretty decent cook."

"You are." He gave another awkward little shrug as he shifted his gaze overhead. "But I'm pretty lousy company."

She sat up and began gathering everything into the basket. In college she'd had a friend who had made remarks like that with regularity. Cassie's role in the relationship had been to disagree and to reassure. *No, Ellen, you don't look fat. No, Ellen, you didn't deserve that grade. No, Ellen, that color doesn't wash you out. No, Ellen, you're not self-centered.* Eventually she had figured out that constant reassurance had been the whole point behind Ellen's constant self-disparagement, and since that was no basis for a friendship, she had ended it.

Reid, however, wasn't looking for disagreement or reassurance. He was simply stating the facts as he'd been taught them.

"Do you mind if I tell you something personal?"

Slowly he sat up, drawing one knee up and resting his arm on it. "You just told me that you're a virgin. How much more personal can you get?"

She smiled. Only about two feet separated them right now, not enough to help her resist the temptation that was deviling her. Scooting closer, she nudged his arm over just a bit and rested her own arm beside it on his knee. She could feel his muscles tighten, could hear the uneven tempo his breathing fell into. He wanted to pull away so hard and so fast that she would fall flat, but she suspected he couldn't bring himself to move. "I like you, Reid," she said softly. "I like you a lot."

As the flush returned hotter and deeper than ever, she pushed against his leg to get to her feet, then offered her hand. He looked at it for a moment, then another, before reluctantly accepting it. She pulled, but doubted that she was really any help in getting him to his feet. He used his own strength and simply held her hand. Even once he was up, he held it loosely, his palm warm, his skin callused, his fingers lean and strong. Tilting her head back, she met his gaze, and she tried to smile, to make light of the moment, but her mouth wouldn't cooperate.

He looked so serious. His eyes were filled with shadows, his jaw set stubbornly. If she didn't know better, she might think he was angry. But she did know better. He was uncomfortable. He was probably searching for a polite way to push her away. He would let her walk into his arms and kiss him as if her life depended on it, no matter how much he didn't want her there, no matter how little he wanted her kiss, because he didn't know how to gently say no. Hadn't he proved yesterday with Tanya that he was uncomfortable rejecting unwanted advances?

For a moment, she considered doing it anyway—taking the few steps that would close the distance between them. Wrapping both arms around his neck. Inching that final millimeter forward so her body was in complete contact with his. Sliding her fingers into his hair, persuading him to bend his head and finally, finally, taking his mouth with hers. So what if he didn't want her to do it? She didn't think he would find her totally repugnant—no man ever had—and who knew? Maybe he even would discover that he liked it. Maybe he would like it enough to want more.

And maybe he wouldn't. Maybe he *would* find her repugnant. Maybe he would rather kiss Tanya or Alicia or any other woman on Serenity than her.

She forced her fingers to go limp. All he had to do was open his hand, and he would be free to walk away. She waited for him to do it, to let go and leave her, but he didn't.

Instead, he raised his free hand, hesitated, then touched her hair. She wished instantly that she'd worn it down this morning, no matter that down was hot, that down was certainly no style for cleaning and painting old furniture. As his palm slid the length of her braid, he looked regretful, as if he, too, wished it were down. When he reached the end, he lowered his hand to his side once again, then finally spoke. His voice was husky, thick and made her think of long nights, wicked games, sex and heat and her big, empty bed. "Don't tempt me, Cassie."

She liked the idea that she could. "How am I tempting you?" she asked, her own voice as husky. "Tell me."

For one brief moment, he seemed torn by what he wanted to do and what he thought he should do. Then he reached for her, his fingers closing around her wrists, using the grip to pull her close, to guide her arms around his back, to clasp her hands together at the small of his back. "Don't let me think I can do this," he murmured, bringing his hands to her shoulders.

They were close now, closer than they'd ever been. When a breeze blew through the arbor, it wrapped the long, loose folds of her skirt around his legs. The lightweight challis caught on denim, hanging for an instant before falling again.

"Don't let me think you might want this." He slid his hands over skin and narrow straps, along her throat to her jaw. "Don't make me think you want..." The rest of his warning was forgotten as his mouth brushed hers once, twice, before settling for a kiss. There was no hesitance, no reluctance, just instant need, instant heat. It made her weak and hungry, robbed her of breath, of thought and reason, of everything except pure, hot sensation. Her nerves trembled. Her muscles tightened. She had never felt such intensity, had never experienced such fierce need. She wanted him to stop before it was too late, before she discovered some secret, hidden, shameless part of herself that would cling to him. She wanted him to never stop.

But he did. After only a moment—or maybe an hour—he drew back. Underneath the tan, his face was pale, his blue eyes dazed. He was breathing heavily, and his fingers, where they touched her jaw, were trembling. For a long time, he simply stared down at her. Then he gave a shake of his head as if trying to clear it. "Don't tempt me, Cassie," he repeated, but this time it wasn't a warning. It was a plea.

A prayer.

It was hot in the classroom, in spite of the open windows and door. Reid sat on the floor, half of an old Sunday *Times-Picayune* spread in front of him and the ugly little half-round table standing at an angle. He had stripped the top and bottom shelves down to bare wood and decided that it wasn't so ugly after all. Now he was using a giant scrub pad to remove the heavy layers of stain and paint from the ornately curved legs and the fluted shelf edges and making very slow progress.

It didn't help that the work was tedious and allowed his mind to wander. It sure as hell didn't help that it kept wandering to Cassie, only a few yards away, barefoot and bent in front of the old dresser with her full skirt tucked tightly between her legs to control the excess fabric. He wondered if she realized that her position pulled the skirt taut across her bottom or that the top of the dress gapped enough around the oversize armholes to offer a glimpse of the swell of her breast. Just a glimpse. Too much. Not enough.

He wanted to see more. To touch. Kiss. Stroke. Claim. Hell, yes, he wanted to claim her, every inch of her, for his own.

He'd spent the first hour in here working to convince himself that he regretted the kiss and the next trying to persuade himself that it had been enough, that it had satisfied her curiosity and his hunger. Then they'd gone to lunch in Karen's backyard, sharing the picnic bench once again, and Cassie had touched him, bumped him and leaned against him often enough to make him break out in a cold sweat. He had finally admitted that the kiss had just been the beginning. Unless he discovered some tremendous new strength, there would be more. No matter how wrong, no matter how selfish on his part, there would be more.

God help him, he might not survive it, but as long as *she did*...

Realizing that he'd quit work completely and was instead simply watching her, he forced his attention back to the table. He had volunteered to do this piece instead of the bookcase, which she had stripped completely in the time it had taken him to do half of one turned leg. He'd completed the leg while she had sprayed the first coat of pale green paint over the wicker dresser. She had completed the first coat of white enamel on the bookcase and was now finishing the dresser's second coat of green, while he still worked on his one piece.

A dozen feet away, she laid the spray can on the floor, then bent lower, until her palms were spread flat on the tile. It was a backache-easing, bone-popping sort of stretch, the kind he indulged in after a long morning under the hood of a car, but he had damn sure never looked that good doing it. She straightened slowly, unfolding, rising vertebra by vertebra to her full height, then came to crouch across the papers from him.

"You know, if I'd had to do it myself, I probably would have painted it," she announced as she watched him work. "I would have just given it a light sanding, then added one more layer of paint."

He shook his head. "You would have had to strip it. There are at least eight or ten coats on here already."

"I wouldn't have the patience to do it right." She blew out an exaggerated sigh. "Want something cold?"

"Yeah. How about a bucket of ice water over my head?" His face was damp with sweat, and so was his T-shirt. His jeans were sticky and uncomfortable, and, like Cassie, he'd kicked his shoes off a long time ago.

"At least you could take your shirt off." She used the hem of her dress to blot her forehead.

"So could you," he retorted without thinking. Then, hearing his own words, he looked up sharply and found her giving him a speculative look. Deciding to bluff it out, he shrugged. "It's private back here. If you didn't tell, no one would know."

"*You* would know." Her voice was soft, full of promise,

and made the muscles in his belly clench. It stirred to life his desire, so recently settled, so long unsatisfied, so impossible to ignore.

"Yeah," he agreed, his mouth dry. "But I wouldn't tell, either."

"It would be our secret, huh?" Somehow her voice managed to get even softer, less substantial, breathless. *He* was pretty damn breathless himself. "Of course, you make this suggestion knowing full well that this is a one-piece dress, that I don't have a shirt to take off."

"And knowing full well that if you did, you wouldn't." Not that he knew any such thing. Again he was simply bluffing, hoping that, since she was young and virginal, modesty would prevail.

She gracefully got to her feet and started toward the back of the room. She'd gone only a few feet past him when abruptly she came back, placed both hands on his shoulders from behind and bent until her mouth was only a breath above his ear. "Someday, Reid," she whispered, "I'm going to surprise you."

He waited until her footsteps faded into the storeroom before murmuring to himself, "You do every day, darlin'. *Every* day."

She returned a short while later with two cups of tepid tap water. He would prefer the bucket of ice water—or seeing her half-naked—but this was better than nothing. He had learned in his life to be grateful for anything more than nothing.

"You're good with your hands."

The familiar words made him stiffen. Jamey had made the same observation one day last fall. The surprise accompanying his words had made it clear that he'd never expected his only son to amount to anything, to ever display any talent that wasn't illegal, to ever do anything for good rather than harm. "I can draw, paint, use a hammer or handle a shovel. I can reglaze a window, refinish a table, build walls or tear them down." Out of habit, his voice turned sarcastic. "I can also pick any lock on this street, hot-wire any car or disarm your

basic burglar alarm. I can break into a place and clean it out
while the owners are asleep in their bed, and I know the fences
who will offer the best prices for the merchandise. Anything
you want—illegal drugs, illegal weapons, somebody killed—
I can send you to the best person for the job. For more than
a few of your standard crimes, I *am* the best person for the
job.''

"Why, you can do just about anything." Her tone was sarcastic, too, and mocking. "You show particular talent for
building those walls, don't you?"

Uneasily he glanced at her. She was giving him the sort of
look he imagined she must give her students when they mis-
behaved, a chiding, chastening look designed to make him feel
about two inches tall.

"It was a simple compliment, Reid. You could have said
thanks. You didn't have to say anything at all." She folded
her hands primly in her lap. "So...who would I go to down
here for drugs?"

"Tommy Murphy or one of the Rodriguez brothers."

"What about weapons?"

"Vinnie Marino, Trevor Morgan or the Rodriguezes." He
gave her a narrow, warning look. "Of course, you go asking
something of Vinnie Marino, he's going to want a lot more
than money in payment."

She didn't look as if the idea bothered her in the least. "And
what do *you* want in payment for your favors?"

His skin heated, as if, in a heartbeat, the temperature in the
room had gone from springtime-warm to blasting-furnace hot.
How many favors would he have to do to earn the payment
he had in mind? Thousands of them? Millions? "I don't want
anything," he mumbled, focusing on the table once more.

"Then you're a much more generous person than I am."
Returning to their earlier conversation, she asked, "Where did
you learn about tools and cars and things?"

He shrugged. "I just learned." He couldn't say how exactly. From time to time in Atlanta, he had helped one neighbor or another work on their cars. He'd had a friend or two

with cars of their own, and he'd read a lot. The rest just seemed to come naturally.

"Oh, I see. We all have an engine-repair gene in our makeup, and yours got magically activated—probably because you're a man—while mine is defective—probably because I'm a woman—which is why I don't notice little things like oil lights, loose belts or low tires."

"Makes as much sense as your version of why wisteria grows on oaks."

She raised her head high. "I suppose you have a better theory."

"Maybe it's an epiphyte, like Spanish moss. It doesn't take anything away from the host, but it doesn't contribute anything, either. It just needs a place to grow. Or maybe it's a parasite. Maybe it's sucking the life right out of that oak, wrapping its woody little tendrils around it until the oak can't breathe or get any sunlight, suffocating it until finally it dies." He'd intended that last part to be a little goofy, like her story, but she wasn't amused, and too late, with a glance at her purple dress, he realized why. Only an idiot would fail to recognize the similarities between them and her silly tale. Apparently he was an idiot, because he'd just twisted it to make the wisteria lady—Cassie—a life-stealing parasite destroying the tree—him—with her very presence. He muttered a heart-felt "Damn."

For a moment, she sat very still, not saying anything, not doing anything. Then, her voice cool, her tone distant, she spoke. "Epiphyte. Now, there's a word I haven't heard since high-school science."

"I came across it somewhere," he mumbled. Bending closer to the table, he traded the stripping pad for a toothbrush and worked to loosen a particularly stubborn bit of paint. When it finally came loose, he glanced up but didn't make eye contact with her. "I didn't mean..." He didn't go on, and she didn't prompt him. With another curse, he tried to focus all of his attention on the table.

After a moment, she returned to work, too, cleaning the

paintbrushes, making sure the lids were secure, then scrubbing bits of green-and-white paint from her hands and arms with a paper towel dipped in mineral spirits. It was the same way they'd spent the past several hours—mostly working, talking a little—but the nature of it had changed. Before, the silence had been easy, companionable. Now it was stiff, stilted. He felt guilty, and she…she probably wondered why she even bothered. She could find plenty of men to spend her free time with, easier men, men more like her, more like everyone's expectations of her. If she gave any hint that she was interested, they would no doubt line up at her door, willing to accept whatever she offered and be grateful for whatever it was.

Intensely hating the idea of Cassie with another man, he finished the last leg with more energy than it required, wiped the entire piece down with mineral spirits, then got to his feet. "Now what?"

She was standing ten feet in front of the dresser, arms folded across her chest, studying it. After a moment, she glanced at him as if his question had just registered and shrugged. "I think that's enough for today. I'll leave everything here for now, then put it in the back room this evening. I'll work on it again tomorrow night."

Not tomorrow after school, when he would be free to help, but tomorrow night, when he would be tending bar at O'Shea's. After the stupid remarks he'd made, she might never again ask him to help with anything. She certainly wouldn't want his advice, but he offered it anyway. "You can't stay over here alone at night." Serenity was safer these days, but just like before, you could never predict when or where violence would occur. All it would take was for Vinnie Marino, Trevor Morgan or one of their buddies to see Cassie alone at the school—not at all difficult with the lights on and the windows and door open. They never missed the chance to harass a vulnerable woman. If they had even the vaguest idea of his interest in this particular woman, *harass* wouldn't begin to cover what they might do.

"It won't be a problem. Karen and Jamey will be only thirty feet away." The words were accompanied by a look that was cool and dismissive, a nonverbal reminder that he was in no position to be granted a say in what she did. Well, damn it, he *did* have a say. Maybe he didn't deserve it. Maybe he had no right to it, but he was going to say it anyway.

"It's a hell of a lot farther than thirty feet to their quarters at the other end of the house. From the living room, Jamey and Karen can't see the carriage house and, unless all the windows are open and everything is quiet inside, they can't hear anything, either. Vinnie and his friends are good at what they do. Their victims rarely get the chance to scream even once. So it *is* a problem—one that I'll discuss with Jamey."

The faint acknowledgment of defeat entered her eyes before she looked away. Jamey might not refuse flat out to let her work in the school at night, but he would insist on being there with her, which would mean sacrificing the few hours he had free to spend with Karen. Cassie wouldn't let him do that.

If she had lost this point, why didn't he feel as if he'd won? Why did he feel like some selfish, mean-spirited bastard who had stolen her pleasure just for the fun of it?

He went to stand beside her, looking, as she still was, at the dresser. "It looks good."

"Yes, it does." After each coat of paint, she'd given it a few minutes to dry, then wiped it lightly with a cloth, removing just enough of the paint to let the white show through. It gave the piece the look of a wash, light and airy, well suited to the wicker's weave. It would fit perfectly in her bedroom with the white bed and the sunny yellow walls. Now all she needed to complete the room was a chair, a big one that could be filled with pillows, that would be just the right place for reading, relaxing or just thinking.

At the same time, they each spoke the other's name. He'd been about to offer an apology, but he swallowed it and waited instead for her to go first.

"I appreciate your help. If I'd had to strip that table myself, it would have taken forever," she said, awkward for the first time since he'd met her. "Now I'll keep the promise I made last week. I won't bother you anymore."

"Honey, you bother me whether you're standing right here in front of me asking favors or pretending that I don't exist."

Looking unhappy and regretful, she continued to stare past him to the dresser. "I'm sorry. I didn't mean…" Then hopefully, "I can move. I can find another place down here. I can stay at Smith's condo until—"

A few strands of her hair had worked free of the braid and curled damply beneath her ear. Reaching out, barely touching her, he lifted them, smoothed them behind her ear, then let his hand slide down to her shoulder, let his fingertips glide down her arm past her wrist, wrapping lightly, just enough to catch, around her hand. "Do you honestly think a few buildings or a few miles will make a difference? It's too late for that, Cassie. You could find a place on the moon, and you would still bother me. You would still be the only thing on my mind. You would still be the only woman I…" At last, good sense and self-preservation caught up with him, stopping the words before they escaped. *The only woman I want. The only woman I fantasize about. The only woman, God help me, that I could need forever.*

After a moment's hesitation, she curled her fingers around his, not tightly, just enough so he could feel the pressure, then gave him a faintly wary look. "But you don't want that. You don't want to be bothered."

He sighed softly. "I don't know what I want." But that wasn't true. He wanted *her*. He just couldn't convince himself that it was all right to have her. He couldn't convince himself that it wasn't desperately wrong, that it wouldn't lead to more sorrow than he'd ever known, more sorrow than she ever should know.

She gave his hand a squeeze, then pulled hers free and stuck both hands deep in the pockets of her dress. "You figure it out, and when you do, let me know. Until then, I'll keep my distance. I won't speak to you. I won't do anything to remind you that I'm around." Turning, she walked to the door, switched off the fluorescent lights overhead, then waited, facing the street, for him to join her.

Leaning against a table, he pulled his sneakers on without untying them, then crossed to the door. She didn't turn or give any indication that she knew he was behind her, not even when he made the second-biggest mistake of his life and slid his arms around her waist, pulling her body against his, followed by the biggest mistake: honesty, pure, harsh and merciless.

"I want you, Cassie. I want you so damn much I hurt with it. But I can't give you anything. All my life, I've been told I'm no good, that I'm worthless, and no matter how hard I try, I can't find any reason to not believe it. I've been in trouble with the cops since I was a kid. I don't have any real relationship with my family. I've got two lousy part-time jobs that any idiot could do, but I'm damn lucky to have them because no one in his right mind would hire me. I don't have any friends, and I've got a whole neighborhood full of enemies. Any way you look at it, I'm a loser, Cassie. It's all I've ever been, and it's all I ever will be. I'm the last thing you need in your life."

She brought her hands up to his wrists and grasped them tightly. "What if I think you're the *only* thing I need?"

"You'd be wrong."

Releasing him, she twisted around to face him. She was smiling, one of those quiet little smiles that robbed him of his ability to reason. "I'm never wrong, Reid. Not about what I want. Not about what I need."

"You could get hurt." That was easier than saying it the other way. *I could hurt you.* No matter how he phrased it, though, the end result would be the same. She could suffer, and it would be his fault. It would be unforgivable and, possibly, unavoidable.

"Maybe. Life's full of risks, Reid. Maybe we'll have an affair and wind up as friends. Maybe it'll end and you'll hate me. Or maybe we'll fall in love and live happily ever after. We'll never know until we try."

Her words brought to mind a conversation he'd had with

Karen last summer. Someday, she had suggested, he might
meet a woman, fall in love and discover that their lives weren't
complete without children. At the time, he'd thought she was
crazy on all counts. He'd known too well that this world was
no place for children—certainly not for *his* children. As for
falling in love, hell, he'd had less personal experience with
love than Cassie had had with sex.

But Cassie was suggesting that loving him was at least
within the realm of possibility. Maybe she was crazy...or
maybe she knew what she was talking about. Maybe someplace thoroughly hidden deep inside him there was something
worth having, something worth loving. Maybe she could find
it, and maybe she could teach him to find the same feelings
within himself.

It was tempting. God help him, it was almost more than he
could refuse. He'd lived a lifetime of never measuring up, of
never being enough, of living alone and unwanted, and now
she was offering to change all that. She was offering things
he'd never believed he would have, things he had never believed he deserved, things he had never even let himself want.
He'd known since he was a kid not to waste his time on impossible dreams. Now Cassie was saying that it was neither
impossible nor a dream. All he had to do was take a chance.
Face the risks.

And if she was wrong about needing him, about the possibility of loving him? If there was nothing for them but an
affair—no love, no happily-ever-after, no future, no nothing?
Well, it wouldn't be the first time he'd lost...though it would
be the worst.

And if there *was* more? The possibility was too important,
too dangerous, to consider.

Life's full of risks, Reid. We'll never know until we try.

With a sigh, he brushed his fingers lightly over her cheek.
"You'll regret this," he warned.

"No, I won't." She sounded so confident, so sure of herself.
He wished he shared her confidence, but he knew better. He'd
made too many mistakes in his lifetime to kid himself about

the enormity of this one. There was one very small chance that this could turn out well, and about a million tremendous chances that it would destroy him. Not very good odds.

But when had life ever given him very good odds?

Cassie closed the classroom door, locked it and started toward the street. Reid fell into step beside her, his jaw set, his expression troubled, his gaze distant. She could easily hate Jamey and Meghan for what they'd done to their son, but Jamey had carried his own blame and guilt for a long time. As for Meghan, Cassie had never laid eyes on the woman, but, yeah, she could hate her. If she was alive. If she hadn't drunk or drugged herself into an early grave.

As they stopped outside O'Shea's and Reid pulled out his keys to open the door, she suggested, "Let's clean up and go somewhere."

"Where?"

"I don't know. We could play tourists in the Quarter or take my car and get out of town. We could go for a drive."

With a shrug, he opened the door and waited for her to go in. "Okay." That was all he said, and not with a lot of enthusiasm. That was all right. She could be excited enough for both of them.

Upstairs he went into his apartment while she scrubbed the foul-smelling mineral spirits and paint from her hands and arms. Dipping a cloth in cool water, she grimaced at her reflection in the mirror. She hadn't bothered with makeup this morning. Her face was damp and flushed, and her hair was working free of the braid and frizzing. She wasn't a pretty sight. No wonder Reid had put his arms around her from behind, instead of face-to-face, there in the classroom.

But what counted was that he *had* done it. It was nothing less than a miracle.

She washed her face, brushed her hair back and secured it with a tortoiseshell clasp, then left the bathroom for her apartment. After knocking at Reid's open door and calling that the bathroom was free, she let herself into her apartment and quickly changed into khaki shorts and a white button-down shirt, both neatly tailored and pressed.

Leaving the apartment, she locked up once more, then sat down on the top step to wait. Only a moment later, he came out of the bathroom, his hair damp, his T-shirt from this morning wadded in one hand. She tried to swallow but couldn't, tried to look away but wouldn't. She had been half-teasing earlier when she'd recommended that he deal with the heat by taking off his shirt. If he'd done it then in those few steamy moments that had followed her suggestion, her virtue would be long lost. They would still be on the floor over there, doing all sorts of things that had never been taught in school.

"Give me a minute to change," he said, coming toward her. If he noticed that she'd gone hot, wondered about her inability to move or recognized the appreciation that surely must be in her eyes, he gave no sign of it on his way into his apartment.

Finally she breathed, expelling the air that threatened to explode her lungs. It was perfectly all right to find the male form appealing. If men and women didn't find each other physically attractive, where would the human race be? Still, she felt like a silly schoolgirl seeing her first devastatingly handsome, sinfully sexy, bare-chested man up close and personal. She was almost too giddy for words.

She—Cassandra Wade, described by all who knew her as overly mature, serious, calm, elegant, refined, cool, distant and aloof—was giddy. Now, there was something that didn't happen every day.

Through the open door, she could hear sounds drifting out—drawers closing, the closet door squeaking, footsteps. She leaned back for a glimpse inside. What little she could see was depressing. Green walls, faded unevenly by the sun that came through the front windows. Gold drapes that looked like something her mother might have thrown away twenty years ago. A sofa as battered and lumpy as her own. One end table, one coffee table and a plain wooden floor in need of a little TLC.

It wasn't the drabness she found depressing, though. It was the utter lack of personality. From her vantage point, she could see absolutely nothing that said Reid Donovan lived there, nothing that said *anyone* lived there. No books or magazines on the tables. No pictures on the wall. No cozy little pillows or throws. No knickknacks, keepsakes or souvenirs. No sign of his artwork anywhere. Nothing. It was about as homey as a ten-dollar-a-night motel room, as if his stay there was strictly temporary, as if he might be moving on tomorrow or the next day.

Those weren't his plans. When she had asked him why he didn't leave Serenity, he had made it clear that this was where he belonged. This was his home. So why didn't the apartment look like it?

He came out of the bedroom and caught her looking. She responded with a smile as she used the banister to pull herself to her feet. "Ready?"

He simply nodded as he locked up. She led the way downstairs, out the French doors and around Kathy's House to her car. As they approached it, she offered him the keys. "You can drive." When he looked blankly at them, she asked, "You do know how to drive, don't you?" According to Jamey, he was one hell of a mechanic. A man couldn't like cars enough to work on them on every day and not know how to drive.

"I can drive," he acknowledged, still refusing the keys. "I went for my first drive when I was fourteen. Unfortunately my friends neglected to mention until the police pulled us over that the car was stolen."

"Did they arrest you?"

He shook his head and circled around to the passenger side. "I outran them. Where I grew up, running wasn't a sport. It was a part of survival. If you didn't run fast enough, you didn't live long enough. I was the fastest of them all."

She opened the door and flipped the power lock, then faced him over the roof of the car. "And did you outlive them all?"

Without answering, he climbed into the car and fastened his seat belt. She followed suit in time to hear his sigh, heavy with sorrow. Was he thinking of all his friends who had died young? No doubt there had been a lot of them—too many. Everyone in her family had lost at least one friend to violence, to drugs and alcohol, drive-by shootings, assaults, robberies, suicides and cold-blooded murder. Everyone except her. Her parents had gotten her away from Serenity before she'd experienced such tragedy.

"A lot of them." He sighed again, a cleansing sort of breath, as they pulled onto the street and drove toward Decatur and away from Serenity. "Anyway, the point of all this is, yes, I know how to drive, but I don't have a license." Glancing at her across the seat, he almost grinned. "Never had access to a car that wasn't stolen, and I figured that taking the test in a stolen car wasn't a particularly good idea."

"You can use mine. You can go tomorrow after work."

"I don't need a license. I don't have a car, and I'm not likely to ever have one."

"You can use mine when you need to go somewhere."

A week ago, his reaction would have been sullen. This afternoon he was amused. "And where do you think I'll be going?"

"Well, let's see... Last weekend you went to lunch downtown. Yesterday you went to Smith's condo, to my parents' house and that great little restaurant, and today here you are, just going for a drive." After stopping for an intersection, she glanced to her left and straight ahead before turning right. "Who knows, Reid, you just might discover that there's a whole world outside Serenity."

He turned his head to gaze at the scenery outside the window. "Honey, I've known that for a long time. It's just not very friendly to people like me."

On that note, he fell silent, and she let him stay that way. She turned on the radio, set to her favorite station, and focused on driving, following a meandering trail that led to a dirt road running alongside Lake Pontchartrain. Finally she parked the car, got out and went to stand in front of it.

After a moment, Reid joined her. "You come here often?" There was a cynical note in his voice as he glanced around.

There wasn't much to see, she acknowledged—the lake in front of them, the interstate some distance behind them, a few fishing boats on the water. There were places along the lake that were truly pretty, but this wasn't one of them. This was simply a place to come, look at the water, listen to it lap against the shore and relax.

"Did you know the lake covers over six hundred square miles?"

He leaned back against the hood and stretched his legs out in front. Long legs, she noted. Being close to five-ten, she had a fine appreciation for men with long legs. "And it's only about sixteen feet at its deepest." He gave her a sidelong glance. "Not the best place for dumping bodies."

She mimicked his position, elbowing him in the ribs as she settled in. "You haven't dumped any bodies."

"No, I haven't," he admitted. Pushing away from the car, his arm brushing hers as he moved, he walked a few yards away to the water's edge. "Why did you bring me here?"

"Maybe so I could have my wicked way with you."

"You're a virgin. What could you know about being wicked?"

She studied him for a moment, listening to his words in her mind. Was he teasing? Merely making conversation? Or maybe issuing a challenge? Reid didn't tease, and he probably wouldn't challenge her for fear that she would take him up on it, would walk across the few feet that separated them, wrap herself around him and prove once and for all that virginal was not synonymous with ignorant. While she might not have experienced much—never anything like his kiss this morning—she wasn't totally oblivious to the things that went on between a man and a woman. For example, she knew that if she got him aroused, he would take care of the rest. He would teach her the rest.

Slowly she straightened, and the look in his eyes grew wary. Underneath the apprehension, though, there was also anticipation. Interest. The same desire she'd seen this morning in the instant before he'd kissed her and, yes, the same regret.

She walked toward him, and he took an involuntary step back. When she got close, though, she didn't wrap her arms around his neck. She didn't plaster her body to his the way Tanya had yesterday. She didn't indulge in an indecent display of hunger and need for hot, hard, wild sex. Instead, she stood near but not near enough and answered his question. "I'll be the first to admit that I don't know enough about being wicked. Guys are funny. Once they find out that you don't intend to complete the act, either they think they can change your mind or they lose interest. Since I never wanted some hormonally influenced boy trying to force me into something I didn't want, I never let things go far enough to make them expect more."

Beside her he was still facing the car—still, she would bet, wearing that vaguely wary look. "What am I supposed to expect?" His voice wasn't quite steady. It was husky and conjured up images of naked bodies in a shadowy room, of heat and hunger, enough need to make a strong man plead and enough satisfaction to make an emotionally reserved woman weep. It was the same voice that had crawled under her skin this morning in the arbor when he had warned her, pleaded with her. *Don't tempt me, Cassie. Don't let me think I can do this. Don't let me think you might want this. Don't make me think you want...*

What should he expect? There were so many answers she could give him. Affection, friendship, love. Desire, passion, sex. An affair, a relationship, commitment, marriage. He could expect what any man might expect from a new relationship. The possibilities were limitless. The potential was tremendous. A doomed affair, a broken heart, a long and happy marriage, a bitter divorce—they all started at the same place, with a man and a woman who felt something special for each other.

But what did Reid know of new relationships—or old ones, for that matter? As a child, he had more or less raised himself, unable to count on the mother who had abused him or the father who had forgotten him. As a teenager, the only people he'd had to turn to were the Morgans and other punks, people with whom he'd had little in common besides a heartbreaking sense of abandonment. As an adult, he knew what it meant to be so desperate for another's touch that sex seemed a fair enough trade. How could he know what to expect from a relationship?

Facing him, she finally answered his question. "Everything, Reid. You can expect everything."

Chapter 6

With a soft nylon brush, Reid scrubbed the grease and dirt from his hands while staring sightlessly at the water. It was one-thirty on Monday afternoon and time to go home. He had worked a half hour past quitting time on a Chevy older than its owner by a good ten years. He often worked overtime, and it usually didn't bother him—after all, what did he have to hurry home to?—but today he'd wished he could have gone home on time.

And what would he have done there? The answer was enough to make him scowl. He would have stood at his living-room window and stared out at the school. He would have watched for some glimpse of Cassie, and he would have indulged in what had become his favorite pastime: erotic fantasies.

It didn't take much at all to make him feel edgy and needy as hell—just the thought of her. The mention of her name. The faint scent of her soap that clung to him after last night's shower. The image of her in her big white bed. In her classroom. Breathless and aroused in the arbor. Just the right thought at the right instant, and his entire body started to throb.

Just the right thought could make his heart ache.

You can expect everything, she had told him. He wanted more of an answer, wanted a precise definition of *everything.* He wanted details, wanted her to run down a list. *I'll go out with you. I'll be friends with you. I'll sleep with you. I'll take you home to meet my family. I'll like you, want you, need you, seduce you, fight with you, forgive you, make plans with you, make a future with you, make a family with you.* It was so much to ask. So much more than he'd ever had…and all that he wanted.

She had made a mistake yesterday mentioning love. Ever since she had raised the possibility, since she had so casually said, *Maybe we'll fall in love,* he'd been trying to imagine how it would feel to have a woman—not just any woman, but Cassie—looking at him the way Karen looked at Jamey. How would it feel to know that he mattered? That he was the most important person in someone else's life? That he could have all those things he'd never had—a wife, a home, a family?

He had gotten so damn greedy. In so short a time, he had gone from accepting that he would always live the way he always had to thinking that maybe he could have more. To hoping. To needing. If it wasn't true, if Cassie was wrong, it was going to destroy him.

As he dried his hands, his rueful expression almost shifted into a smile. It was easier to believe in all her possibilities when she was with him. It was easier to believe that miracles could happen and dreams could come true when his very own walking, talking dream was in front of him, insisting they could.

After clocking out, he left the garage and headed home. It wasn't a long walk, a half dozen blocks. From the moment he turned onto Serenity, he could see all the way to its end, a concrete barrier in the middle of the last block. Years ago the city had divided the street in half, tearing out several blocks, cutting off the neighborhood from one of its only two ways in and out. A lot of people in the surrounding area—and some from the neighborhood itself, including Jamey—thought the city should have done the same thing at this end, cutting off Serenity from the rest of the city and protecting the rest of the city from Serenity.

A few blocks past O'Shea's, Trevor Morgan's current ride was parked in the street, its rough idle audible from a distance. The way the sun was shining, it was impossible to see who was in the car, but it wasn't difficult at all to recognize Vinnie Marino as he came out of the gray house that had once been home to Cassie's family. Reid couldn't stop the edgy little shiver that crept down his spine as his former partner got into the car and it pulled away from the curb. Unless he turned down the next side street, there was no way he could avoid being seen by the men in the car. Since last fall, he'd been trying really hard to avoid them. The surest way to get into trouble of one sort or another was getting within speaking distance of his old buddies.

He forced himself to continue walking, crossing the street, stepping onto the sidewalk on O'Shea's block. Trevor always liked to take it slow through the 'hood, to announce their presence to one and all and publicly flaunt their arrogance. By the time they drew even with Reid and Trevor brought the car to a stop, they were only a few yards this side of the bar.

On the other side of the car, Vinnie climbed out and rested his arms on the roof. "Hey, Reid. We don't see you around much. Seems you're spending all your time over there with them church people." He jerked his head back to indicate Kathy's House behind him.

For a lot of people down here, their only experience with do-gooders was through one religious group or another. They were used to churches butting in where they weren't wanted and didn't belong, and they automatically assumed that Kathy's House was just more of the same, but they were wrong. The people at Kathy's House didn't preach. They advised, listened and Karen gently nudged, but none of them preached.

"I've been busy."

"We've got a job to do this week for Mr. Falcone. We could use some help. Why don't you come with us?"

"I can't."

"Come on, Reid," Vinnie coaxed while, from this side, Trevor stared at Reid from behind a pair of dark glasses. The set of his mouth was hard, his manner menacing. Before Ryan's murder, Reid had always thought there might be hope for Trevor. He was just a kid, after all, not even yet twenty. He hadn't shared his brother's goal of one day being a hotshot in Falcone's organization. Like Reid, for the most part, he'd just been going along, doing what his big brother did and having a good time. Reid had thought that someday the kid would wake up and realize that going along and having a good time were no way for a man to live. Looking at him now, though, Reid saw no hope.

"You owe us," Trevor stated flatly.

Owed them for what? Taking him in all those years ago? He had earned his keep, had paid his share of the rent more regularly than either Ryan or Trevor. He had done his share of jobs and committed his share of crimes. He didn't owe them anything, not for walking away, not for siding with Karen, not for turning his back on them. "I don't owe you," he disagreed, his tone mild, "and I'm not interested in your job." He started to turn away, but Vinnie's next words stopped him.

"Yeah, all you're interested in is that redheaded bitch your old man married and her pretty little teacher friend."

Slowly turning back, he fixed a cold, deadly gaze on the other man. In all the years they had run around together, he never had liked Vinnie. Ryan had liked the criminal life for the money, the prestige and the reputation as a man not to be messed with. Trevor had followed his brother into it. But Vinnie didn't care so much for the money, the reputation or the fear. He just liked hurting people. It gave him the same sort of rush other people got from booze or drugs. "Getting fixated on Karen got Ryan killed," Reid reminded him, his voice harsh for all its softness. "Are you going to make the same mistake, Vinnie?"

Marino opened his mouth to respond, then glanced to Reid's right and apparently thought better of it. Slapping his hands on the roof of the car, he slid in, calling as he did, "We'll see you around, Donovan. You'd better be looking for us." He gave one last bang on the roof through the open window as the car resumed its slow journey.

Jamey was standing somewhere off to his right, Reid knew without looking. Everyone in the neighborhood was intimidated by Jamey, even the baddest of the bad. Reid wasn't even sure why. In all the years he'd lived on Serenity, Jamey had never gotten into a fight, had never been the reason behind anyone's arrest, had never done anything to earn the sort of respect he'd gotten. He had made threats and given warnings, but he'd never been forced to carry through because everyone had been afraid of him. Ryan and Vinnie had routinely backed down from him. Reid had always backed down, except for the one occasion when he'd punched him. No one had had the nerve to find out if he would make good on the threats.

For a long time, Reid had been convinced that he would. Now he wasn't. Oh, he had no doubt that Jamey would do whatever was necessary to protect the things important to him—O'Shea's, Kathy's House, Karen, Cassie and the others—but Reid suspected that a great many of those times over the years, Jamey's threats had been all bluff.

"Getting rid of those two would sure go a long way toward cleaning up Serenity."

Reid finally turned and saw his father leaning against the wall at O'Shea's. "I could have handled this myself."

"I didn't say anything."

"You didn't have to say anything. Just coming out here was enough."

"You have many run-ins with them?"

Reid shook his head as he started toward the bar. "I usually manage to not be around when they are."

"That's probably good advice for everyone." Jamey turned

into the first set of doors, walking past empty tables to the bar. Reid followed and sat down on the end barstool. "You want a drink?"

"No, thanks. I'll get one when I eat."

Jamey pulled up a stool on the opposite side and made himself comfortable. "What are your plans for the afternoon?"

"I never have plans." But that wasn't entirely true today. At odd moments during the morning, he'd found himself thinking about Cassie's apartment and his own, about that look on her face when he'd caught her looking around curiously. He'd been satisfied for more than six months with the place where he lived, but lately he'd found himself thinking that he might like it better if everything weren't quite so shabby. He'd lived in tattered, worn-out, run-down places all his life, and there was no reason for it, not when a few coats of paint could make all the difference in the world.

"I was wondering…" Feeling the weight of Jamey's gaze, he broke off. Was he really about to ask permission to repaint the apartment? He, who hadn't put a single nail in the wall, who hadn't moved a piece of furniture, who hadn't done a single thing to make the place look like someone was living there?

Yeah, he was. Why shouldn't he? It was Jamey's apartment, granted, but there was no way his old man was ever moving back in, not with Karen across the street. He had agreed to Cassie's paint job without any hesitation, and, hell, Reid *was* living there and had been for months.

"Wondering about what?" Jamey asked when the silence had dragged on too long.

"If I could paint the apartment."

"You can do whatever you want with it. It's your place."

He said that last part so casually, as if it were understood. Well, Reid had never understood it. He had never had a place to call home with any sense of permanence. With Meghan he had always known that, usually sooner rather than later, she would quit paying the rent and they would be evicted if they didn't sneak out in the middle of the night first. On Serenity, his grandmother had told him up front that his welcome in her home would soon run out, and with the Morgans, any time Ryan had wanted to kick him out, he would have.

"Like I told Cassie, Karen's got gallons of paint over in the workshop. Before you buy anything, see if she's got what you need."

"I will. Thanks." Sliding to the floor, Reid circled the bar and went upstairs. Instead of going straight to the bathroom for a shower, though, he let himself into the apartment and stopped in the middle of the living room. *It's your place.* It was still the same shabby place, but those three little words made a difference. He could hang some of his sketches on the walls. He could rearrange the furniture, could even get rid of it and bring in new pieces. He could build those shelves he'd wanted in the closet. He could put his mark on the apartment and make it his own place.

And if the day came when Jamey asked him to leave, at least for a time it really would have been *his* place.

"Hi."

Startled, he turned to see Cassie standing in the doorway. She wore a denim skirt that reached practically to her ankles with a skinny white top underneath a chambray shirt that was unbuttoned and tied at her waist. Her hair was pulled back from each side and fastened with a clasp, leaving the rest to fall down her back. She looked pretty and cool, and she made him hot.

She stood there, hands together, waiting for him to speak. He asked the first question that came to mind. "Why aren't you in school?"

"It's recess. Jaye's watching the kids while I get my camera. We're going to take pictures for a class portrait."

"Recess," he repeated, feeling thickheaded and dim-witted. Instant arousal could do that to a man.

"You know, the break in the middle of classes when the kids get to go out and play."

He shook his head to clear it. "The only part of school I excelled at. I was very good at playing."

She came a few steps closer. ''I bet you were. I bet you still are.''

One swallow wasn't enough to clear his throat. He tried again. ''If my clothes weren't dirty, maybe I could show you.''

Another few steps brought her right in front of him, with her gaze focused on his shirt. He knew without looking that oil stains and dirt were smeared across the white cotton. He was a mechanic, working mostly on old engines. He couldn't do it without getting plenty of dirt on himself. Cassie wasn't the least bit put off by it, though. Grasping the hem of his shirt, she began tugging it upward, and he let her. Even though every protective instinct—every brutally honest instinct—he possessed was warning him to stop her, he stood there, unprotesting, and let her pull his shirt over his head and down his arms before dropping it on the floor.

The smile she gave him was enough to make his mouth go dry. ''There. Easily solved. The real problem is how much you can show me in the six and a half minutes before recess ends.''

For a long time, he simply looked at her, hearing a clock ticking in time with the suddenly audible thud of his heart. At least a minute passed before he drew a deep breath and moved. He had to force himself to touch her, even though he wanted to. He wanted it more than he ever could have imagined, but he was so unused to getting what he wanted.

He settled his hands at her waist and gave a tug. She came willingly the last step and laid her hands right above the waistband of his jeans. He wished he had all the time in the world, wished he could untie the knot in her shirt and slide it off, wished he could see her in just that thin little ribbed top that clung like a second skin. He wished he could stroke her, tease her, make her tremble, whisper sweet promises in her ear, cover her breasts with wet kisses and undo every button on that long skirt to allow him access for a few tormenting caresses.

But for those things, they needed all night, at the very least, and all they had was recess.

Slowly he slid his hands up, molding his palms to the shape of her as they moved across her rib cage, over her breasts, not hesitating long enough to see, feel, remember, before moving up the long, elegant line of her throat to her face. Then he kissed her. Light kisses, sweet and lazy, not too passionate, not too deep, but so damn intimate. They made him hot all over, a slow, achy heat that spread and intensified. It was the sort of heat—the sort of need—that could drive a man crazy, but only a little at a time.

From somewhere outside, noise penetrated his mind. He would have ignored it, would have stayed lost with the woman in his arms, if Jamey hadn't added his amused voice from the bottom of the stairs. "Hey, Cassie, your public's waiting."

Reluctantly Reid ended the kiss, drawing back, then kissing her once more before raising his head. The rushing in his ears started to fade, and he could better hear the clamor outside. Pulling her with him, he moved close enough to the window to see the entire student body of the Serenity Street Alternative School lined up along the fence in front of Kathy's House, all laughing, giggling and calling their missing teacher's name.

"Well, darn," she muttered, drawing a deep breath. "I've got to go." Then she offered him a dazzling smile. "Maybe we can continue this later. I'll be back by four. Will you be here?"

"Yeah," he answered, needing his own deep breath. "I'll be here."

When Cassie stepped onto the sidewalk, camera in hand, a cheer went up in the school yard. She waited until she was in the middle of the street, then lifted her skirt in a deep, flourishing curtsy that made the kids laugh. Once she was on the opposite sidewalk, she glanced back at O'Shea's, at one second-floor window in particular. She couldn't see Reid, but she knew he was there. She could feel him.

Jaye sent the kids running toward the arbor, then waited for Cassie just past the gate. "I don't blame you for being late. He *is* cute," she remarked, taking the camera.

"Who?"

"Don't play innocent, child. You know good and well who I'm talking about. Reid. The rebellious son. The reluctantly doting stepson. The next-door neighbor. The notorious bad boy." Jaye grinned. "What were you two doing up there?"

"I was getting my camera. I forgot where I put it when I unpacked. I've only been living there a couple of days, you know. I'm not totally settled yet."

The other teacher subjected her to a long up-and-down look. "You're right. You do look unsettled. Of course, if I ran into tall, blond and dangerous every time I left my apartment, I'd be unsettled, too."

"Reid's not dangerous. He's nothing like Vinnie Marino and the rest."

"Oh, darlin', you *are* innocent. Marino, Morgan and those other little thugs...all they can do is steal you blind and take your life. Reid, though...that young man can break your heart." Jaye's expression turned bitter. "You tell me which one's more dangerous."

She didn't wait for an answer, but turned instead to the kids, separating her own class from the younger bunch. If she had waited, Cassie might have told her the truth: that Reid had already broken her heart. Every time they talked, every time he confided some incident from his past, every time he got a certain look—a scowl, longing, boyish embarrassment—her heart ached. And every time he touched her, each time he kissed her, each time he got certain other looks—arousal, amusement, need—the ache went away, replaced by an emotion too strong, too sure, to mistake and too important to put a name to.

Apparently Jaye's experience with heartache had been of a different nature. Cassie wondered about the particulars. She didn't know much about her fellow teacher. She wasn't even sure how Karen knew the woman. All of the volunteers had some connection to Karen's old social-worker days, except for Susannah Sinclair, whose husband had been best friends with Karen's first husband, and Cassie, who'd heard of Karen

through Jolie. Actually, though, Cassie knew all she needed
to know about Jaye: that she was dedicated, she was wonderful
with the kids and she could afford to live on the salary Karen
could afford to pay. She knew that she liked the other woman.
What else mattered?

Getting what they were hoped were two decent photographs
took a half hour of class time and an entire roll of film. By
the time they were satisfied and herded the kids back inside,
there was less than a half hour left in the school day. Cassie
used it for reading aloud and was grateful when Jaye's knock
at the door signaled the end of class. After seeing the kids
home, cleaning the room and grading a stack of papers, she
gathered her things and headed across the street. As she cut
through the bar, she wondered if Reid would be upstairs, as
he'd promised, or if sometime in the past ninety minutes, his
version of common sense had kicked in and sent him running
to the nearest exit.

At the top of the stairs, as she fumbled with her books,
papers, camera and keys, she got her answer. She knew the
feeling of anticipation racing down her spine, knew the look
that was responsible for it. She didn't turn around but unlocked the door and swung it open as she commented, "I half
expected you to be gone."

"I got as far as the bottom of the stairs."

"Why did you come back?"

In the heavy silence that followed, she finally turned to face
him. He was leaning against the doorjamb, wearing clean jeans
and a T-shirt. His damp hair and the sweet fragrance of her
bath soap indicated that he'd taken a shower in the hour she'd
been gone. The familiar scent made her smile. He'd taken to
using her soap, and she had begun using his. She liked the
clean, no-nonsense smell, liked being reminded of him every
time she caught a whiff of it. Apparently he felt the same.

Or maybe he just liked the scent of jasmine.

At last he shrugged. "I wanted to see you. I wanted..."
Another slight, helpless shrug.

Wanting. In her life, she had almost always gotten what she

wanted. She'd had a safe place to grow up, a stable home, parents who loved her, siblings who doted on her. There had never been any question that she would finish high school and go to college, that she would have the ability to support herself comfortably without having to resort to the physically demanding, low-paying jobs that were often the only option for so many women. She'd had friends and boyfriends, had been given respect and acceptance and allowed pride and dignity. She'd had the luxuries of time, money, love and security. She had been blessed.

It had been a different story for Reid, though. Through most of his life, he'd been denied the very basics that every person had a right to. He'd done without a decent education, without true friends, respect, pride and security for so long that he no longer expected them. But he wanted to be here with her. He wanted...

She smiled faintly. He wanted exactly the same thing she wanted.

Crossing the hall, she reached past him, nudged him aside and closed the door to his apartment, then retraced her steps and went into her own place. She left the door open behind her and laid everything she carried on the couch before turning to see if he'd followed her. He hadn't, not quite. He had come to the top of the stairs, though. Only one more step would bring him to the doorway. Only another after that would bring him into the room. "Please come in."

For a moment, he still hesitated, then he walked into the apartment and closed the door. That simple act seemed to shrink the room by half and draw the air right out of it. Suddenly she felt warm, and her chest was too tight to manage a deep breath. But that was all right. What did she need with air when she and Reid were alone in her apartment and he was looking at her as if she was the most important woman in his life?

Breaking the stillness, he reached behind his back to secure the lock, then slowly moved toward her. Cassie felt a tremendous urge to skitter away, and she almost gave in to it. Instead, she swallowed hard, nervously smiled and remained where she was. She wasn't scared. Whatever happened in the next few minutes—the next few hours—she trusted Reid. She trusted him with her heart. She could certainly trust him with her body.

He stopped a breath or two in front of her and caught her hands. Her palms were damp, her fingers gone cold in spite of the day's heat. He held them tightly for a moment, his bigger hands wrapping completely around hers. "Don't be afraid."

"I'm not. I've never been afraid of you."

That brought a rueful smile from him. "I've been afraid of you since the first time I saw you." Then the smile faded, and he became heartachingly serious. "I would never hurt you."

"I know. I would never hurt you, either."

He accepted it with another of those little shrugs, as if he weren't quite convinced but didn't figure it was worth arguing. "You said we could pick up where we left off later. I believe your hands were here—" he placed them at his waist, and she automatically curled her index fingers through the empty belt loops of his jeans "—and mine were..." Just as he'd done earlier, he started at her waist and slid his hands upward, but this time he moved oh, so slowly, lingering on her breasts long enough to make her nipples ache, long enough to spread heat and need and make her shudder, then along her throat, finally reaching her cheeks. He cradled her face in his work-roughened palms, his thumbs gently stroking, and he bent his head until his mouth touched hers. "Here," he finished, his voice little more than a whisper before he kissed her.

It was the sweetest kiss she'd ever experienced—gentle and restrained, delivering plenty and promising so much more. It made the nerves in her stomach tighten, made the butterflies there kick into aerobic high gear. In need of support, she released her hold and slid her arms around his waist, snuggling close to him, leaning against him. His body was strong and hard, his arousal particularly so. The feel of it, so long and powerful against her belly, fascinated her...and scared her, too. She'd meant it when she said she had never been afraid of him, but what they were about to do…she was afraid of that. No matter how much she wanted it, no matter how wonderful she knew it would be, she was scared. It was so important. For both their sakes, it had to be so special.

As she became utterly content with the kiss, the intensity changed. It became harder, more demanding, stealing what little breath she could catch, sending an incredible weakness through her body. Her muscles were taut, her nerves quivery, and her skin rippled with a raw, edgy sensation that wasn't entirely comfortable but was more than desirable. She had naively believed that she was familiar with arousal before, but she had never experienced anything like this. She had never felt so feverish, so fluttery and purely womanly, so wanton and selfishly greedy. She had never felt so passionate, so far from serene, so close to losing control.

When he ended the kiss, she clung, unwilling to give up such pleasure. Only the certainty that there was more to come, so much more, gave her the strength. He drew his hands down her body, making her burn everywhere he touched and shiver everywhere else. At her waist, he began unworking the knot in her shirttail, slowly loosening the fabric, taking his own sweet time for no reason, she suspected, but to make her nerves hum with impatience. In an effort to hurry him along, she leaned forward and pressed a kiss to the base of his throat. He swallowed hard, and his fingers fumbled.

Liking the response, she kissed him again, this time moistening his jaw with her tongue. He muttered a soft curse that ended in a groan as she kissed his ear. Between them his hands became motionless, their task forgotten. Still teasing him with little kisses, she brushed his hands away and untied the knot herself, then raised his hands to her shoulders, inside the shirt. He pushed it down her arms, sweeping it off and letting it fall, then gripped her upper arms and forcibly moved her a few steps back. He looked adorable, clearly aroused and, at the same time, clearly determined to give her every chance to back out. "Are you sure…?"

"Yes." She offered nothing else—no reassurances that she knew what she was doing, no declarations of love that he would find difficult to accept, no promises of no-strings-attached that she couldn't keep. Just a simple statement of fact. She was sure. She wanted this—wanted *him*—more than he could imagine. More than she could find words to express.

He studied her face for one long moment after another, then gave a sigh. It brought her relief because he wasn't going to walk away. It seemed to bring him confidence that she spoke the truth.

Before they went any further, she cleared her throat. "I am sure, Reid, but I, uh, I'm not...not prepared. I know most single women are—at least, most of my friends are—but I've never done it before, so why would I be? Even though I know it's important to use something, I wouldn't even know what to get—"

He cut off her nervous words with a kiss, his tongue dipping into her mouth, before answering. "It's all right. I'm prepared." Claiming her hand, he pulled her across the living room to the bedroom. The windows were open, a light breeze lifting the sheer white curtains, bringing the faint scents of flowers, springtime and sunshine into the room. Her dresser was still across the street in the school's storeroom, along with the bookcase she intended for this room, leaving her with no furniture at all besides the unmade bed. With its thick white comforter spread haphazardly and a half-dozen fat pillows tumbling all over, it dominated the room. Under the circumstances, she thought with a smile, it would dominate even if it were surrounded by clutter.

Reid stopped beside the bed and looked at her. In his eyes was appreciation, uncertainty and a lot of desire. Reaching out, he hooked one finger underneath the thin strap of her tank top, then let it slide down beneath the fabric, teasing the swell of her breast, until he reached her arm. "I like this," he murmured, his voice husky.

The tank certainly left little to the imagination. It fitted so snugly that she rarely wore it and never without a shirt or jacket over it, because it left her feeling so exposed. Exposed, she knew now, wasn't necessarily a bad way to feel. In a few more minutes, she was going to be much more exposed and loving every second of it.

Loving every second with him.

Still stroking beneath her shirt, he came closer and bent his head. Just before his mouth made contact, she tilted her head back, leaving his kiss to fall on her jaw. Her eyes drifted shut, the better to enjoy the pure, sweet sensations from his mouth and hands—the pleasure so new, the need so intense, the pain so unexpected. By the time he undressed her and laid her on the bed, her entire body was trembling. By the time he stripped off his own clothes and joined her, she was beyond waiting, beyond sweet words and gentle seduction. A great throbbing emptiness had consumed her, making her ache, reducing her to pleading for relief.

Reid moved between her legs, his hands planted on either side of her head, supporting his weight above her. He looked so serious, so intense, as if he, too, were empty and in need of filling. "It might hurt," he warned before moving, and it did, despite his gentleness. For just a moment her body burned, then pain gave way to satisfaction. He filled her, stretching her, and it felt so sweet, so strange and yet natural.

For one long moment after another, he remained motionless, giving her body a chance to adjust to his. It was an effort for him, evidenced by tight muscles, ragged breathing and the rigid set of his jaw. She quickly grew impatient as the initial satisfaction gave way to stronger need. She wanted more. She wanted to feel him move inside her, to thrust and withdraw and thrust again, to treat her to that sweet, foreign pain of needing and not having, then to ease it, to bring her satisfaction that could make her weep.

"Please, Reid," she whispered, and he trembled so fiercely that she felt it deep in her belly. "I want..." That was all she could say. It was enough.

Falling into an easy, ever increasing rhythm, he used his mouth, his hands and his body to coax her, to tantalize and torment her. He taught her new meanings for pleasure and pain, and when it grew to be too much, when the entire experience became more than she could bear, he taught her a brand-new, breath-stealing, heartaching meaning for satisfaction.

And love.

It was a slow night in the bar, a fact for which Reid was grateful because he was far too preoccupied with the apartment upstairs where he had left Cassie in bed. He'd wanted to stay there with her, had stayed there, just watching her, marveling over her, until he risked Jamey coming upstairs to find out why he was late taking over the bar. He had never been so reluctant to leave a bed or a woman before, but he had forced himself to get dressed and leave with a sweet kiss and a promise for dinner later.

That had been over an hour ago, and he had spent the time waiting restlessly behind the bar. He had served a few drinks, wiped a few tables and tried to distract himself with the newspaper, but he'd had little luck. All of his attention was focused upstairs, listening for the slightest creak, for the sound of running water or the light tread of steps on the stairs. He kept picturing Cassie as he'd left her, naked, drowsy, long legs tangled in the covers, long hair tumbling across the pillows. He kept remembering the way she had felt underneath him, the way her body had resisted, then welcomed him, the way her muscles had tightened and quivered, the way she had looked so soft and incredibly satisfied when they were done. It had been so damn hard to leave her, but as soon as he got off work, he could go back to her.

He managed a faint smile. That was a new experience in his life—having someone to go home to. Knowing that Cassie would be waiting for him, that she would wonder if he was late, that she would miss him if he didn't show. In all his life, there had rarely been anyone to notice, and never anyone to care. But she cared.

Movement across the room caught his attention. He looked

that way as a slender woman, her arms filled, came through the doors. She didn't glance at any of the customers, but came straight to the bar, stopping directly in front of him.

"Hey, Alicia."

She didn't return his greeting until she'd climbed onto a bar stool and settled the baby she held more comfortably. "I don't see you around much, Reid."

"I'm easy to find." It wasn't as if he had many places to go. His life was about as simple as it could get. If he wasn't at the garage or the bar, he was in his apartment or, lately, with Cassie. Anyone who wanted to see him easily could, but he doubted that Alicia really wanted to. Since Ryan's murder last September, she had become even more isolated than Reid. She had quit her job, cut off her friends, holed up in her grandmother's apartment with the baby and rarely come out. She was a little hopeless, Cassie had said Saturday, but that was an understatement. As someone who had lived without hope for the better part of his life, he recognized utter hopelessness when he saw it, and he saw it all over Alicia's face.

Opening the cooler, he took out a couple of sodas, poured one into a glass and slid it across the bar to her. "How's the baby?"

She didn't glance at Sean, didn't shift him from where he slept with his head on her shoulder. "He's fine. He's crawling and teething."

"He must keep you busy." Even as he said it, he knew it wasn't true. Her grandmother had confided in Karen that *she* was taking care of Sean, that Alicia just wasn't able. All Alicia did was grieve. There were days when she didn't bother getting out of bed, times when she couldn't rouse herself enough to care that the baby was hungry or needed changing. Karen and the center psychologist had visited her a number of times, but they'd had no success. She wasn't sick, Alicia had insisted. She was just so very sad.

"I'm going to California," she said, both her words and her blunt, abrupt manner surprising him. "I have an aunt in

Los Angeles who said I can stay with her. I'm going to start over there.''

Reid stared at her. Leaving Serenity had long been one of her goals, but after Ryan's death, he had figured she would never make it. She would stay here forever, mourning what she'd lost, building Ryan into far more than he'd ever been in reality and living the rest of her life with the illusion. If she did get out, he'd thought she wouldn't go more than a few miles from the place where Ryan had lived, certainly no more than a few miles from the place where he was buried. But California and starting over... That was quite a change.

And the queasiness deep in his stomach warned him that she planned to make it alone. It was written in her lifeless eyes, in the thin, hard set of her mouth, in the lack of caring that shadowed her face. "When are you leaving?"

"Tomorrow."

"What about Sean?"

For a moment, she avoided the question. Instead, she held the baby out, the sudden movement waking him. "You want to hold him?"

He stared at the kid, his bare feet dangling a few inches above the bar. He had never held a baby before, had never gotten closer than being in the same room with one. After a moment, though, he took the baby, cradling him awkwardly in his arms. As babies went, he was a cute one, dark eyed and dark haired, like his parents. He had his father's leanness, his mother's delicacy and a solemn, wide-eyed look all his own. He wasn't very big—not even an armful—but he seemed healthy and content to lie where he was.

Reid looked from the baby to his mother, who was staring guiltily at the bar. "You're not taking him, are you?" She was going off to California to make a new life for herself and leaving her baby behind. Granted, her grandmother loved and pampered him, but she was an old woman. Sean needed a mother, as well as a great-grandmother. He needed someone young enough to play and keep up with him, someone whom he could reasonably count on being there for him now, in five years and in fifteen years. He needed someone to love him the way only a mother could. "You're leaving him here and going off without him."

When she looked up, her eyes were damp, her expression sorrowful. "I love my baby, Reid, but I can't take care of him. Losing Ryan was like losing myself. Every time I look at Sean, I think of his father. Every time I remember the day he was born, I remember that it was also the day his father died. It's all I can do to get out of bed, to dress myself, to remember to eat. I can't take on the responsibility of a baby, too. I just want to go off somewhere and be alone until it quits hurting."

"And he's supposed to wait? He's supposed to stay here and live with a woman who's too old to take on the responsibility of a baby and wait for you to deal with your grief?"

"I'm not leaving him with my grandmother. She would happily take him, but you're right. She's too old. It's too much responsibility." The quaver disappeared from her voice and was replaced with grim determination. "I'm going to ask Karen and Jamey to adopt him."

It was rare that he heard a suggestion regarding *anything* that struck him instantly with such a feeling of rightness, but this one did. It had long been one of Karen's greatest sorrows that she couldn't have children. She was the most giving, loving and maternal person he'd ever met. She had eased the emptiness in her life by mothering others—kids, neighbors, friends. She'd even made a pretty good effort at mothering *him* even before her marriage to Jamey gave her legal status. But all that was a poor substitute for having a child of her own, a baby to nurture and protect, a son to live in her home, to brighten her days and call her Mama. She would be the best mother in the world, ten times better than old Mrs. Gutierrez, a hundred times better than Alicia.

The fact that Alicia recognized that fact made her pretty damn special.

"Have you talked to them yet?"

She shook her head. "I'm going to tonight. I thought it would be easier if I didn't take Sean with me, so it wouldn't look as if I were using him to persuade them. He's a sweet baby. He could change anyone's mind.''

Except hers. This was hard for her. He didn't need to see or hear the tears to know that. She was nothing like Meghan. She wasn't abandoning her son. She was saving him.

"I'll keep him while you're there," he volunteered, even though she hadn't asked, even though she could easily take the baby down the street to her grandmother's place, even though he knew less than nothing about taking care of a baby.

"I'd appreciate it." She slid to the floor, then set the diaper bag on the bar. "I'll be back soon." She rushed out of the bar as if he might change his mind, leaving him alone with three customers and one solemn, wide-eyed baby.

"What do you think, Sean?" he asked, his voice little more than a whisper. "We just might wind up as brothers."

Brothers. In age he was better suited to be the baby's father. In fact, he and Ryan had been born only a few months apart. Reid had never given any real thought to fatherhood, though, other than a general acknowledgment that he wasn't a candidate for it. What did he know about being a father, about accepting responsibility for another life, about loving and nurturing? Damn little.

But he was learning more every day. Cassie was teaching him. She could teach him about parenting, too, especially if the baby to be parented was her own. *Their* own.

"Hey, Reid. What are you doing?"

The soft, husky voice came from behind him, sending a shiver down his spine. After all that time spent straining to hear the slightest sound from upstairs, he'd let Cassie walk up on him without hearing so much as a creak on the stairs or a footstep in the hall. He turned to face her, standing where the hallway opened into the bar, wearing the same clothes he'd stripped off her this afternoon and a satisfied smile that was at odds with the shyness in her eyes. Shifting the baby to one arm, he reached for her, and she came willingly, stepping into his embrace, tilting her head for his kiss.

He had never known how much pleasure a man could find

in simple kisses, had never realized how wickedly innocent and sweetly intimate they could be. Kissing Cassie could overwhelm him. It could make him want and could satisfy some small bit of that hunger. It could stir a pain that was pure pleasure. It could make his arousal strong and his will weak. It could even make him think that maybe he did know what love was. Maybe it didn't matter that he'd never experienced it firsthand. Maybe he could recognize it, believe in it, feel it anyway. Maybe he could take it on faith.

When he ended the kiss, they were both breathless. He was hard, and she was flushed and dazed. He brushed a strand of hair from her face, then quietly asked, "Are you all right?"

Her smile was so womanly, so full of promise and sinful satisfaction that it should be illegal. "I'm fine." Reaching out to stroke the baby's hair, she asked, "Is this Sean?"

He nodded.

"He looks comfortable. Of course, I've always thought that in your arms was a nice place to be. Where is Alicia?"

Pulling her over to a private table behind the bar, he sat down. She drew the opposite chair closer and sat, too, her knees bumping his, her hair brushing his arm as she bent near the baby. When he finished telling her about Alicia's decision, she sat quietly for a moment, then sighed. "It's a tough situation. My heart goes out to all of them."

"Do you think Karen will say yes?"

"She'll want to. She deserves a chance to be a mother."

"But?"

"What if Alicia changes her mind? What if she gives Sean to your folks and they make him a part of their family, and then she comes back and says, 'Hey, everything's okay now. I've got myself straightened out and I want my baby back'?"

It would be devastating. It would take Karen about thirty seconds to fall irrevocably in love with Sean. Whether she'd had him six years, six months or only six weeks, it would break her heart to have to give him up.

"Then there's Jamey."

"What about him?"

Cassie's smile was infinitely gentle. "He thinks he's a lousy father. He believes he caused you tremendous harm with his neglect, and he feels very guilty for it. He might not be willing to try again, to put another child at risk."

"It's hardly the same situation. He's not seventeen anymore. He's not being forced into marriage with a woman he doesn't even like, much less love, all because of a kid he never wanted. He loves Karen. He wants her to be happy. He can learn all the things he didn't know the first time." With a shrug, he awkwardly added, "I think he'd probably make a good father."

Still smiling, Cassie leaned back in her chair. "I think it takes a hell of a son to admit that." Her words made his face flush with heat and somehow made him want her even more. She didn't give him a chance to say or do anything about it, though, but went on. "What kind of father do you think you'd make?"

He looked down at Sean, whose yawn enveloped his entire face. A week ago, even a few days ago, Reid would have retorted that it didn't matter what kind of father he would be because there was no way in hell he was ever going to bring a child into the bleak, hostile world of Serenity. But things were rarely one hundred percent totally so. Serenity wasn't totally bleak or hostile, just as he wasn't totally worthless. Maybe the neighborhood was poor, and crime and despair were serious problems, but there were isolated areas of love, satisfaction and security. There were places where people were happy and not anxiously waiting to escape. Karen and Jamey had created just such a haven across the street. Shawntae Williams and her mother had one, too, that offered a warm, loving home for J.T.

He could be part of such a place. He could live with love, satisfaction and security. He could help make a place where a child would be safe and protected, where they could all be happy and care nothing about escaping Serenity.

With Cassie's help, with her guidance, he could be part of a home.

With a soft sigh, Sean's eyes fluttered shut, and he drifted off to sleep once more. After watching him for a moment, Reid met Cassie's gaze and gave an answer to her question that made her smile. "I think I could be a damn good father."

Chapter 7

It was midnight and a quiet night on Serenity. Cassie stood
at the window in her living room. There was no activity on
the street, no cars, no loud music or angry words. Lights were
on in an occasional apartment, but most were dark and still.
Kathy's House was dark except for a single light filtering
through from the back. No doubt, Karen and Jamey were in
their bedroom, debating the choice Alicia had given them tonight. It was one Cassie wouldn't want to face. Whatever they
decided could break their hearts.

The image of Reid holding the sweet little boy in his arms
downstairs earlier had been enough to break *her* heart. There
was something so touching about strong men and innocent
kids, something especially so with this particular man, who
couldn't remember ever being cuddled, fussed over or protected himself. He had a vein of tenderness in him that even
he hadn't suspected was there. But *she* had.

Downstairs shadow fell over the sidewalk as the four sets
of French doors were closed and the lights switched off. She
had stayed in the bar until eleven, when she'd come up to take

a shower and get ready for bed. She hadn't invited Reid to join her, and he hadn't asked, but she knew he would come to her.

The stairs creaked, and she swallowed hard. Anticipation. The next time would be better, he'd told her this afternoon, when they'd collapsed in a tangle, their bodies slick with sweat, her entire body humming with satisfaction so sweet.

If that was the case, she might not survive.

As he reached the top of the stairs, she watched him over her shoulder. He came inside, closed the door and locked it. Next he switched off the lamp, leaving the room dark except for the light through the windows. As he approached her, she felt a shiver and hugged herself tighter, but she didn't go to meet him. She remained where she was and waited.

He came to stand behind her, sliding his arms around her waist, ducking his head to kiss her throat. He was already aroused, and so was she. She didn't know if it was what was sure to follow or simply Reid himself. Maybe all he had to do was walk into the same room, and she got turned on. Maybe that was what being newly in love was like.

"You look pretty in white." His whisper tickled and made her move deliberately, enticingly, against him.

The cotton gown she'd pulled on after her shower was the closest she ever got to frilly. Sleeveless, beribboned and laced, it was femininity subdued. It was pretty, and tonight she had wanted to look pretty.

He kissed her ear, his tongue sending shivers through her. "Tell me to go home."

"I'd rather tell you to take me to bed."

"I don't want to hurt you."

"I'll be hurt only if you leave me here alone."

"I'm talking about..." His mouth only a breath above her ear, he murmured exactly what he meant in words intended to explain and scandalize. They did both—and turned her on. So did his hands, slowly unfastening the buttons that secured her gown from neck to waist.

"I'm not sore," she insisted as he slid one hand inside the

fabric. He proved her wrong, though, when he began stroking her breast, each lazy stroke ending on her nipple. She wasn't sore, exactly, but achy. Needy. Unsatisfied. Their clothes provided an unwelcome barrier, his hardness pressed against her was an unbearable temptation and the little bit of attention he paid her breast was a too subtle version of what she needed.

Slowly he turned her. She let go of the curtain and leaned back against the window frame as he began kissing her forehead, her cheek, her jaw, her throat, all the way down to the nipple he had just caressed to a peak. His mouth closed around it, and her eyes fluttered shut. His teeth gently nipped, and her throat grew tight. Such sensation from no more than a kiss. She could feel it in her chest, curling tightly in her belly, pooling heated and damp between her thighs. He suckled hard, and her body grew hotter, her muscles trembled and her legs grew weaker.

Abruptly, his breathing ragged, he lifted his head and took her mouth, fierce, frantic need driving him. He opened his jeans, and she lifted her gown, the soft fabric bunching around her hips, giving him access, letting her feel the long, heated length of him probing, sliding—

"No." His protest was harsh. It took a moment to penetrate the daze of hunger, longing and pure, raw need that enveloped her, another moment for her to open her eyes and see him staring down at her from only inches away.

"Yes," she whispered, reaching for him, trying to pull him closer, trying to pull him deep inside her.

He raised his hands to her face in simple caresses that could seduce her as easily as the most intimate touches. "No, Cassie," he whispered. "Not like this. Not without..." His thumb slid across her lips, coaxing them apart, then he kissed her briefly. "We're not going to risk your future because we're too impatient to do this right."

"If it gets any more right than this, I don't think I can stand it." Then she offered a halfhearted protest. "It's not the right time for me to get pregnant."

"I'm not worried about that." One more kiss. "We're not

going to risk your life, darlin'. Come on.'' Taking her hand, he led her across the room and into the bedroom, straight to the bed.

Moonlight shone through the windows, spotlighting the single plastic packet that he'd left on the sill earlier. Cassie picked it up, turning it in her hands, studying it curiously. When she looked up, Reid was watching her. When he held out his hand for the packet, she closed her fingers around it and offered her sultriest smile. ''Soon,'' she promised.

Sliding one strap, then the other, off her shoulders, she let the gown fall to the floor, then stepped out of it. She took a step toward him, and he took a step back. A few more steps, and the bed was at his back. He couldn't retreat any farther. Clumsily she managed to hold on to the condom and pull his shirt over his head, to slide her hands inside the waist of his unfastened jeans and guide them off, too. At last he stood naked in front of her, his body strong, his skin smooth and golden in the yellow moonlight and his arousal...

Swallowing hard, she touched him, brushing the flat of her palm against him, wrapping her hand around him. The skin was soft, the flesh intimidatingly hard. Each time she touched him, his body betrayed him with some small response—a shudder, an involuntary thrust, a deep, strained groan. Each time she touched him, her own body responded—hunger intensifying, pain sharpening, emptiness threatening to engulf her.

Finally he caught her hand, forcing it away from his body. ''No more,'' he demanded through clenched teeth. ''You're going to make me... I want to be inside you... *Now*, damn it.''

She tore open the packet, removed the contents and examined it.

''Like this.'' His voice was gritty, barely controlled, as he positioned the thin roll properly in her grip, then guided her hands to his groin. Swearing once, he helped her work the sheath into place. The instant she finished, he reached for her, pulling her onto the bed with him, lifting her into place above him, sliding her down, slowly and steadily down, until he filled her, until they were thoroughly, intimately joined.

She sat motionless, savoring, enjoying, loving the way they felt together. But all too soon, it wasn't enough. She needed more, needed him moving inside her, needed to witness once again the sheer power of his completion, needed to feel once again the sweet satisfaction of her own. She needed stimulation, torment, pleasure, release. She needed everything. "I don't know—"

"Like this." His hands on her hips, he coaxed her to move, helping her set an easy, erotic rhythm, rising, sinking, thrusting forward, pulling back, arousing him with the same taut movements that further aroused her. When she was close to finishing, when her body was tight and her muscles were trembling and the pleasure had become too much to bear, he took over, holding her hips steady, thrusting his own against her, filling her deeper, harder, faster. The end came in a bright, explosive rush, like a million fireworks bursting into brilliant light, leaving them quivering, helpless and incredibly, heart-stoppingly satisfied.

Long minutes passed before he withdrew, longer minutes before she moved to lie beside him. She thought of all the things she would like to say—*Thank you. You were well worth waiting for. I want you. I need you. I love you.* But, in the end, when she finally roused herself to speak, she didn't say any of them. She simply leaned forward, pressed a kiss to his cheek and whispered, "Good night, Reid."

There was something to be said for ending a long period of celibacy, Reid thought Tuesday afternoon. He couldn't remember the last night he'd slept so soundly or the last morning he'd awakened so rested. He couldn't remember ever awakening beside a woman without a great deal of regret or facing a day with something very close to pleasure.

Of course, he'd never slept or awakened beside Cassie. He had never faced a day knowing that, when it was over, he would make love with her again. He had never had such reason for hope.

The thought made him grin. He was feeling optimistic today—*he*, Reid Donovan, who'd never had much reason for hope. He was feeling as if the world couldn't possibly be a better place than it had been last night. Than it would be again tonight. As soon as he saw Cassie.

He finished scrubbing the grease from his hands, then clocked out. He had three hours to pass before she was due home. Even with a half hour for his afternoon shower, he would still have plenty of time for a solitary lunch and a quick walk to the nearest pharmacy. Last night had exhausted his meager stash of condoms. Supplying more was the least he could do.

He had expected her to ask why he had just happened to have condoms with him yesterday afternoon, but she hadn't, most likely because she'd been distracted by other things. Maybe she hadn't asked because she thought he was the sort of man who always carried a couple. At one time, that had been true. He had always been prepared. But that was a long time ago. He wouldn't have had the two they'd used yesterday if Karen hadn't given them to him.

Safe sex was one of the lessons they were trying to teach at the women's center. His stepmother hadn't asked if he was practicing it, but had simply given him the condoms, along with one of their pamphlets. For the first time since he'd met her, she had been too uncomfortable to pry. He had been uncomfortable, too, too much to tell her that he was practicing abstinence. He had accepted the offering, and, in an odd way, he'd been touched by it, because it supported Karen's claims that she really did care about him. He'd had a hard time believing it until then.

Sometimes he still did.

He walked past Serenity and into the Quarter proper, where he made his purchase at a corner drugstore before turning back toward Decatur. He hadn't gone more than a dozen feet when a man and a woman, both wearing suits, both obviously cops, stepped onto the sidewalk ahead and stopped. He stopped, too, puzzled, uneasy. Neither of them made a move toward him.

He wondered if they would let him walk past or if they would stop him if he tried. How serious would they be about stopping him? Would they simply block his way or take him down and handcuff him? He'd been in that position plenty of times before— spread-eagled against a rough brick wall, his arms bent up so far behind him that his shoulders threatened to dislocate, or facedown on the pavement with some two-hundred-pound cop balancing his weight in the middle of Reid's back. It was usually uncomfortable, sometimes painful and always shameful.

The man directed a nod somewhere behind Reid, and immediately he heard a car approaching. Keeping his hands loosely a few inches from his sides, he turned as a gray sedan pulled to the curb beside him. The two men in the front seat remained there, but the passenger in back climbed out and advanced with credentials in hand. Reid didn't need to look at them to know the man was with the FBI. He'd met the guy twice before, over on Serenity. Both times had been purely social situations—Karen and Jamey's wedding and the grand opening of Kathy's House—but there was nothing social about his manner now. This was business, and the knowledge made the muscles in Reid's stomach tighten.

"Reid Donovan? I'm Remy Sinclair. Would you come with us?"

Reid glanced at the other agents again. They had moved closer, cutting off any chance of escape in that direction. But he wasn't going to run, even if that was exactly what he wanted to do. He was a grown man, for God's sake, and he hadn't done anything wrong—at least, not lately. He had no reason to run. "Why?"

"We'd like to talk to you, and we would prefer not to do it here on the street. Get in the car, please."

He looked at the car, at Sinclair, then the other two. All the time he'd been running with the Morgans, he had expected to be arrested every damn day, every time he saw a cop, every time someone came to the door. He had been prepared for it then. Hell, he hadn't even cared. He'd had nothing to lose then.

But he did now. He had a job. A place of his own. A stepmother who worried about him and a father who had at least started to forgive him. He had Cassie.

But maybe not for long.

When he hesitated, Sinclair reached out but didn't actually touch him. "We just want to talk, Reid. Please get in the car."

Uneasily aware that he had no choice, he sidestepped the agent, walked over to the car and climbed in. After Sinclair got in, the driver pulled away from the curb. The other agents got into a second car that turned in the opposite direction at the first intersection.

"How is Karen?"

He looked warily at Sinclair. "She's fine."

"Everything okay at the women's center?"

"Yeah." The pointless questions grated on Reid's nerves. Sinclair's wife, Susannah, was one of the nurses at Kathy's House. No doubt, she kept him informed of everything that went on there.

A moment or two passed in silence. Reid stared out the window, trying to figure out where they were going. Not to any police station that he knew of, not to the jail or downtown to the FBI's or U.S. Attorney's offices. In fact, the driver seemed to have no particular destination in mind. He was driving just to be driving. Maybe they really did only want to talk.

"You used to run around with Ryan Morgan and his gang," Sinclair commented at last. "Why did you stop?"

"It's hard to run around with a dead guy."

Sinclair ignored his sarcasm. "Ryan's death hasn't made any of the others straighten up, get a job and try to live right. Why did you?"

"Because I didn't want to die. Because it was a stupid way for a man to live. Because Karen seemed to think I could do better." Reid exhaled heavily, then admitted something he'd never told anyone else. "Because of my father." At the grown-up age of twenty-six, he'd decided that he wanted whatever relationship he could have with Jamey. It would never be a normal father-son thing, but maybe they could at least speak civilly to each other. Maybe he could quit antagonizing his old man, and just maybe Jamey could quit hating him.

"While you were with Morgan, you did a number of jobs for Jimmy Falcone, didn't you?"

A chill swept over Reid. Such casual mention of such a dangerous man was guaranteed to put every self-protective instinct he had on alert. Falcone wasn't a man to cross. People who did that died—like Ryan. Sinclair himself had been the intended victim of two murder attempts by Falcone's people. Nobody but Jimmy knew exactly how many others had angered him and paid for it with their lives, not even his employees who shared the responsibility for the killing, because people who knew too much about Jimmy's business became a liability. They lived looking over their shoulders and guarding their backs.

If they lived at all.

"A few," he answered, his voice unnaturally flat and cold. "Nothing important."

"But you did work for him. He knows your name. He knows your reputation."

Reid nodded.

"What I'm about to tell you is confidential," Sinclair said. "You can't tell anyone—not your father, not Karen, not your girlfriend."

Did they know about Cassie, or did they just assume that he was seeing someone? A study of Sinclair's face persuaded Reid that it was just a guess. After all, Sinclair was best friends with Cassie's sister and rich prosecutor brother-in-law. If he knew Reid was involved with her, he wouldn't approve. He wouldn't be looking so harmless.

Sinclair traded glances with the front-seat passenger before stating, "We have a cooperating witness within Falcone's organization."

Cooperating witness. Nice name for a crook willing to sell out another crook to save his own hide. "Does he know that the last cooperating witness you had with Falcone has spent the last few years in a federal prison?" Of course, Nick Carlucci hadn't been your run-of-the-mill cooperating witness. For one thing, he hadn't been very cooperative, and he'd had no interest in saving his own hide. What he'd had was a personal vendetta against his boss that he would have done anything to settle. When he pleaded guilty to a long list of felony charges and went off to prison, he had thought he'd settled the score, had thought that his testimony against Jimmy would send the old man away for the rest of his life. He'd been wrong.

Ignoring his question, Sinclair went on. "As you can probably guess, since Falcone got burned by Carlucci, the old man's gotten paranoid. He keeps a tight rein on everyone around him. We have the witness in place, but now we need a reliable method of passing information back and forth, someone that Falcone wouldn't suspect, someone who wouldn't sell out our witness to gain Jimmy's favor."

And they wanted him to be that someone. The suggestion was laughable. He'd worked too damn hard to break his ties with all those people to simply waltz back in because the FBI asked him to. Besides, who the hell did they think they were dealing with? There was nothing in his background to make them think he was reliable or trustworthy, nothing to suggest that he wouldn't happily sell out their witness for the rat he was. Hell, he'd never been more than a small-time punk, and now he wasn't even that. He was nobody—but he was too smart to betray Jimmy Falcone.

"I'm not interested."

Again Sinclair went on as if he hadn't spoken. "The job wouldn't entail any illegal activity. According to our informant, you could get hired as a driver and start tomorrow. You wouldn't be breaking any laws. You wouldn't be taking part in any crimes. You wouldn't have access to anything damaging to Falcone, so he wouldn't watch you as carefully as he watches the rest of his employees. Of course, your true reason for being there would have to remain a secret from everyone. As far as they're concerned, you have to let them believe that you couldn't leave the life behind, that going straight was too hard, that you tried and you failed.''

It wasn't laughable anymore. Sinclair wasn't kidding. They'd given some thought to this. They honest-to-God wanted him to throw away the past six and a half months—the toughest, loneliest months in his life—to do this job for them. To Sinclair it was so simple. *You can't tell anyone. It's got to be a secret. Let them all think that you really are a loser. Betray their faith, disappoint them, disillusion them, lose them.* And when it was over, what would he have for his trouble? Nothing. Worse than nothing, because for the first time in his life, he actually had something.

''You've got to be crazy.''

Sinclair didn't speak.

Trying to quiet the panic building inside him, Reid took an unsteady breath. ''Look, it's been hard getting away from all that. I'm not going back. I'm not getting involved again, not for any reason, not for anyone.'' After all, they couldn't make him do it. They couldn't force him to lie to Cassie, Karen and Jamey. They couldn't make him give up whatever little bit of progress he'd made since last fall. They couldn't compel him to destroy his future all for the sake of their damn job. They had asked, he had refused, end of story.

Not quite.

The front-seat passenger handed a file back to Sinclair, who opened it, pulled out a photograph and passed it over. The subject was a woman, elegantly dressed, smiling, wearing diamond earrings and a stunner of a diamond necklace. She was pretty—auburn haired, fair skinned, blue eyed—but there was a hint of toughness that stopped her from being beautiful. She looked like a woman who had lived life hard, but had eventually prospered and done well for herself.

Obviously she was connected to the case. The witness? Jimmy had always liked his women pretty and well dressed.

He thought thousand-dollar dresses and precious gems could disguise a lack of refinement, just as he thought his own five-thousand-dollar suits kept people from seeing him as the low-born thug he was.

If she *was* the witness, he acknowledged silently, Sinclair was taking a risk identifying her to him. How did he know Reid wouldn't leave here and go straight to Jimmy? What made him so sure Reid could be trusted with the knowledge? Obviously something did. There was more to this request than he'd heard yet. Maybe it was part of a deal. Maybe it was leading to an ultimatum: *Do this for us, or go to prison. Do this, and we'll forget all those crimes we've tied you to. Do this or else.*

He tried to return the photo, but Sinclair wouldn't take it. "I can't do it," he repeated, a note of desperation slipping into his voice. "Everyone on Serenity is just waiting for me to screw up. No matter what I do, they don't trust me. They're convinced that I'm no good, and they're waiting for me to prove it to them. I've had to work damn hard to get where I am. I have too much to lose. I *can't* do this. Find someone else."

"I'm sorry, Reid," Sinclair said, and he truly looked regretful. "I know it's tough. But we can't find someone else. We need *you.*"

"Why me?"

"She asked for you."

"I don't even *know* her. How could she ask for me?"

"You know her. You just haven't seen her for a while."

Reid looked at the picture again. The woman was older, probably in her forties. If the roots were any indication, the auburn hair wasn't natural. Her own color was probably brown. The eyes were really blue, though, as blue as his own.

As blue as his own. Reid became still, staring at the picture with rapidly growing dismay. In recent years, he had come to believe that any family resemblances were shared strictly between him and Jamey. They were both tall, with blue eyes and blond hair. But there had been other blue eyes in the family.

It had just been so damn long since he'd seen them that he had forgotten about them.

You know her. You just haven't seen her for a while.

His hand trembling, he laid the photograph on the seat but continued to study it. Was there something familiar about the smile? The set of the jaw? The way the nose was a little crooked?

"No." He shoved the picture away, knocking it to the floor, then turned to stare out the side window. It wasn't true. He was just seeing things, just letting his imagination run away with him.

Beside him, Sinclair sighed. "I'm sorry. I wish there were some other way. I wish there were someone else. But there's not. We need your help, Reid." He broke off, then finished in a softer voice. "Your mother needs your help."

After another half hour, they let Reid out where they had picked him up. He took the few necessary steps to reach the sidewalk, then simply stood there, numb and sick with frustration. It wasn't *fair*. Meghan had walked away from him without a single regret when he was a kid. What right did she have to come back now, to expect him to give up everything for her, to destroy everything he'd worked so hard for? Damn her, what right did she have to take Cassie from him?

Apparently she thought the fact that she was his mother gave her those rights. She had stressed it to Sinclair as if it meant something—and damn her selfish soul, it did. He just wasn't sure it meant enough, that the part of him that had always loved, wanted and needed Meghan was as strong as the part that loved Cassie. He wasn't sure he could risk his relationship with Cassie—wasn't sure he could risk his entire damn life—to help Meghan get out of trouble.

They would understand, Sinclair had insisted. Once the case was over, once the truth came out, everyone would understand and everything would go back to the way it was before. Reid wished he shared his optimism, but he'd never had much experience with understanding and forgiving. Karen probably would understand. She gave him credit for being a better person than he was, anyway. Jamey, though, was a different matter. He was trying now, but whatever was between them was so fragile that seeing Reid go to work for Jimmy Falcone, taking his orders and his dirty money, could do irreparable harm. One more disappointment might be more than Jamey could overcome. He very well might decide that, whatever Reid's reasons, he just wasn't worth the effort.

Like Karen, Cassie thought he was better, too. She was a sweet, forgiving person, but how forgiving? When he refused to answer her questions or concede to her arguments—and she would have plenty of both—what would she do? Turn her back on him? Lose faith? Give up hope? She would undoubtedly put him out of her life. She despised Jimmy Falcone and everyone who did business with him. She would hate what she thought Reid had become. Of course, when she found out the truth, she would be apologetic, but that didn't guarantee that they could pick up where they'd left off. She might have come to her senses by then. She might have met someone else. She might have simply quit caring. After all, Sinclair had admitted that they might be talking about a long-term commitment.

What Sinclair hadn't admitted was that the truth might never fully come out. If the FBI wasn't able to put Falcone away once and for all, there was no way Reid could admit to anyone besides Cassie and his parents what he'd done. If he did, Falcone would want to send a message—and he was damn good with deadly messages. The rest of the neighborhood would still look at Reid with distrust, convinced that he was nothing more than the loser they'd always believed. They would still be intimidated by or scornful of him. They would never accept him.

A tourist leaving a nearby bar bumped into him, jarring him from his grim thoughts. He watched the guy stagger away, then looked back at the bar. He wasn't much of a drinker, but today he deserved a beer—or three or five. Today he deserved to dive headfirst into the biggest, cheapest bottle of booze he could find and not come out again until his problems were solved.

It didn't look like that was going to happen any time in the near future.

He walked through the double doors, grimacing at the foul smells of cheap liquor and overpowering cigarette smoke. Like O'Shea's, this bar wasn't much of a tourist spot, although the guy who'd bumped him obviously hadn't cared. This place catered to hard-core drinkers, to people with plenty of sorrows to drown. He'd always felt at home in such places, but never more so than today.

He paid for a beer at the bar, then carried it to the darkest corner booth and slid in. He didn't have to do what Sinclair asked. He wasn't obligated to Meghan. For the life she had given him, the way she had treated him, the day she had abandoned him, he owed her less than nothing. So what if she was in trouble over in Dallas, where she'd spent the past eight years? So what if she was facing indictment on a number of charges stemming from her involvement in Jimmy's prostitution and drug businesses? So what if she could go to prison or worse? None of that should mean anything to him.

But it did. Damn it all, there must be something terribly wrong with him, because it did.

He drained half the bottle, then slumped back on the bench. After eleven years, Meghan was back in New Orleans, but she hadn't come back for him. She probably hadn't even given him a thought until she'd come up with her brilliant plan to involve him in her troubles.

He had thought about her—had wondered whether she'd been done in by the life-style she had preferred over him. He had imagined her still living that life, still drinking heavily and partying hard, still trying on every guy who came along for Mr. Right. He'd even imagined her finding Mr. Right and living the good life in a pretty little house in some pretty little town.

He hadn't imagined her taking a job as a prostitute. Oh, there had been times when she'd traded sex for money, but it hadn't been business, merely desperation, and the men had been acquaintances, not customers. But, according to Sinclair, that was how she'd supported herself for at least eight years—first working for Jimmy in Houston, then running the business for him in Dallas. Now she was still with him. Living with him. Right here in New Orleans.

Ex-prostitute. Madam. Gangster's mistress. Mom. He smiled bitterly. He had felt a great many things for Meghan over the years. Today he was ashamed. Today, somewhere deep inside, some small part of him hated her. Some part wished she would disappear from the face of the earth. Some part wished she had never existed.

And some part... Scowling, he raised the bottle to his lips and finished it in one deep swallow. The sour taste didn't make the admission he was about to make go down any easier, but at least it took the edge off the self-disgust that accompanied it.

Some stupid, damn-fool, idiotic, abandoned-child part of him was going to help her. Wanted to help her. Needed to help her.

Whatever the cost.

As Cassie cut across the yard after school, Karen called to her through an open window. "Come inside for a minute, will you? I have a message for you."

Changing direction, she climbed the steps to the veranda, then stepped into the broad hall where the receptionist sat at her desk typing. Three toddlers were at play in what had once been the gentlemen's parlor, while their mothers sat across the hall where the formal parlor had been turned into a waiting room. With a smile for everyone, Cassie made her way to the small, cramped room that served as Karen's private office, taking a seat in front of a battered gray metal desk.

Two tall windows looked out on the front lawn and provided ventilation that did little to dispel the afternoon heat. At least the fan on top of one file cabinet provided a slightly cooling breeze. In another few weeks, Cassie was going to need one of those for her classroom and another for her bedroom. She made a mental note to put out the word and see what the family could round up.

"How was class?"

"Fine. We're making progress in the reading and math departments." Except for J.T., the others in her class who had attended school before this month hadn't learned much and had, she suspected, been labeled slow by teachers with too many students, too many obligations and not enough help. Most of the kids, it seemed, had spent their time in school doing busywork. They had colored a lot of pictures and played a lot of games. But things were different at the Serenity Street Alternative School. They were learning to read, write and count, as well as lessons in social and survival skills. Most importantly, Cassie sometimes thought, they were also learning to dream.

In the past twenty-four hours, she'd become quite a dreamer herself. At odd moments through the day, she had caught herself indulging in dreams of Reid—erotic ones, tender ones, happily-ever-after ones. She had been impatient for the end of the school day to arrive, to get home, to see him, kiss him and do whatever she wanted with him. She was still impatient, but she hid it well as she waited in front of Karen's desk. "You look as if you've had good news."

Karen grinned. With her T-shirt celebrating New Orleans and her electrified red hair that curled wildly in every direction, she looked younger than Cassie had ever felt. "I do. Remember the grant from the Griswald Foundation that we applied for?"

Cassie nodded, even though she couldn't recall any specifics. A place like Kathy's House required a lot of funding, and much of it came in dribs and drabs. Karen was always applying for grants or corporate handouts.

"It looks like it might come through. Serenity Street will have its first business that doesn't involve liquor in more than ten years."

Now Cassie remembered. The actual recipient of the grant

would be Mrs. Williams, Shawntae's mother, whose goal was to open a small corner grocery in the neighborhood. The Griswald Foundation helped small businesses get off the ground with grants, loans and advice. Once the store was up and running, Karen hoped to get other businesses to follow. She wanted to make Serenity a real neighborhood again, to make life easier for the people who lived there and more appealing to anyone who might be persuaded to invest there. She wanted to revitalize the place, and the Griswald grant would be a big step forward. "When will the final decision be made?"

"A few weeks, probably. Keep your fingers crossed." Her boss slid two yellow slips of paper across the desk. "Your messages."

The first was an invitation to dinner at Jolie's. Ordinarily Cassie would be eager to spend an evening with her favorite sister and family, but ordinarily she wasn't still settling into a job they thought she never should have taken or deceiving the entire family about her new living arrangements. Ordinarily she wasn't in the still-new-and-giddy phase of an intimate relationship that she was ardently hoping would develop into something committed and long-term with a man about whom they were sure to have second thoughts.

The second message was from her mother and pretty much the same—an invitation to a cookout on Saturday with all the family. She viewed it with far more enthusiasm, though, because of something her mother had added: "And bring that nice young man of yours." Of course, Jolie and Smith would be there, too, but in the crowd, they would have little opportunity to form more than the most superficial opinion of Reid. Her mother liked him, so they would have little choice but to also like him.

"And who is this nice young man of yours?"

A blush warming her cheeks, she smiled as she tucked the messages in her purse. "Reid helped me move some stuff from my mother's house. She was impressed."

"Good. How's it going over there? You two getting along?"

She considered giving a blunt, no-room-for-doubts sort of answer, something along the lines of *How would you like to be my mother-in-law?* Instead, she simply smiled and shrugged. "We're fine." She studied her boss's Cheshire-cat grin that hadn't diminished one bit since she'd come into the room and suddenly remembered Alicia. "Reid told me about Alicia's plans. What did you and Jamey decide?"

At last the grin faltered, and Karen's eyes grew bright and damp. "We're in the market for a crib," she replied, her voice quavering.

A warm rush of pure pleasure swept through Cassie. "Wonderful. Sean couldn't ask for better parents."

"That's what Alicia said. Jamey's not so sure. Frankly neither am I. I'm full of talk and advice, but I don't have any real experience with babies. I hold them from time to time here in the office, and I change an occasional diaper or hold a bottle, but I don't know anything about being a mother."

"You'll learn," Cassie assured her, then gently teased, "I know this place that offers parenting classes that'll teach you everything. By the way, for what it's worth, Reid thinks Jamey will make a good father."

A tender look appeared in Karen's eyes. "It's worth a lot. Thanks."

"Where is Sean?"

Karen gestured to the floor, and Cassie stood up to look. In the corner behind the desk, room had been made for an old-fashioned cradle, one that usually sat in the waiting room, and Sean, stripped down to his disposable diaper, was sleeping soundly on his stomach. His face was turned to the side, his long lashes brushing chubby cheeks. He looked adorable, and he made her feel all soft and mushy inside.

"Has Alicia left?"

Sadness shadowed Karen's face. "We spent this morning in an attorney's office, and she caught a bus this afternoon. She was heartbroken to leave him, but at the same time..." Sighing, she shook her head. "Adults have a tendency to discount young love, to suggest that because a couple is young, what they feel can't possibly be as intense as what we feel, but that's not always true. Ryan's death broke Alicia's heart. She thinks living without him will be easier in a different place, a place that doesn't remind her every day of him.''

"Will it be?'' If anyone around here understood what Alicia was going through, it must be Karen. Her first husband, Evan Montez, had been a cop killed by some lunatic who'd kidnapped a young girl. For a time after his death, Karen had remained in New Orleans, in the house she had shared with him, seeing the friends they had known as a couple, before moving back to her family's home a few hours away. Of course, since Evan had been from the same town, it must have held its own memories of him, but at least they hadn't been recent.

"It depends. Some people need to distance themselves from the memories. Some people find tremendous comfort in them. Some people find no comfort either way. Alicia will have to find out what works for her.''

"I hope she does.'' Cassie stood up again. When her boss also got to her feet, Cassie hugged her. "I'm happy for you, Karen.''

"I'm happy for you, too.'' When Cassie drew back to look at her, the older woman shrugged. "Reid deserves someone special.''

They certainly agreed on that.

With a series of goodbyes on her way out, Cassie left the office and the house and hurried across the street to O'Shea's. She stopped behind the bar to give Jamey a hug and congratulations before asking, "Is Reid upstairs?''

He shook his head. "He hasn't come in yet.''

"Is that unusual?'' Reid had gotten off work over three hours ago. She had assumed he would come straight home, had assumed that he would want to be there when she got in.

"Sometimes he runs errands or gets something to eat. He'll be here soon. It's been almost seven months since he started working here, and he's never been late even once.''

Of course he hadn't. He took his responsibilities seriously.

He was grateful for the jobs he'd gotten at a time when few people were willing to hire him, and he was conscientious in performing them. He would come home soon.

She chatted with Jamey just to pass a few minutes, then went upstairs to her hot and stuffy apartment. She left the door open and raised all the windows, then changed into shorts and a tank top. After pulling her hair back in a ponytail to get it off her neck, she settled with the papers she'd brought home to grade on the sofa—because it was comfortable, not because she could see the top of the stairs from there. She was having trouble concentrating because it was hot and her mind was numbed from a full day of schoolwork, not because the stairs remained silent and unused. She was distracted because of the messages from her family, Karen's news regarding the grant and the unexpectedly strong maternal longings Sean had stirred in her, not because Reid was late coming home.

When, after an unbearable wait, she heard the first creak of the stairs, she had to stifle the urge to throw the papers aside, jump to her feet and rush to the door to greet him. Instead, she pretended to be calm and serene. She continued to make corrections on the math papers in her lap and watch the door from the corner of her eye.

Reid came to the top of the stairs, noticed her open door, stopped and for a moment looked at her. He was dressed the same as usual, in jeans and a T-shirt, and he carried a small paper bag in one hand. He didn't smile, speak or greet her in any way. He simply looked, then turned and walked away.

Her welcoming smile frozen on her face, Cassie laid the papers aside and went into the hall. "Reid?" Had he had trouble while he was out? Maybe Marino and Morgan had harassed him or some cop who'd known him from his reckless days had rousted him. Maybe there had been a problem at the garage or he'd gotten some bad news.

He was almost to the bathroom when he stopped. He didn't turn around, though.

"What's wrong?"

"Nothing."

When she slipped past him, then turned to look at him, his face gave nothing away. He looked tough, cold, but he often had—though not lately. Maybe he was feeling shy about what had happened between them yesterday afternoon and again last night. But he hadn't been shy when he'd awakened naked in bed beside her this morning. He hadn't been at all shy when he'd gotten up, gathered his clothes and headed for a shower.

Feeling uneasy and anxious inside, she tried to smile. It wasn't a great success. "Weren't you even going to say hello to me?"

For a moment, he avoided looking at her, and she thought he was going to brush her off without a word, as if what had happened had meant nothing to him, as if *she* meant nothing to him. Then, unexpectedly, a sweet, faint smile touched his mouth, and he raised one hand to her cheek. Bending his head, he kissed her. "Hello," he said with that same smile when he raised his head. "I'm running late, and I really do need to take a shower." He moved past her, went into the bathroom and closed the door.

Something was definitely wrong. Was it her? Did he regret making love to her? After all, even though they'd met last fall, they hadn't really known each other long. Had their relationship progressed too quickly from getting acquainted to getting involved to getting naked for his comfort? Or maybe the fact that she'd been a virgin bothered him. Maybe he was afraid that she would make demands now, that she would expect some sort of commitment.

If so, he was right. While she certainly didn't expect a proposal of marriage or an engagement ring, she did expect a monogamous relationship. But that wasn't so much to ask. He'd been uninvolved for months. It wasn't as if he were being forced to choose between her and someone else.

She was still standing in the hall, still brooding, when the door opened again sometime later and he came out. He hesitated when he saw her—wearing nothing but a towel around his hips, he probably felt modest—then he came out into the hall.

Forcing a smile and a cheery tone into her voice, she said, "I was kind of hoping you would be here when I got home."

"I had a few things to take care of after work."

He passed her and went to his door. She followed. "We have some time before you have to go back to work. Want to share an early dinner?"

The look he gave her was long and measuring. What had he expected her to suggest instead of dinner? A quick romp in the sack? She was up for it if he was—but, sadly, he wasn't.

He unlocked the door with the keys he held in one hand, then ran his fingers through his hair. "Listen, Cassie..."

The muscles in her stomach knotted. She'd heard a few *Listen, Cassie*s in her life, usually followed by something she didn't want to hear. *I've met someone else. There's this girl back at school. I don't want to see you again. Let's be friends.*

"I just want some time alone. I've got to go to work soon, and I thought I'd read the paper and do some cleaning." He shrugged awkwardly, as if he were lying and knew she knew it. "I'll see you later, okay?"

Forcing her smile to stay in place through sheer will, she nodded. "Sure. Of course. Later." She didn't point out that he didn't have a newspaper—the towel certainly left no place to hide it—or that his apartment was rarely in need of cleaning. Instead, still nodding, she backed away to her own apartment, went inside, closed the door and leaned against it.

If she were a poorer judge of character, she might think she'd just gotten the brush-off. She might think that now Reid had gotten what he wanted—what young women were taught that young men *always* wanted—he was dumping her. In fact, in spite of her good judgment, deep inside she wondered if maybe, just maybe, that wasn't the case. Reid had been alone all his life. The past few months had been particularly lonely for him, and there she was, offering whatever was necessary to ease that loneliness. He would have to be crazy to turn it down, even if it hadn't meant much to him. Even if it had only been...

Tears seeped into her eyes as one of his comments over the

weekend slipped into her mind. *Sometimes you find yourself needing to be touched, even if it means having sex with someone to get it.*

Maybe, for Reid, yesterday had been one of those times.

Maybe she had mistaken loneliness for affection, basic human need for desire. Maybe he had thought that relieving her of her virginity was a fair trade for fulfilling that need for physical contact. Maybe the entire act had meant nothing to him.

Maybe *she* meant nothing to him.

Chapter 8

The sky was overcast as Reid finished dressing Wednesday morning, but the cloud layer blocking the sun did nothing to lessen the intensity of its heat. It was a muggy, miserable morning, feeling more like July than March. It was a good day for stretching out somewhere in the shade—or better, considering his foul mood, for taking refuge in a dim, smoky bar and enough booze to bring on blessed oblivion.

Falcone would send someone to pick him up around ten, Sinclair had said when Reid had called him last night and told him he would take their lousy job. The job Meghan had secured for him as her driver wouldn't be difficult. He would take her wherever she wanted to go—mostly shopping, according to Sinclair, which didn't surprise Reid. If she hadn't developed a taste for the finer things Jimmy's money could provide, she wouldn't be the Meghan that Reid remembered, sometimes loved and lately hated.

The job would allow him to spend a great deal of time with her and would give him reason to be taking packages in and out of Falcone's house. No one would suspect that a few of those boxes might contain papers, tape recordings or film. No one would suspect anything at all, she had assured Sinclair. Her loyalty to Jimmy was unquestioned, just as Reid's loyalty to her should be.

Loyalty. The word made him feel sick. What had she ever done to deserve his loyalty? She'd been a lousy mother who had run out on him a long time ago. She hadn't loved him, hadn't protected him and hadn't ever, not even on one occasion, put his needs above her own. Even now, here she was living in the same city with her only son, and yet, if it weren't for her legal problems, she never would have spared him a moment of her thoughts.

But she was his *mother.* She had given birth to him, had fed him, clothed him, sheltered him—for a time, at least. Clearly the relationship meant nothing to her, but it counted for something—for too much—with him. Hadn't he stayed on Serenity all these years in part because of her? Hadn't he nurtured a few pathetic dreams in those early years about her discovering that she missed and wanted him, about her coming back for him? Hadn't he spent half of his life taking care of her and looking out for her and too much of the other half worrying about and missing her?

He was a fool. There was no denying that. Any man worthy of the name would turn his back on her, just as she had always turned her back on him. No man in his right mind would risk every decent, caring relationship he had to help the one person who'd done the most damage in his life. No man with an ounce of pride, dignity or self-respect would cause a woman like Cassie even a moment's pain for the sake of a woman like Meghan.

But that was exactly what he intended to do. Maybe, when it was over, he could make things right with Cassie. Maybe she would still want him, Jamey would forgive him and Karen would understand. But right now he had to help Meghan. She was his mother. He had no choice.

He took up a place at the front window to watch for Falcone's car...and for Cassie. It was almost time for her and

Jaye Stephens to bring the kids outside for ten minutes of play, releasing tension and burning off pent-up energy. Sometimes she played with them. Other times she watched from the shade of a tall live oak. Once last week, she'd sat in the arbor with Tanya's niece on her lap for a few quiet minutes of one-on-one time. He'd wanted that for himself last week, to share a few minutes of quiet intimacy with her, and he'd gotten it. He wanted more—would always want more—but he might never get it again.

She had come downstairs last night to fix her dinner and offered to cook for him, too, but he'd said no. Not *No, thanks*. Not *I'm not hungry*. Not *I feel so damn sick inside that I can't eat a thing*. Just *No*. Short, blunt, rude. It had brought that wounded, rejected look into her eyes again that left him feeling damned to a certain hell.

He hadn't seen her again since then. She had taken her dinner upstairs and hadn't come down again. Her door had been closed, her apartment quiet, when he'd come up after closing up the bar, and she had left for school this morning without knocking at his door. Standing in the living room, listening to the sounds of her leaving, he had told himself that he was glad, that he didn't want to see her this morning and sure as hell didn't want to talk to her, but he had lied. She wasn't more than a hundred feet away right now, but already he missed her. He wished he'd accepted her offer of an early dinner yesterday, wished that instead of moping around the apartment until time to relieve Jamey in the bar, he had spent that hour or so in her apartment, in her bed. He wished he'd spent last night with her, just one last night, and had gotten one last kiss from her this morning.

Across the street, the two classroom doors opened almost simultaneously, and kids raced into the yard. Jaye carried a chair out with her, positioned it near the brick wall and stretched out comfortably to watch the children. Cassie came out last and headed for the side steps leading to the veranda.

For the first time, he noticed that Karen was there, seated in a rocker with Sean Morgan—soon to be O'Shea, according to Jamey's announcement in the bar last night—in her arms. Jamey was standing beside them, bending over the baby. They looked like the perfect family, Reid thought, hating the lump in his throat that was equal parts sentimentality and resentment. He was happy for them, but it was tarnished by bitterness. How different would his life have been if Jamey had been even half as eager to have him as he was to have Sean? If his father had ever given a damn about him, he would have tracked Meghan down when she fled New Orleans. He would have reclaimed his son and given him a decent home with at least one parent who cared, and now, all these years later, Meghan wouldn't be able to come back into Reid's life and use guilt and what should be meaningless ties to coerce him into helping her.

But Jamey hadn't given a damn. He had come home and discovered his wife and son were gone, and he had been relieved, happy to be freed from the marriage and the fatherhood that he'd never wanted. Now, twenty-six years later, he had a new wife and a new son. Soon—unless he was a more forgiving man than Reid had seen evidence to suggest—he would have no use for the old one.

Reid became aware of the car before it drove into sight. The engine was finely tuned, a far cry from the shake-rattle-and-sputter of Trevor Morgan's car. Nothing but the best for Jimmy Falcone and his current whore, Reid thought bitterly as he picked up his keys and left the apartment. Immediately, though, he was ashamed of the thought. Whatever Meghan was doing with Jimmy and why were none of his business. All he had to do was the job the FBI had given him and get out with his life intact.

The car was parked in front of O'Shea's when he unlocked the French doors and stepped outside. Across the street, some of the kids were still playing, but most of them had stopped and come to the fence to stare at the obscenely expensive steel-gray car with its heavily tinted windows. Jaye was staring, too. On the veranda, Karen looked worried and Jamey was scowling. He might not recognize the car—it wasn't Jimmy's usual long, black limo— but no doubt he suspected who the owner was. Who else had the nerve—or confidence—to send an eighty-thousand-dollar car into a neighborhood like Serenity?

A man got out of the front passenger seat and opened the rear door. Reid stopped, unable for an instant to make himself move forward. This was his last chance to say no, to back away or walk past, to run hard and fast in any other direction. This was his last chance to stay in Jamey's good graces, and Karen's, and J.T.'s, who was standing at the fence watching him with a look of solemnity that no kid his age should wear. It was his last chance to keep Cassie in his life—Cassie, who had separated herself from the others and was watching him with a stark, disbelieving look.

It was his last chance to save himself.

And he threw it away for a chance to save his mother.

He crossed the sidewalk to the car, then stood motionless a moment, his gaze locked on Cassie. She was gripping the railing so tightly with both hands that, if the wood were protected by fewer coats of paint, it might crumble, and she was looking at him, silently, eloquently pleading. He wished he could tell her not to worry, wished he could assure her that everything would be all right. He wished he could beg her to trust him, no matter what, but he couldn't. If Falcone's people were going to trust him, according to Meghan and Sinclair, then his own people couldn't. They had to believe the worst.

Even if it damn near killed him.

The man waiting by the door shifted impatiently, but Reid didn't look at him. He drew a deep breath, then climbed into the back seat. The guy closed the door and got in, and the driver pulled away from the curb. At the end of the block, he turned, then drove slowly past Kathy's House again, giving Reid too much time to examine the expressions of the three on the porch. Karen looked shocked, paler than usual and afraid. Jamey's surprise was quickly giving way to the cold, bitter, scornful anger Reid knew so well. As for Cassie, she couldn't even bring herself to look. She was leaning against one of the posts that supported the roof, her head bowed, her hair falling forward to hide her face.

The last face Reid saw, though, was the one he thought might haunt him the most. It was J.T., by himself now, standing on the sidewalk in front of the gate. Although J.T.'s mother's first rule of survival for her son had long been to stay away from Reid, they'd been friends anyway for a long time. Judging by the look of disappointment on the kid's face, Reid knew they wouldn't be friends any longer.

Scowling, he slumped back in the seat. He damn well hoped Meghan and Sinclair appreciated what he was doing, because it was a sure bet that no one else did.

It was a leisurely drive across the river to Falcone's estate. A tall stand of perfectly groomed shrubs extended a mile along the road, divided in thirds by two electronically controlled security gates set into granite pillars. Behind the shrubs was a twelve-foot-tall iron fence, wired for sound and monitored twenty-four hours a day. There were two armed guards at each gate and a number more on the grounds. The place was a fortress for the rich and well connected.

That included his mother. As of this morning, the well-connected part, at least, included him, too.

The gates swung open as the car approached. The driver bypassed the main house and went around back to the garage instead. There, once again, the passenger opened the back door, and Reid stepped out, glancing around with curiosity. He might have worked sporadically for Falcone in the past, but he'd never been invited to his estate, where even the garage was a damn sight more luxurious than any place on Serenity. It was filled with cars of the sort Reid would never get his hands on, not unless he resorted to stealing again. There was the limo in an oversize bay at the end, a Jag, a classic hardtop T-bird and a twin except in color to the Mercedes he had just arrived in. Each of the cars was in showroom condition, treated with more care than most people in Falcone's life.

Reid turned back to the man who'd opened the door. "So what do I do now?"

In reply the man gestured toward the house. Reid turned and found himself face-to-face with his mother for the first time in eleven years.

Her appearance wasn't a total shock—he'd seen Sinclair's photo, after all—but it left him staring. She bore about as much resemblance to the woman he remembered as the Jag did to Trevor's gray-primer Ford. She was slender instead of too-much-drugs-and-booze skinny. Her hair was tinted auburn, short and sleek, instead of brown, long and unkempt. Her skin was clear, and her blue eyes were bright and alert in a way that he'd never seen. The unhealthy, scrawny, trashy look he remembered was gone, replaced by an air of good health and good living with a veneer of the best sophistication money could buy.

She was a stranger.

He was putting his life at risk for a *stranger*.

"Hello, Reid." Walking with grace across the cobblestone drive in spite of her heels, she came straight to him and slid her arms around him in an expensively perfumed embrace. He stiffened, disliking the contact, resenting all the times he would have done *anything* to get such a hug from her, remembering all the times he'd gotten the back of her hand instead.

Wisely she kept the embrace brief, pulling back after only a few seconds, then sliding her arm through his and starting toward the house. "Come along. We'll find someplace quiet where we can talk."

She drew him past the biggest swimming pool he'd ever seen, through the center of a flower-filled gazebo and into the house. It was huge, about ten times more space than she and Jimmy could ever need, and intimidatingly quiet. He felt as if he were in a museum as he followed her through inlaid-marble halls, past one elaborately decorated, antique-filled, high-ceilinged room after another. She finally settled in what was probably the only room in the house where he could feel reasonably comfortable, a sitting room with windows, plants and wicker furniture of such quality that it shared little in common with most of the stuff he'd seen. Not even Cassie's wicker dresser—

His mouth tightened. He hadn't helped her move the dresser to her apartment or finish the other pieces. Monday afternoon they'd been too busy in bed, and yesterday he'd been out feeling sorry for himself. He might never get a chance to see the dresser in her bedroom, might never get a chance to set foot in her apartment—or her life—again.

Meghan arranged herself on a chaise while he took a seat nearby. "You've grown up."

"A kid does that in eleven years."

She laughed. "It's been a long time. Not long enough to make you forgive me, was it?"

He didn't reply.

"You would realize that I did you a favor if you weren't so stubborn. I wasn't much of a mother." She admitted it freely, without guilt, without regret. "You were better off with your grandmother."

"My grandmother kicked me out after a few months. I lived on the streets."

"Oh." For a moment, she sounded disconcerted, then with a wave of a manicured hand in the air, she dismissed his pronouncement with a flash of bright red nails. "You would have been on the streets with me, too. I had a few tough years after I left you here."

"Obviously your luck has changed." His luck had changed, too, every bit as dramatically as hers. Now, thanks to her, the pendulum had swung back. He was back where he'd started, working for a man who gave corruption a bad name and with less reason to hope than he'd had in a long time.

Meghan took exception to his dry statement. "I worked hard for everything I have."

"Yeah. I heard what kind of work you did to get where you are now."

She gave him a cool, measuring look. "Considering what kind of work you've engaged in—when you've bothered to work at all—you hardly have room to criticize.'' She paused to shake out a cigarette and light it, then abruptly announced, "You look like your father."

There had been a time when he'd fiercely resented every O'Shea trait he'd recognized in himself, from his height to his blond hair to a few unconscious mannerisms. That time was months in the past, though. If he had to take after one of his parents, Jamey was the better choice.

"You two ever settle things?"

"We were working on it. You've *un*settled them all over again."

She smiled thinly. "How is he?"

"Fine. He's married now."

"And your grandmother?"

Even though he hadn't been close to the old woman, even though she had kicked him out on the street, his resentment grew at Meghan's careless question. "She died years ago."

There was a flash of regret in her eyes, but it disappeared as quickly as it had come. She was so self-absorbed that she couldn't conjure up more than a passing remorse for her own mother's death. What the hell was he doing here? It meant nothing to her that her mother was dead, nothing that she was disrupting her son's life to the point that he might never get it straight again. Since the bonds between mother and child were so obviously missing from her life, why the hell was he here? Why was he helping her? Why did he care when she didn't?

Because that was the way it had always been. To her, he had been a burden from the moment she'd known of his existence. He had ruined her plans, her future and her life. He had forced her into a marriage she'd never wanted and had been her excuse for everything that had ever gone wrong. It was his fault that she'd been eighteen, divorced, uneducated and on her own in Atlanta, that she'd never been able to make anything of herself, that one man or another hadn't wanted her, that she'd had to resort to drugs or booze to find any pleasure. To him, she had been his mother. She'd been his entire world.

She had never wanted him, but he had always needed her. She had always neglected him, but for as long as he could remember, he had taken care of her. He had fed her when she was too sick to eat, had put her to bed when she was too drunk to find her way, had lied, cheated and stolen for her. Now here he was, trying once again to help, but this time would be the last. Once he was finished here, he would never see her again. He would never need her again. He would have Karen, who, in six months, had been a better mother than Meghan had ever been, and that would be enough.

Depending on the generosity of Jamey's and Cassie's spirits, Karen might have to be enough. She might be the only one to forgive him.

Abruptly Meghan rose from the chair and tapped him on the shoulder. "Come on, let's go shopping. If you're going to work for Jimmy Falcone, you have to dress better than that. We'll buy enough to get you started—my treat. After that, you're on your own."

He followed her out of the room. He'd known his clothes wouldn't be suitable, though his jeans were relatively new and unfaded and the blue-and-white-striped button-down shirt was starched and pressed. He'd seen how Jimmy's people dressed—in well-cut suits usually roomy enough for a holster or two underneath—but, hell, he was a garage mechanic and a bartender. Just how many suits did they expect him to have in his closet?

After a stop to pick up her handbag, she led the way to the garage, where she literally snapped her fingers in the direction of one of the men lounging there. "Give Reid the keys to the burgundy Mercedes. If Mr. Falcone asks, tell him we've gone shopping."

The man tossed a set of keys to Reid. He approached the car slowly. He had never driven a car that could compare to the Mercedes before—had never even wanted to until that moment. Circling behind it, he started to open the driver's door, but stopped when Meghan, standing impatiently on the opposite side, gave him a chiding look.

"You're being paid to be my driver, Reid. My driver *always* opens and closes the doors for me." She said it with just the right amount of snippiness, as if she had long been accustomed to such courtesies. Not a bad trick for someone who had many times found the fare for the city bus out of her reach.

He went around the car, opened the door, waited until she slid inside, then closed it again. Once again he returned to the driver's side and got in, inserted the key and turned it. The engine sprang to life, smoother and more powerful than any he'd ever gotten his hands on. Driving this car would be pure pleasure, even if his reasons for doing so weren't.

As he backed out of the garage, he met Meghan's gaze in the rearview mirror. "I hope Jimmy is well insured."

"Why? I heard you worked in a garage as a mechanic. Surely you're a good driver."

"I'm a great driver." He shifted into gear, then glanced at her over his shoulder. "But I don't have a license."

Cassie sat at the top of the steps leading to the front door of Kathy's House, her arms resting on her knees. It was after five-thirty, and the women's center was closed for the day. She was considering summoning the energy for a heavy sigh when, beside her, Karen gave just such a sigh. Cassie couldn't bring herself to echo it. It sounded entirely too sad already.

"I don't understand," her boss said for the hundredth time since this morning. "What business does Reid have with that man?"

"Reid's done business with Jimmy Falcone off and on for years."

"But not now, not for months! He's tried so hard, Cassie. He's done so well. Why would he start dealing with him again?" After a moment, she answered her own question. "Maybe it's been too hard. Maybe he just got tired of trying. Maybe he just wants to be accepted someplace exactly the way he is."

She had accepted him, Cassie thought numbly. She had accepted him right into her bed—not that he'd been eager to return. Maybe this was somehow her fault. He'd made love with her Monday night, had come home Tuesday acting odd and evasive and had gone off with Falcone's people this morning. Maybe *she* was somehow responsible for whatever had happened, for whatever choice he had made.

Wouldn't that be quite an ego stroke? Other women drove their men crazy with love or, at the least, lust, while she drove hers to crime.

She hadn't been home yet, though she was heartsore and soul weary. After making it through the day on autopilot, she had come to Kathy's House to find out if Karen or Jamey had heard anything, to commiserate and to delay going home to her empty apartment and brooding the night away. She couldn't bear seeing Reid's apartment and knowing he wasn't there—worse, knowing he was with Falcone. She couldn't bear her own apartment, filled with belongings he had helped her move, and especially her bed, where they'd made love, kissed and cuddled and finally slept.

But she couldn't delay forever. She either had to beg a spot on Karen's couch, return to Smith's condo or go home. Home was where she belonged. If Reid went looking for her, that was where he would look.

Bolstering her confidence with a deep breath, she reached across to stroke Sean's dark hair. "He has an explanation, Karen," she said determinedly. "There's a perfectly good reason for whatever he's doing."

"And what could that be? We're talking about a young man who's been breaking the law since he was about five, who's given up everything he had to go straight, who's had to endure prejudice, fear and contempt, who's had to fight for every bit of respect or acceptance he's gotten, who's now getting involved with the most notorious, most dangerous criminal in the entire state. What perfectly good reason could there be for that?"

Cassie didn't answer. She couldn't. All she knew was that

she had to believe in him. She had to have faith. Jamey's was fading, and Karen's was wavering, but she must believe that the man she loved wouldn't do what he was doing without a reason. Maybe he didn't love her. She could accept that. Maybe he didn't care much about her at all. It would surely break her heart, but she could accept that, too. But she couldn't accept that he had returned to his old life. She couldn't accept that he would again get involved with his old boss. She could *not* accept that he would throw away all that he had worked for. He *must* have a reason, and she would wait until he could give it.

"I've got to go home." She picked up her books from the step and cradled them to her chest. "Don't jump to any conclusions, Karen. Let's see what Reid has to say."

"Sure. Of course." Karen gazed down at Sean, who was contentedly chewing his fingers, then sighed softly. "There was a time when I first got involved with Jamey when I wasn't thrilled about the idea of being Reid's stepmother. I'd always wanted a child, for as long as I could remember, but not a grown stepson whose life had been so troubled. Of course, we don't get to choose the families of the people we fall in love with, but now I can't imagine anyone I would want as a part of our family more than Reid. I wish he were my own, but I couldn't love him more if he were, and I worry about him. I'm really worried about him."

"Trust him," Cassie said quietly. "You did it when no one else did. Don't quit now." With a faint smile for a goodbye, she followed the sidewalk through the gate, then crossed the street and went into O'Shea's. Behind the bar, Jamey looked too angry for the reassuring kind of conversation she'd just shared with Karen, so Cassie merely offered him the same sad smile and went upstairs. She put her books down, then went down the hall to the bathroom, where she bent over the sink and splashed water over her face. The cool water washed away the grit and sweat of a day's un-air-conditioned work, but it didn't make her feel any better. It didn't wake her from the bad dream her day had turned into.

She was reaching for a towel when her gaze settled on the wicker wastebasket she'd moved in with her. On top of a pile of dirty makeup-remover pads and an empty shaving cream can was a small brown paper bag, the same bag Reid had been carrying when he'd come home yesterday. Hesitantly she bent and fished it out, then pulled open the stapled top.

There was a box of condoms inside with a sales receipt dated and time-stamped yesterday afternoon only twenty minutes after Reid had gotten off work at the garage. At 1:20 he'd been planning ahead, making certain he was well prepared for whatever he might do, and *who* he would have done it with, she knew, she wanted to believe, was *her.* But less than five hours later, he had walked right past her as if she were a stranger, and he had lied to avoid spending time with her. He had withdrawn from her, just as a turtle drew into its shell when threatened. Who—or what—had threatened Reid?

Maybe Jimmy Falcone.

She dried her face, then took the bag with her when she left the bathroom. She hadn't gone three feet when she heard footsteps on the stairs that brought her to an abrupt halt. Instinctively she stuffed the bag into one of the deep pockets of her dress, then waited for Reid to appear. When he finally stood at the opposite end of the hall in front of her, she felt a queasy little fear deep in her stomach.

If she had passed him on the street anywhere besides Serenity, she might not have recognized him. His hair was shorter, and in place of his usual jeans and sneakers, he wore a suit—an expensive, elegantly cut, dove gray suit. He looked like any of a thousand young businessmen in the city, though far more handsome.

He looked like a stranger.

He was carrying a handful of garment bags, no doubt holding similar suits, and a large shopping bag, probably filled with shirts, ties, maybe more shoes. God help them, he had taken a job with Jimmy Falcone.

He didn't notice her until he'd set the shopping bag down and shifted the suit bags to his left hand so he could reach his keys. For a moment, he stiffened, and then he looked away as if he were ashamed to be seen by her.

Slowly she began moving toward him, walking in a wide circle around him. "Nice clothes." Her voice wasn't calm, but it was steady. "Whoever knew mechanics and bartenders were paid so much?"

He unlocked the door but didn't open it. "Cassie—"

She waited at her own door for him to continue. When he didn't, she coaxed him. "Go on. I want to hear whatever you have to say. I want to know how you can justify going to work for that man."

There was momentary surprise on his face when he turned around. "How did you...?" Then his expression turned sullen. "It's just a job."

"'Just a job'? Doing what? Who do you have to rob? What do you have to steal? Who do you have to threaten, intimidate or maybe even kill?"

Laying the garment bags over the shopping bag, he took a few steps toward her. "Damn it, Cassie, you know I wouldn't—"

She reached out, clasping his wrist, feeling the fine fabric of his coat crinkle under her fingers. "Reid, Jimmy Falcone represents everything you've worked so hard to get away from. My God, he had your best friend killed!"

He pulled free of her and backed away. "It's just a job. I'm just a driver. There's nothing illegal about it. I just chauffeur his latest..." He faltered, and his cheeks turned pink before, with his scowl deepening, he went on. "His latest woman around town on her shopping trips."

"And today she shopped for you. How sweet." Her voice trembled. "Reid, you can't work for that man. He's dangerous. He kills people. He destroys people's lives. Even if you aren't doing anything illegal—"

"*Even if?* You don't believe me, do you? You think I've gone back to the old life, don't you? You think I was dirty so long that I don't have the willpower to resist. You think I'm so weak that all it'll take to make me tumble is being around someone else who's dirty."

Her throat was thick and tight with tears. "I think you've had it so tough for so long that you could get used to the good life really fast. I think you could come to accept doing whatever it takes to keep it."

"And what's wrong with that?" he demanded. "I've been poor all my life. What the hell is wrong with me making some money for once in my miserable life? You know what Jimmy pays for a week of driving around town in his fancy car? More than I make in a month at the garage and downstairs combined. I'd have to be a fool to turn that down."

"No, Reid. You'd have to be a fool not to." She reached out hesitantly but didn't touch him. "Why are you doing this? Why are you risking everything you have for that man?"

He stared at her for a moment, his blue eyes wintry cold. "I've got two lousy jobs that no one else would take for such lousy pay, and a cheap, shabby apartment that I can be kicked out of any time O'Shea takes a notion. That's all I've got, Cassie, and you think I should give a damn about losing it?"

"What about the people? Jamey, Karen, your new stepbrother. Your boss at the garage who gave you a chance. The people at the center who admire what you've tried to do. What about J.T., Reid? What about me?"

The set of his jaw grew stubborn. "What about you, Cassie? You wanted to be my friend and a hell of a lot more...as long as I lived the way you wanted. As long as I was the loser and you were the bright, generous do-gooder. As long as I was properly grateful and you were able to feel charitable and superior. Now I've found a job that I like, where I don't have to work twelve hours a day, where I can make enough money to live a decent life. I'm not the loser anymore. I'm not poor. I don't have to live in this dump because I can't afford anything better. I can go where I want and do what I want. Now suddenly you're not so willing and eager, are you? You're as damn quick to judge me as everyone else. What does that say about you?"

"So I was treating you like a charity case, and you were..."
Cassie's voice quavered again, and she couldn't get it under
control. "You were just using me until something better came
along." She tried to smile but couldn't. "I'm sorry. I was
wrong. You're not the fool here. I am." With that, she closed
and locked the door, walked straight into her bedroom, curled
up on the bed and cried. She cried until she was all cried out,
and then she did what she always did when she had trouble.

She went to Jolie.

After their marriage, Jolie and Smith had lived in her house
for as long as it'd taken them to find a bigger place that they
both appreciated. They'd settled on a sprawling Creole cottage
in an older, established neighborhood and had had the whole
place renovated just in time for the birth of their first child,
who had since been joined by twin girls.

Cassie parked behind Jolie's red 'Vette, climbed the steps
to the high porch and rang the doorbell. When Jolie answered
with a daughter on one hip and another clinging to her right
leg, she looked worn, frazzled and blank. "Was the invitation
for tonight?"

Now it was Cassie's turn to look blank, until she remem-
bered the dinner invitation her sister had extended through
Karen. She shook her head. "It's tomorrow, but I don't think
I can come. Is this a bad time to talk?"

Jolie laughed. "Oh, darlin', this is as good as it gets. Come
on in. What do you mean, you don't think you can come to
dinner tomorrow?"

"I just can't." After closing the door behind her, Cassie
bent to pick up the child balancing on her mother's foot. The
twins were far from identical, although they both had their
father's dark hair and quiet personality. Claire had inherited
Smith's blue eyes and was chunky, while Mary Rose was slender as a reed with hazel eyes all her own. Three-year-old Patrick, engaged in a high-decibel battle against evil elsewhere in
the house, was his mother's clone, with blond hair, green eyes
and more energy than Cassie's thirteen students combined.

Jolie led the way to the family room at the back of the

house, where she deposited Mary Rose on the floor. Cassie set Claire down beside her, then wandered to the tall windows overlooking the backyard. It was a lush, private haven, elaborately designed with tall trees and sheltering shrubs, with plenty of beds for flowers and plenty of grass for the kids. It was a far cry from the yard Jolie had grown up with—a patch of bare dirt surrounding the ugly gray Serenity Street house—or even from the postage-stamp yard she'd had at her little yellow house. If anyone deserved such drastic changes, though, it was Jolie. She'd earned them.

"You're a hard woman to get hold of," Jolie said from somewhere close behind. "Mama and I have left a dozen messages on your machine in the last couple of days. Don't you ever check it?"

For a moment, Cassie felt blank until remembering the answering machine she'd deliberately left in the condo. When she'd moved to Serenity, she had intended to use the machine to keep up her pretense, at least until she'd broken the news to the family, but in her few days there, she'd forgotten all about it. "I...I've been kind of busy."

"What's his name?" Jolie appeared in Cassie's peripheral vision, slender, beautiful and serene. It was funny how things had changed. All her life, Cassie had been the Wade stuck with the serene label, while Jolie had been the one with passion. Now, in spite of the three demanding toddlers, she looked as if her life couldn't possibly be more tranquil, while Cassie had suddenly uncovered her own passion.

She didn't try to evade her sister's question or brush off her curiosity. Serene or not, Jolie was still the best investigative reporter the city of New Orleans would ever see. No one kept secrets from her unless she chose to let them remain secret. Besides, confiding and seeking advice had been Cassie's reason for coming over. "Reid," she said, hearing the faint tremor in her voice. "Reid Donovan."

Jolie's voice softened. "Tell me about Reid Donovan."

"He's Jamey O'Shea and Meghan Donovan's son. He's handsome as sin, sweet and misunderstood. He's a good mechanic and a great artist, and some of us on Serenity care a great deal about him.''

"Including you."

"Especially me." Drawing a deep breath, she turned to face her sister and smiled unsteadily. "Oh, and one other thing— he just started a new job. As of this morning, he works for Jimmy Falcone."

Reid sat on the bed, his back against the rusted bars of the headboard, his legs stretched out in front of him. He had put away all the clothes Meghan had insisted on buying, taken a shower and knocked at Cassie's door a half-dozen times before finally settling in here. He had handled her badly, which wasn't surprising since all he'd wanted to do was wrap his arms around her tight and trust that she could make everything better. He should have been calmer, but right from the start she'd made it clear that she didn't believe he could possibly be doing anything legal, and he had reacted the way he always did: defensively. Sullenly. He had said nasty things and had let her believe that she meant nothing to him. He had hurt her, and God would surely make him pay.

Meghan had suggested that he take the paycheck she'd passed on for Jimmy—a generous welcome-to-the-family gesture—and find himself a new place to live, some decent little apartment a world away from Serenity. His initial response had been negative, but now, after seeing the look Jamey had given him when he'd walked through the bar and the run-in with Cassie, he thought that maybe Meghan had the right idea. He could save himself a world of hurt if he stayed away from Serenity until this was all over and done with, until Remy Sinclair could help him convince them that it had all been part of the FBI's plan.

But if he left for however long this damn thing took, there might not be a place for him to come back to. If he removed himself totally from their lives, they would find it easier to forget and move on. As long as he left here every morning and came back here every evening, they would have to acknowledge him. They couldn't just wash their hands of him.

Feeling weary and sore, he got up from the bed and pulled on a T-shirt and shoes. It was nearly six-thirty, time for him to take over downstairs. He doubted that Jamey expected him to show, doubted even more that his old man wanted him to, but he headed that way anyway. Tending bar would be an easier way to spend the evening than moping over Cassie.

As he walked down the hall between the stairs and the bar, Jamey looked but didn't say a thing until Reid moved past him and picked up a clean towel from the stack under the bar. "What are you doing?"

Reid tried to check his frustration. "What I've done every weeknight since last September—working. You have a problem with that?"

Jamey shrugged. "It's a lousy job for someone who wears a suit and drives a fancy car for Mr. Jimmy Falcone."

Gritting his teeth on a curse, Reid stared off at a distant wall until he could respond with some measure of calm. "You want to fire me? Go ahead. You want to kick me out of your place upstairs? It won't be the first time." But it would definitely be the worst.

His old man started to turn away, then swung back. "Why are you doing this? Wasn't your life tough enough without you going out looking for something to make it tougher? Wasn't it already hard enough without you giving everyone the best reason in the world to distrust you more than they ever did?"

"What I do is my own business, O'Shea, not—"

His voice ominously low, Jamey interrupted. "Don't call me that."

O'Shea. For years that was all Reid had called him—except to his face, when, with all the bitter anger of the punk he'd been, he had preferred *bastard.* Using his father's last name—the last name *he* had been denied—had been one way of distancing himself, of never letting himself forget how far from a real father-son relationship they were and would likely always be. It hadn't been until recently that he'd been able to call him Jamey. He couldn't even imagine ever reaching the point where he might call him Dad.

"What I do is my own business," he repeated. "If you're angry about it, that's your problem. You deal with it."

Jamey walked to the end of the bar, then turned back to look at him. "I'm not angry with you, Reid," he said tiredly. "I'm just disappointed as hell."

As he walked away, Reid wished he could say the words didn't hurt, wished he could pretend that he was so accustomed to such remarks that they just rolled off his back. After all, hadn't he lived most of his life with his mother's indifference and his father's contempt?

But he couldn't pretend. He was already lying to everyone else, but he couldn't lie to himself. His father's simple, quiet words did hurt. They hurt so damn much.

The evening passed in a blur. None of the customers seemed in a better mood than he was. No one wanted to talk. No one wanted anything but to drink his drinks in peace. For a moment, he considered joining them—filling a dozen glasses or more with samples of every beer and liquor Jamey had in stock, pulling a chair up to a table and methodically emptying them. But getting drunk never solved anything. Meghan had taught him that.

Seeing her today had been a letdown. It wasn't that she'd changed. She had always been self-centered and shallow. His own expectations had let him down. Even though he had accepted eleven years ago that she'd made a deliberate choice to remove him from her life, he had imagined a hundred different reconciliations, every one of them involving great emotion on her part. In every little dream, she had discovered some previously untapped and limitless source of love for her only son, and she had been driven to return to him, to make amends with him and make a happy, loving home for him. They had been the foolish dreams of a foolish child.

He no longer expected love from her, but he would have liked some little regret. He would have appreciated some hint

of gratitude for the help he was giving her or some acknowledgment of the sacrifice he was making for her. All he'd
gotten, though, had been an impersonal hug, offered for effect,
and a long day of Meghan discoursing on Meghan.

It hadn't been the reunion of his dreams, but it had taken
care of those dreams, once and for all. He wasn't a kid any
longer. He didn't need the mother who was never going to be
there for him. All he needed was to know that he'd treated
her fairly, that he had done what he could before walking away
from her. Once this mess was over and she had betrayed
Jimmy to the best of her ability, there would be nothing left
between them.

At the other end of the bar, the phone rang, a rare occur-
rence. When he answered, a voice belonging to a woman who
embodied the ideal mother responded. "This is Rosemary
Wade. I understand I can reach my daughter at this number."

He wondered how she had come to that understanding. As
of yesterday, Cassie hadn't confided her change of address to
anyone in her family for fear of their reaction. Today she was
probably wishing she'd never made the change in the first
place. She would have been better off if she'd stayed in her
expensive condo and far away from *him*. "Hold on, Mrs.
Wade," he said quietly. "I'll see if she's upst—"

"Oh, I know she's not there right now. She just left her
sister's a few minutes ago. I was just calling to confirm—
Reid?"

"Yes, ma'am."

"So she *is* living there. When you two came to the house
last weekend, you were helping her move in there, weren't
you?"

"Yes, ma'am." He felt guilty for the lie she'd been told,
though he hadn't been the one to tell it. Hell, he'd hardly said
anything at all to the woman.

"Is she safe there?"

Safe from everything but *him*. "Things have gotten better
down here. It's not a place where she should be living, but it
could be worse."

"Oh, that's reassuring."

"I'm sorry. I didn't mean..." Seeing a slender figure cross the street out front and head for the bar, he felt a rush of relief. "She just came in. Do you want to talk to her?"

"Of course I do."

Cassie came across the bar, pointedly ignoring everyone in it. When she was only a half-dozen feet away, he spoke. "Telephone, Cassie."

She hesitated until he laid the receiver on the bar and went to the other end. Finally she climbed onto the stool and picked up the phone. He tried not to listen to her end of the conversation, tried even harder not to watch her, but he couldn't stop. She was so damn beautiful, and he wanted to say so damn much to her. He wanted to hold her. He wanted her to save him.

When she finished with the call, she hung up and simply sat there for a moment, her head lowered. He stood ten feet away, drying a glass that might not have been wet to start, and tried to think of anything to say. At last he settled on the obvious. "You finally told your family that you've moved."

She glanced up, looked as if she were going to say something obnoxious, then shook her head. "Yeah, I told them. They weren't thrilled."

"What did you expect? They worry about you."

Her eyes darkened a shade or two. "Is that supposed to make a difference? Like it makes a difference to you that Jamey, Karen and I are worried about you?"

He carefully set the glass down, laid the towel beside it, then approached her. "Cassie, it's just a job. I'm not doing anything illegal. I've just been hired to drive this woman around. That's all I'm doing."

"No. What you're doing is breaking your parents' hearts."

He knew it was stupid to go closer. It was crazy to touch her hand. It was downright lunacy to look into her eyes, and it was madness to ask the obvious question, but he asked anyway. "What about you?"

Turning her hand over, she gave his a squeeze, then pulled

free and circled the bar. There she looked back. "Don't worry about my heart, Reid. You've already broken it."

He followed her into the hall, catching hold of her again, pushing her back against the wall and holding her there with his body. She didn't struggle, didn't try to get away, not even when his mouth pressed against hers. Instead, she brought her hands to his shoulders. She moved against him—not struggling, not trying to get away, but trying to get closer. She even started to open her mouth to his tongue, but stopped, leaving him with a kiss that couldn't begin to satisfy his need.

"Damn it, Cassie, don't shut me out!" he whispered fiercely before kissing her again, but she resisted. He could have coaxed her, could have pleaded or begged for that one small concession. He could have done any of a dozen things until he felt the dampness of the tear that had slipped down her cheek. Filled with sorrow, he ended the kiss and let her go. His silent curses echoed her footfalls on the stairs.

Damn Jimmy Falcone. Damn Remy Sinclair and especially Meghan. Most of all, though, he damned himself for the biggest fool who'd ever known and lost a woman like Cassie.

Chapter 9

Traffic was light on Interstate 10 as Reid drove toward New Orleans. In the back seat Meghan was staring out the window, her expression decidedly bored. In the week he'd been driving her, she had apparently bought everything her heart desired in New Orleans and was now expanding her horizons. She had chatted all the way to Baton Rouge this morning about the shops where they would go, the things she would buy, the money she would spend. On this return trip, the Mercedes's trunk was filled with boxes and bags from the city's most exclusive stores, Jimmy was about eight thousand dollars poorer and Meghan was moody. Funny how, after so many years apart, Reid still recognized the mood that once would have resulted in a weepy attempt to drown her sorrows. Personally he had favored her mean, angry binges. Getting knocked around had always been preferable to her endless melancholy tears.

For the first time since leaving the last outrageously expensive store, she spoke. "Do you have any fond memories of me?"

He looked in the rearview mirror to find her watching him, her expression as idle and disinterested as if she had pointed out that there were clouds in the sky overhead. After a moment, he shifted his gaze back to the road. "No."

"Go on, answer truthfully," she said, a hint of bitter laughter in her voice. "Don't spare my feelings." Then she gave a great sigh. "None at all? No Christmases, no birthdays, nothing?"

"We never celebrated Christmas or birthdays." He was twenty-six years old, and he'd never had a Christmas tree or a birthday cake. Last year's Christmas gift from Karen was the first he'd ever received. "Which memories do you think I should treasure? All the times you hit me? The times I went hungry because you spent the food money on drugs? The nights I spent alone while you were out partying? How about the times I broke into our old apartments to steal our stuff after we'd gotten evicted yet again? Or maybe—"

"All right, you made your point. Living with me wasn't easy. I never wanted a baby, you know. That made it easy for me to blame you whenever something went wrong. When I left your father to go to Atlanta, I should have left you, too. Jamey would have provided you with more stability than I did."

"He never wanted a baby, either," Reid reminded her, even as the image of Karen holding Sean in her lap and Jamey leaning over them came to mind.

"Maybe not, but he would have dealt with the disappointment better than me. He would have accepted his responsibilities. He's good about that. You must get it from him."

Reid ignored her description of him as a disappointment and focused instead on her last words. "I must get what from him?"

She waved her hand, her nails a brilliant scarlet flash in the mirror. "Your sense of responsibility. Obligation. That's why you're here. Because I'm your mother and for some odd reason, you think that's supposed to mean something."

"It's supposed to," he agreed, then dryly added, "Of course, the money doesn't hurt."

Her smile came slowly. "Spoken like a true Donovan. Of course, that first part was more like a true O'Shea. Your father was always looking out for others."

"While you were always looking out for yourself."

"I *have* to look out for myself. I don't have a husband, family or friends to turn to, and I can't count on guilt over a lousy mother-son relationship to work with you again, can I?"

He gave a shake of his head. Not a flicker of emotion crossed her reflection in the mirror. No regret, no dismay, no sadness. But he wouldn't feel regret or dismay once he'd seen her for the last time. Sadness, maybe—after all, he'd had those dreams of a loving mother for a long time—but mostly only relief. He would be relieved to watch his mother walk away and know that he would never see her again, and *that* was reason for sadness.

"So what are you going to do with all this sweet money Jimmy's paying you? Got a girl to spend it on?"

His hands tightened around the steering wheel. He'd hardly seen Cassie in the past week. She had come through the bar last evening while he was working, carrying the little table that he'd stripped for her, now all sanded, stained and polyurethaned. A second trip had brought the bookcase, painted a high-gloss white. He had offered to help her with the dresser, but she had politely turned him down. She could handle it, or she and Karen could, or she and Jamey. She and anybody else in the whole damn world except *him*.

He sighed heavily. "I was seeing someone until last week."

"What? She didn't approve of your new job?"

"No."

"You're kidding. You're a chauffeur. You drive a car. What's to disapprove of?"

"Well, let's see. I've been in trouble with the law since I was a kid. I've spent the last seven months trying to get straightened out, and then I go and take a job as a chauffeur to the mistress and business associate of the most powerful organized-crime boss Louisiana has ever seen—who happens to have been my boss a few years back when I almost wound up in prison. What could she possibly disapprove of?''

He got a glimpse of another casual, dismissive wave. ''What does she do for a living that she can afford to be so high and mighty?''

''She teaches kindergarten through third grade at the Serenity Street school.''

''Oh, how sweet.'' Her sarcasm made the muscles in his jaw clench. ''You know, Reid, opposites might attract, but they don't live happily ever after. Your little schoolteacher friend might have a lot of fun with you now, but when she settles down, it's going to be with someone who's just like her—someone educated. Someone who hasn't been in trouble with the law all his life. Someone she wouldn't have to be ashamed of with her family and friends.''

The muscles tightened even more. She was only putting his own fears into words, but he hated hearing them, especially hated hearing them in that smug, confident voice of hers. Damn it, mothers were supposed to offer reassurance, encouragement and comfort, not destroy hopes and confidence. But Meghan freely admitted that she was a lousy mother, which apparently exempted her from common courtesy.

''What—no argument?''

He wanted to insist that Cassie wasn't like that. She wasn't ashamed of him, and she didn't care that he'd been in trouble. She was just worried that he was going to get into trouble again, but it wasn't going to happen. All the money in the world couldn't make him go back to a way of life that always had been and always would be his greatest shame. Spending time in Jimmy's big, expensive house didn't make him any less appreciative of his own little apartment, shabbiness and all. That life held no appeal for him. Everything he wanted, everything he loved, could be found on one block of the poorest street in New Orleans's poorest neighborhood.

By the time they crossed the Mississippi River and reached Jimmy's estate, it was nearly six-thirty and he was feeling anxious. He was supposed to relieve Jamey at O'Shea's in another five minutes, but there was no way he could make it—and no way Jamey would be interested in hearing his excuses. In spite of his claim to the contrary last week, his old man was angry and seemed more so every time Reid saw him. Every evening when he walked into the bar, Reid half expected to get fired, but it hadn't happened yet. He would like to think that his father was giving him the benefit of the doubt, but it was more likely that Jamey cared more about spending time with his wife and new son than he did about what was happening with his other son. He could tolerate Reid's presence in the bar as long as it gave him time at home with Sean.

He parked near the back door, as Meghan had instructed, and made two trips upstairs with her purchases. He was on his way out to move the car to the garage, then get one of the men hanging out there to give him a ride home, when Meghan called his name. It was echoed from the doorway leading into Jimmy's private study. He turned and saw Meghan coming down the stairs with a bag before settling his gaze on his boss.

In all his years in New Orleans, he'd had little face-to-face contact with Jimmy Falcone. Even in the past week, he'd been in the house two dozen times and hadn't seen the man. He was always shut up in his study, taking care of business elsewhere or meeting with associates over lunch at his favorite restaurant.

He was a little guy with graying black hair whose dress was always impeccable, his behavior almost always so. To look at him, no one would ever guess that he'd grown up poorer than dirt in a family that had long been considered the trashiest in the parish. People who hadn't known him back then couldn't even begin to imagine how far he had come, and all it had taken was determination, hard work, ruthlessness and an utter disregard for any life but his own.

"How do you like your job, Reid?"

Reid shrugged and avoided looking at him by watching Meghan instead. "It's fine."

"He's not thrilled with the company he's required to keep,"

she said, coming up to slide her arm through Jimmy's, "but he's quite taken with the car. He's a mechanic, you know. Engines impress him, much more than wayward mothers."

"That seems only reasonable," Falcone said mildly. "Any problems?"

Reid shook his head.

"Are you okay on money?"

A nod.

"I understand you're still living on Serenity. I have a number of guest cottages here on the estate. If you would like to take advantage of one..."

Before he had a chance to refuse, Meghan did with a less than charming laugh. "He's quite happy on Serenity. It seems he's got a thing for some little schoolteacher there. He wants to stay close to her." As a flush heated his face, she offered the bag she was carrying. "You mixed up the bags. These shoes are yours."

They had spent a good portion of the day in various shoe stores, but all the purchases had been hers. Beyond a cup of coffee while she shopped for lingerie, he hadn't bought a thing. Of course, there probably weren't any shoes in the bag. Like the package she'd given him earlier in the week, this one undoubtedly contained information for Sinclair. Just as he'd done before, he would take it home, call the FBI agent and arrange to meet him somewhere crowded. The first time he'd caught a glimpse of cassette tapes, a notebook and a roll of film, and for a moment he had let himself hope that it would be enough, that whatever information she was providing was damning enough to let Reid off the hook. Apparently it hadn't been, because he was still here and she was passing this new stuff along.

Of course it hadn't been. His life couldn't be that easy.

He accepted the bag with a muttered thanks, then forced his gaze to meet Falcone's. "It's been a long day," he said stiffly. "If there's nothing else, I'd like to get home."

"By all means, go on. I'll see you again soon. We'll talk."

He had to swallow hard on the queasiness that assaulted his stomach. "Talk?"

Jimmy's smile was broad and warm and didn't quite reach his eyes. "Sure, about my plans for you. You don't think I'd keep Meghan's son working as a mere driver forever, do you? It's hardly a job for family. Prove yourself at this, and we'll find something else for you. Something better, something that makes use of your best talents."

Reid's responding smile was sickly and sure as hell didn't reach his eyes. "Yeah, we'll talk." And when that day came, damn Meghan and Sinclair to hell, he was getting out. He was going home and begging Cassie's and Jamey's forgiveness, and he was never doing anything like this again, not for anyone.

One of the men gave him a ride back to the Quarter. He would have taken him all the way to Serenity, but instead Reid asked to be let out at Jackson Square. He had to make arrangements to pass whatever was inside the box to Sinclair. The sooner he did that, the sooner they could examine the contents and—please God—the sooner Reid could quit this damn charade.

It took the agent twenty minutes to get to the meeting place they had agreed to on the phone, a crowded bar on Bourbon Street. Sinclair removed the contents from the shoe box, then gave the bag and box back to Reid for appearance's sake. He asked a few pointless questions—"How are you doing? Do you have any problems?"—then left less than ten minutes after he'd come.

Did he have any problems? Reid thought grimly as he walked home. More than he could count. More than he could handle.

It was a quarter to eight when he walked into the bar. Old Thomas and Virgil were seated at a table near the door, and Eldin drank alone in the corner. Karen and Shawntae sat at a table near the bar, drinking sodas and doting over the baby in Karen's arms, and Jamey was behind the bar, drawing a beer for a man whose name Reid had forgotten.

He touched Karen on the shoulder as he passed, but he didn't speak, didn't look at her. He didn't take his gaze from Jamey, who looked as formidable and unforgiving as he ever had. "Give me five minutes, then you can go home."

"Take all the time you want. I'd hate to impose on your busy schedule."

The sarcasm in his voice made Reid stiffen and stirred to life the queasiness in his stomach that hadn't settled until long after he'd left Falcone's. "I had to work late. I'm sorry."

"Is that supposed to make everything all right? You don't come in, you don't call, you just blow off everything else because your crooked boss asks you to, and 'I'm sorry' is supposed to make up for it?"

Behind him a chair scraped as Karen stood up. "Jamey—"

Reid ignored her. "What do you want me to say? What do you want me to do?"

"For starters, you can quit."

"*Jamey.*"

He ignored her, too. "You can quit Falcone's job, or you can quit this one. It's your choice."

Reid stared at him. He'd been expecting this, hadn't he? Of course...yeah...not really. Deep inside he had hoped, had let himself believe, that his father trusted him enough to let him keep this small part of his life intact. It wasn't much. It wasn't Sunday family dinners or halfway friendly conversations, but as long as Jamey let him keep this job, as long as he trusted Reid with his business, there was reason to hope.

Now it didn't look as if there was.

Karen came closer, cradling Sean in her arms. "Reid, if it's money, maybe Jamey can give you—"

"It's not the money." He looked at the baby, as comfortable and contented as any child could ever be. Someday Sean would understand. He would grow up with parents who would do anything in the world for him, and he would be willing to return the favor, to risk his future to protect theirs. Not that Reid's situation was even remotely similar. Meghan wouldn't

lift a finger to help him if he was in trouble, but he had to try
to save her from prison, where she rightly belonged.

Just as Cassie had told him last week, he was a fool.

He turned back to his father. "I can't quit." It was meant
to be a simple statement, but it came out more like a plea. He
wanted to plead, to beg for trust, love and forgiveness. He
wanted...damn it, too much.

Jamey's expression turned as hard as stone. "I'll leave your
final check on the bar in the morning. You can leave your key
when you pick it up."

Not only was he losing his job, but the apartment, too. The
thing he had feared since the day he'd moved in had finally
happened: Jamey was kicking him out. Feeling raw and achy
inside, Reid took the few steps necessary to circle the bar and
come to a stop in front of his father. "Don't do this," he said,
embarrassed that all he could manage was a thick whisper that
quavered unsteadily. "Please..."

After staring him down for a long, still moment, Jamey did
the one thing he'd always done from the very beginning, the
one thing Reid could always count on. He turned his back and
walked away.

With the radio tuned to her favorite station, Cassie was
perched on top of a ladder in the hall when she became aware
of the slow, heavy treads on the stairs. For just an instant, her
pulse quickened at the thought of seeing Reid. In the next
instant, she felt a surge of panic that tried to send her running
to the bathroom for cover. She wasn't up to seeing him, knowing that she couldn't touch him, kiss him or change his mind.
She certainly wasn't up to being tantalized by what she
couldn't have, not as long as he continued down his dangerous
road.

She focused narrowly on the crown molding she was painting, taking no care to protect the ceiling or walls. They would
be painted next, deep salmon for the walls and bright white
for everything else. She had started with her door, propped
open now for the paint to dry, and worked her away around

to the bathroom and halfway back up the opposite side of the hall. It was a big job, but it gave her something to do and gave the living quarters a badly needed lift, even if it did nothing to lift her spirits.

When he reached the top of the stairs, Reid looked as if his spirits had dropped about as far as they could possibly go. She couldn't remember ever seeing a more exquisite expression of sorrow, and it made her ache. Balancing the brush on the can, she climbed down the ladder, wiped her hands on a towel and slowly approached him as he fitted the key into his door. "Reid?"

He stopped but didn't look at her.

"What's wrong?"

He rested his forehead on the door for a moment, then faced her with a reckless smile that would have been much more effective if it hadn't been so unsteady. "Nothing's wrong. Everything is exactly the way it used to be. Jamey's pissed, he doesn't trust me and he doesn't want me around."

"What are you talking about?"

"I have until tomorrow to find a place to live. He wants me out of here."

She brushed his hand away from the key, turned it, then swung the door open. "Are you surprised?" she asked quietly as she reached inside to flip on the overhead bulb. She wasn't, although she did feel a tremendous regret. Anyone could see that Jamey was worried sick about his son, but he had a hard time expressing it without anger and guilt. He had long blamed his failures as a father for Reid's problems. Now there was disappointment, too, because Reid had done so well for so long before jumping back into trouble with both feet.

"Yeah," he admitted bitterly, "I'm surprised. I thought he really did—"

When he didn't go on, she finished for him. "You thought he really did care, and he thought you really were a better man than this. You were both disappointed." She walked into the apartment, laid out in exactly the same plan as her own, but so dreary and ugly. What a stark contrast between the places where he spent his days and this place where he spent his nights. Where he would spend one more night. "Jamey loves you, Reid. We all do. We're all disappointed."

"What did you say?" He stood in the doorway, staring at her as if she'd suddenly started speaking a foreign language. Maybe she had. Maybe he truly didn't understand the concept of love. When you'd lived your entire life without it, maybe at some point it became impossible to learn, recognize or appreciate.

Feeling chilly in spite of the muggy warmth in the apartment, she hugged her arms to her chest. "I said your father loves you. Karen loves you. I…" She had to swallow hard. All her life she'd dreamed about meeting the perfect man and, in the most impossibly perfect and romantic setting, admitting her love for him. Reid was far from perfect, and so was the setting, but she had to say the words anyway. It was time—maybe past time. "I love you."

In those silly, naive dreams, her declaration of love had always been met with equal measures of joy and passion. Reid looked unbearably sad. "You don't even trust me."

"I do. I have from the beginning. I trusted you enough to make love with you when I'd never done it with any other man."

"Do you trust me enough to do it again right now? Or does the idea of getting intimate with someone who works for Jimmy Falcone turn your stomach?" He didn't wait for her answer, but came to her, taking hold of her arms, pulling her up close against him. The elegant suit could do nothing to disguise the strength of his body or the power of his arousal. It could do nothing to convince her that with him, naked and as intimate as two people could be, wasn't exactly where she wanted to be.

He slid his arms around her and kissed her temple, her cheek, her jaw, before finally taking her mouth. Controlled and ignored for more than a week, her need was fierce, painful, threatening. All the sorrow, heartache and fear of the past week were forgotten, lost in hunger and desire and the desperate need to believe just once more in him, in herself, in them.

He buried his hands in her hair as his mouth pressed harder, greedier. After a moment, he slid his palms over her breasts, down to her hips, around to her bottom. He lifted her to him, so close, so tight, and rubbed against her with teasing, tormenting slowness, as if he couldn't wait to slide inside her, as if their clothing weren't an impossible barrier, as if he needed her right here, *right now*. She didn't protest, didn't try to retreat, because she needed him, too. She needed him desperately, in ways she'd never known, in ways only he could satisfy. She needed him—

"Reid, please don't— Oh. I'm sorry."

Karen sounded embarrassed. Reid, who stepped back so suddenly that Cassie thought she might crumple without his support, looked it. His face was flushed, and his eyes were shadowed with shame and that heartbreaking pain. He turned away to the window, Cassie stayed where she was in the center of the room and Karen hovered uncertainly in the doorway.

"I...I'm sorry," Karen murmured. "I didn't realize... I didn't mean to..."

"It's all right." Reid's voice was so flat and dull that Cassie never would have recognized it sight unseen. "She wasn't planning to let it go any further than that. Having sex with a reformed punk is one thing, but doing it with someone still in the business is different, isn't it, Cassie?"

It *did* make a difference, but she would have done it anyway. If Karen hadn't interrupted, she would have willingly, eagerly, gone into the bedroom with Reid and spent the entire rest of the night making mad, passionate love.

For the last time.

Finally finding the strength to move, she crossed the room to him, laid one hand on his shoulder, whispering a farewell. "If you ever change your mind, you know where to find me."

His body tensed, and he raised his hand to cover hers. To hold hers, she hoped. To remove it from his shoulder, he proved.

With a tight, teary smile for Karen, Cassie left the apartment and went into her own. She left the door propped open, shut off the lights and curled up in the corner of the couch. She couldn't see across the hall, but she could hear. Karen sounded as unhappy as Cassie felt. Reid sounded even more so. If this job of his—this job he liked, where he earned good money and could do what he wanted—was so damn wonderful, why was it making him so miserable?

The money wasn't the draw. He had worked too hard to earn his father's respect, much too hard to build a relationship with him, to throw it all away for money. Besides, if the money were so important, he would have been out of the apartment and away from Serenity a week ago. If it were worth sacrificing his family and her, he would be out spending some of it, buying himself a better life, enjoying the rewards of working for a man like Falcone.

She didn't believe he'd simply given up, that trying to go straight had become too hard. He'd made such progress. People had begun to accept him. Besides, he was tough and stubborn. His entire life had been hard. He wouldn't give up anything he really wanted just because it didn't come easily.

That left blackmail. Threats. An offer, as the old gangster movie had put it, that he couldn't refuse. He had done a number of jobs for Falcone in the past, and no doubt the bastard had documented every one of them. Maybe he was now using that information to force Reid to do his bidding. After all, with Ryan Morgan dead, Falcone needed someone bright and reasonable to take over down here, and Vinnie Marino missed on both counts.

Across the hall, Karen's voice was pleading. "He's so worried about you, Reid."

"Firing me and kicking me out of here... Yeah, I can see he's really worried."

"He gave you a choice."

"He gave me *no* choice. I can't quit that job."

"Why not? Why is it so damn important to you?"

Cassie held her breath, hoping that he would confide in

Karen. After all, she had been a major force in his decision to get away from the Morgans and Falcone in the first place. She had offered him respect and friendship from the start, without criticism, without reservation, and he loved her for it.

After a long silence, Reid finally answered, defeat heavy in his voice. "It just is. Why isn't that enough for you?"

"Dealing with a man as dangerous as Jimmy Falcone requires a better explanation than that."

"I don't have a better explanation to give you."

Karen's voice began trembling. "I know you, Reid. I know you hate what's happening between you and Jamey, between you and Cassie. I just don't understand why you're letting it happen. Why are you doing this to the people who love you?"

There was another long silence, then, "I'll be out of here tomorrow. You won't have to worry anymore. I won't be your problem anymore."

Cassie felt the first tear slip down her cheek, tickling along the way. She wiped it dry before it reached her mouth. She had cried more tears for Reid than for every other male in her life combined. Considering the hurt she felt right now, there were many more tears still to come.

The passage from March into April was barely noticeable. The daytime temperatures climbed a few degrees higher, the nighttime lows didn't drop quite as low and the number of tourists in the Quarter just about doubled. Otherwise, everything remained the same in Reid's life: intolerable.

He had found an apartment in the building next door to Kathy's House and just far enough down from O'Shea's that he could see the side windows that marked Cassie's bedroom. He could have moved anywhere in the city, Meghan had chided, and she had laughed when he'd replied that he didn't want to live anywhere in the city. He wanted to stay on Serenity. It was where he belonged, even if no one else shared his opinion. He was just a masochist at heart, she had decided, and he was beginning to agree with her, because it hurt like hell every time he passed O'Shea's and the women's center, every time he saw Cassie, Jamey or Karen, every time he looked at the places he was shut out of. It hurt—and it made him bitter.

They talked about loving him, but not one of them had the slightest bit of trust to offer. Maybe he didn't deserve their trust. But even he, with his vast inexperience, knew that love without trust wasn't much. It was a start—more than he'd ever had before—but it wasn't enough.

It was Wednesday morning, the beginning of his third week on Falcone's payroll. Outside it was unusually humid with the threat of a storm darkening the sky. Inside it was pretty damn uncomfortable, too. After using a damp bath towel to blot the sweat that dotted his face, he ran a comb through his hair, then picked up the starched and pressed shirt hanging on the doorknob. He missed going to work at the garage, missed the jeans and T-shirts and the familiar comfort of dealing with engines, which he understood far better than people. He missed the bar, too, with its familiar routines and regular customers.

Most of all, he missed Cassie.

If you ever change your mind, you know where to find me. Her words last week had given him hope...for a minute or two. He believed she'd meant them at that moment, but who knew about this week, next week or next month? By the time this charade was finally over, who knew if she would still give a damn about him? He certainly didn't.

The sound of a horn on the street below drew his glance to the window. Jimmy was still providing taxi service, which made Reid's life both easier and harder. It would take some effort to make it to the estate every morning on his own, but at the same time, the presence of the car and driver on Serenity twice every day seemed like rubbing salt into a wound. It made it impossible for anyone to forget that he was working for Jimmy.

The driver this morning was Vince Cortese. Vince was from Serenity Street, and he'd known Jamey, Meghan and Nick Carlucci growing up. He'd worked for Falcone since he was a kid and was, according to Meghan, one of his most trusted employees. He was one of the very few, Reid had learned, who was allowed to call both the boss and the boss's mistress by their first names. No standing on formality for Vince. Then again, he was the only one of Jimmy's employees who had gotten shot protecting his boss and had gone to prison for him once, too. Reid couldn't even begin to imagine what kind of business association could buy that kind of loyalty.

The drive passed in silence and much too quickly. He didn't want to go to Falcone's, didn't want to set foot inside his house or spend even an hour with Meghan. Maybe it was Cassie and Jamey or his complete disillusionment with his mother. Maybe it was his general distaste for what he was doing or, hell, maybe it was just the damn weather, but the closer they got to the estate, the edgier he felt, the tighter his muscles knotted, the queasier his stomach got.

As they passed through the gate, Vince spoke for the first time. "Better grab a magazine or book before you leave this morning. Meghan has an appointment at the salon, then she's meeting Jimmy for lunch at Brennan's. This afternoon, of course, she'll be shopping."

There was a sarcastic bite to his last words. Reid knew most of the employees disapproved of Meghan's free spending of Jimmy's money. He disapproved himself every time he followed her through store after store and every time he carried bag after box to her room. Her closet and dressing room were bigger than his entire apartment and were filled to overflowing with more clothes, shoes, handbags, cosmetics and jewels than one woman could need. She was looking ahead, of course, to the days when Jimmy and his generous support were gone, stockpiling every single item she might want or need in the future. No doubt, she was also building herself a tidy little nest egg with the cash allowance Jimmy gave her every week. She didn't intend to let the fact that she'd betrayed her boss and lover affect the quality of life she had become accustomed to.

Vince parked near the door, and Reid followed him inside. One of the servants usually announced his arrival to Meghan

while he waited in the kitchen. He always had time for coffee
and a roll before she finally wandered in or sent for him, plenty
of time to wish like hell that he was someplace else or, better
yet, someone else. Someone whose only knowledge of Jimmy
Falcone came from stories in the newspaper. Someone who
thought places like Serenity existed only in cities like New
York and Los Angeles. Someone whose mother would never
in a million years consider prostitution or a position as a gangster's mistress acceptable occupations.

But he wasn't someone else and, in all honesty, wouldn't
want to be. Maybe Reid Donovan didn't have much, but he
valued what he did have: a stepmother who would always
forgive him, a father who might not, a stepbrother who might
never know him and a chance, just a chance, with the woman
who'd taught him everything he knew about love. He wouldn't
trade those things for the world.

As he was finishing his coffee, Meghan swept into the room
in a cloud of perfume, perfectly dressed, perfectly made up.
She looked less in need of a visit to a salon than any woman
he'd ever seen, but need mattered little. Pampering did.

Remembering Vince's recommendation, he picked up the
newspaper he'd started to read, opened the door for her, then
followed her to the car. Beyond a few terse directions, she
didn't speak once they'd left the estate. She was in one of her
moods—had been the past few days. Sometimes she hardly
seemed to notice his presence. Other times she was decidedly
bitchy. He didn't know what was bothering her and didn't
want to know. She'd dragged him deeply enough into her
problems already.

At the salon, he settled into a chair near the door while
Meghan disappeared into the back for what she called the
works—a cut, color and style, new nails in the same full-alert
red and who knew what else. This was the same place she'd
brought him on his first day for a haircut—for a mere fifty
bucks—and the same place where he'd spent too much time
in the past two weeks waiting. A couple of hours, a couple

hundred dollars, and she came out looking only marginally different than when she went in.

He read the paper and a magazine from a nearby rack, paced the length of the room and turned down an offer for coffee from the receptionist. The last thing he needed this morning was more caffeine in his system. He checked the clock every fifteen minutes, until finally, after three restless hours, he approached the desk. "Can you tell me how much longer Ms. Donovan will be?"

The woman checked the appointment book, then excused herself to ask the stylist. In less than five minutes, she returned with a puzzled look on her face. "Ms. Donovan left over two hours ago."

Reid stared blankly at her. "What do you mean, she left? She came with me. I've been waiting for her. How could she..."

"She left by the back door. Over two hours ago." The woman offered an apologetic shrug. "She told Bridget she was meeting someone."

He felt uneasy—hell, bordering on panicky. He did *not* want to go to the restaurant and inform Jimmy Falcone that his mistress had slipped off to meet some unknown person. And whom could she be meeting? She didn't have any friends. She was too self-centered, had too little to offer anyone else. A man? Maybe she was having an affair. Jimmy would take a sexual betrayal as personally as a business betrayal, but it wouldn't be the first stupid thing Meghan had done. Or maybe it wasn't an affair but business. Maybe she'd had something so important to pass along that she'd scheduled a meeting with Sinclair. But, damn it, if that was so, why hadn't she told him? Whatever her reason, why had she left him hanging out to dry?

"Look, I need to talk to Bridget—"

The door opened, letting in a rush of hot, humid air, the faint scent of approaching rain and a familiar hard-set face. "She's late for lunch," Vince announced.

Reid looked past him to the limo double-parked out front.

At least he didn't have to go to the restaurant...but at least they wouldn't have killed him in the restaurant. He knew all too well that that was a very real possibility. Whatever conclusion Jimmy reached regarding her disappearance, if he suspected for a moment that Reid was somehow involved...

Swallowing hard, he turned to Vince and, in a less than steady voice, said, "She's not here. She took off a couple of hours ago."

The next few minutes were among the most anxious of Reid's life. He was grilled by Vince, right there in the salon lobby, then left standing on the sidewalk with one of Jimmy's bodyguards, listening to the rumble of thunder, while Vince broke the news to their boss. When he climbed out of the limo, he left the door open for Falcone to issue one terse order— "Get in here"—then closed it with unnecessary force behind Reid.

Since he'd come to live on Serenity, Reid had believed that no one could pack more icy contempt into a look than Jamey, but Falcone had him beat hands down. Reid couldn't move, could hardly even breathe, under the weight of his soulless, dark gaze.

"Where did she go?" His voice was as cold, as malevolent, as his eyes. If Reid hadn't already known that this was a man capable of cold-blooded murder, he would know now.

"I don't know."

"You're her son. She must have told you something."

"I'm her son," he agreed, "the one she walked away from eleven years ago without a single regret. The one she never gave a thought to until she was suddenly stricken with some belated—and apparently short-lived—maternal impulse."

"If she cares so little for you, why did she ask me to hire you?"

He shrugged, hoping it looked more casual than the jerky way it felt. "Who knows? Guilty conscience, maybe?"

Falcone laughed. "Meghan doesn't have a conscience. You and I both know that."

The door swung open again, and Vince joined them in the

car. "The stylist says she came in, made a phone call, waited about fifteen minutes, then left the back way. When the woman went outside to have a cigarette, she saw Meghan walking to a car with a man—tall, blond, older than the kid."

Once again Falcone fixed that nerve-stripping gaze on him. "Sound like anyone you know?"

Another unnatural shrug. "My father. But he and Meghan hate each other. He doesn't even know she's back in town."

"Anyone else?"

He shook his head even as he thought the answer: Remy Sinclair. That would explain Meghan's mood the past couple of days. Either she'd found something really important or she had believed that Jimmy was growing suspicious, and she had called Sinclair for help in getting out. It would also explain—beyond the fact that she'd never felt a moment's concern for anyone besides herself—why she'd left without a word to Reid. It had probably been Sinclair's idea. If they had both taken off, Jimmy would have gone looking for them both. This way Reid would appear to be exactly what he was: an easy-to-deceive sap. As long as Jimmy believed that, Reid was safe…and he was out of this mess.

"You've spent a lot of time with her lately. Did she mention any friends?"

"No."

"Does she have any family?"

"Just me."

"Where would she go?"

"How would I know? Yeah, I spent some time with her, and she talked a lot. You spent time with her yourself. You know that if it didn't concern Meghan, it didn't interest Meghan." His surge of irritation felt completely believable. "So how does it feel to have her run out on you? She's pretty good at it—but then, she practiced on *me* first. She left me with nothing when I was fifteen, and I've got even less now." He gave an angry shake of his head and half whispered, "Damn her."

Falcone studied him for a long moment, then gave a nod,

apparently the driver's signal to pull away. As he did, the rain began to fall—not a sprinkle or a gradual buildup to a downpour, but a full-fledged, thunder-and-lightning torrent that dampened Reid's hopes of being able to get out and walk away—walk home. Those hopes were washed away completely by Falcone's next words.

"Come stay at the house, Reid. We'll see what we can do for you."

Chapter 10

Recess couldn't have come a moment too soon on Thursday morning. Maybe it was something in the air—spring fever or relief that yesterday's line of thunderstorms had moved on—but Cassie had never seen thirteen such rowdy, restless kids in her life. Only two hours into the school day, her patience was unraveling and her nerves were frazzled. She needed to dismiss class for the day and go home. No, not home. Anywhere but there. In the past week, she had found her pretty little apartment too pretty, too little, too depressingly confining. She needed to get away from Serenity, away from all the hopes and dreams that had brought her there, away from the unhappiness that now held her. Away from her obsession with Reid.

She'd spent too many of her evenings this past week standing at the window watching his apartment. She'd seen him over there a few times, nothing more than a shadow with more substance than the shadows around him, looking back at her. The frustration was enough to make her pull her hair, stamp her feet and scream, *Why?* Why was he doing this? Why was

he letting Falcone take away everything good in his life? If
the man was threatening him, why wasn't he asking for help?
Why wasn't he doing everything in his power to protect himself and the things important to him?

But only Reid knew the answers to those questions, and he
wasn't talking.

"Miss Cassie?"

She looked up from the workbook untouched in front of her
and saw J.T. standing in the open doorway. He looked serious
and on edge. "What is it, J.T.?"

"Someone wants... Reid wants to talk to you." His message given, he spun around and ran off.

Cassie sat motionless for ten seconds, twenty, then slowly
pushed her chair back and started toward the door. She saw
him before she reached it, standing on the sidewalk outside
the iron fence. He was wearing charcoal gray slacks and a
white shirt with the sleeves rolled back, and his tie was loos-
ened around his neck. Even after two weeks, the suits still
seemed foreign to her, but she had to admit that he couldn't
possibly look any handsomer unless he was naked. She missed
the faded jeans, though, and the snug-fitting T-shirts. She
missed the Reid she'd fallen in love with.

There was a car parked on the street behind him, a Mercedes
in a deep, rich burgundy. The trunk was open, and Vince Cortese, one of Serenity's few claims to fame—or should that be
infamy?—was waiting there. As she approached, she could see
the garment bags in the trunk, the same ones Reid had brought
home after his first day on the job, the same ones he'd carried
across the street a week ago to his new apartment.

"Moving again?"

He took a step toward her. "For a while."

"Where?"

Guiltily he shifted his gaze to the ground. It was the only
answer she needed. He was moving to Falcone's estate. The
old man had built a half-dozen guest cottages on his property
to house his most trusted employees. Cortese lived in one.
Nicky Carlucci had lived in one, too, until he'd turned on his

boss and wound up in prison. Now Reid would be living there. That was awfully accommodating of Jimmy for a mere driver who swore he wasn't doing anything illegal.

She curled her fingers around an iron fence post. Her knuckles whitened, and her forehead wrinkled with the scowl she summoned to keep her pleas at bay. "So why are you here? Did you come to say, 'Goodbye... It was fun... Thanks for the sex, but I won't need you again'?"

He came closer. She tried to back away, but too soon he was right in front of her, sliding his arm around her waist, pulling her to him with greater strength than she could resist. She tried, but not too hard. She didn't want to frighten the children playing nearby, didn't want to give Jaye any reason for alarm. "Let me go."

"I can't," he said simply, and she knew in her heart he wasn't talking about right this minute. Despite his messages of the past two weeks to the contrary, he did care about her—might even love her—and that knowledge almost made her melt. "Go ahead. Act angry."

His voice was little more than a murmur, soft and intimate. To counteract the longing that was killing her inside, she pushed hard against him. "I'm not acting. I *am* angry. Why are you doing this? Why won't you tell me what's going on? Why won't you trust me?"

"I do trust you. That's why I'm here." He bent to kiss her, but she twisted her head away. She couldn't allow it, not in front of the kids, not here, not now. But he didn't seem to mind that his kiss landed high on her jaw instead of her lips. In fact, he wasn't really at all interested in kissing, she realized even as his mouth brushed across her ear.

"I need your help, Cassie," he whispered, and the urgency in his voice had nothing to do with need or desire. "Stay angry. Don't show any surprise. When we leave, go inside the house and call Remy Sinclair. Tell him Jimmy's not convinced that he can trust me and he's insisting that I move to his place where he can keep tabs on me. Ask him what the hell I'm supposed to do now— and don't tell anyone. It's got to be a secret—just you, me and Sinclair, okay?''

Remy Sinclair. Susannah's husband, Jolie's friend and FBI agent. The muscles in Cassie's stomach knotted, and her lungs grew too tight to breathe. It was Remy's fault that Reid was in this mess, the FBI's fault that the past two weeks had been so miserable. Damn them, what had they had done? What had they forced Reid to do? All this time, she had wondered if he was being coerced into working for Falcone, and she'd been right, except that it wasn't his crooked boss doing the arm twisting but the damn government. They—the cops, the *FBI*—had put his life in danger.

Dazed and dumbfounded, she didn't resist when he tried once more to kiss her. Standing limply, one hand clinging to his shirt, the other still wrapped tightly around the iron bar, she accepted his kiss and his tongue, and when he brought his hands to her face, she darn near purred and rubbed against him. When he drew back, though, with his teeth coming together on her lip, the little jolt of pain cleared the haze from her mind, reminded her of his admonition—*Stay angry*—and gave her the strength to shove him away. "*No.* No, don't do this. I can't..."

He looked dazed, stumbling back a step or two before catching himself. He reached out to touch her, but, nervously aware that Vince Cortese was watching with both interest and amusement, she slapped his hand away. "Come on, Cassie," Reid coaxed, speaking in a voice loud enough for the other man to hear. "Don't be this way."

In an effort to hide the trembling that was rapidly spreading through her entire body, she hugged herself tightly and focused her narrow scowl on him. "You made your choice two weeks ago when you went to work for that man. Go away, Reid. I don't want you coming around here again."

That made Vince laugh and propelled him into action. He slammed the trunk of the car, dusted his hands, then walked around to the driver's side. "Come on, Donovan. We don't have time for this." He laughed again. "Don't worry about it, kid. You want a woman, Jimmy's got a *lot* of women. You don't disappoint him, and maybe he'll give you one.''

With the faint beginnings of a regretful smile, Reid gave her one last, lingering look, then walked away. He climbed into the car, slammed the door, and Vince drove away. She stared after them until the car was long out of sight.

"Cassie? Cassie, are you okay?"

Startled, she turned to find the kids straggling back into the classroom and Jaye, looking worried, a few feet behind her. She tried to swallow, but couldn't, tried to breathe deeply but couldn't do that, either. All she could do was stand there, numb, too worried to be relieved, frightened now in a way that she hadn't been before. It was one thing for Reid to voluntarily take a job with Falcone, to place himself in the path of temptation. The danger there was to his reputation and his efforts to live a respectable life. It was another thing entirely to betray Jimmy, to take that job with the sole purpose of bringing him trouble. Jimmy Falcone killed people who caused him trouble.

Jaye was waiting for an answer, but all Cassie could do was stare at her, her fingertips touching her mouth, her reaction to Reid so strong that she swore she could still feel his mouth on hers. Then, with a great shudder, she lowered her hand and knotted it into a fist. "Yeah... No, I'm not. Can you watch my kids for a minute?"

Without waiting for an answer, she walked away, straight into the house and down the hall to Karen's office. Jethro was asleep inside the door, his long black body filling half the available floor space. A blue-and-yellow quilt filled the other half, with Sean lying there. Behind her desk, Karen looked up and automatically smiled, then swiftly grew serious. "What's up, Cassie?"

"I have to go somewhere. Can someone take my class until I get back?"

"Of course. What's wrong?"

"I can't..." Letting the words trail off, she left the office. Karen moved quickly, though. Before Cassie reached the veranda, her boss, with the baby in her arms and Jethro stumbling over her feet, had caught up with her, catching her arm.

"What's wrong? Is it your family?" Abruptly her face paled. "Is it Reid?"

"Reid's fine. I'll be back as soon as I can." Pulling free, she returned to the school, retrieved her purse from the bottom desk drawer, then left again.

Less than twenty minutes later, she was being escorted to Remy's office by a gray-suited young man who'd probably had life a hundred times easier than Reid but didn't wear the clothes as well.

Remy wasn't alone. Her brother-in-law was standing in front of the agent's desk, looking grim and very prosecutorial. Ignoring Remy for a moment, she fixed her attention on Smith. "So you're in on this, too."

Her accusation brought a wary look to his eyes. "In on what?"

"You're part of his idiot plan—" she flung her hand in Remy's direction "—to make Reid go to work for Jimmy Falcone."

"No one made Reid do anything." Remy gestured toward the chairs that fronted his desk. "Sit down, both of you. What do you know about our plan, Cassie?"

"I know you forced Reid to take a job with Falcone. He never would have done this on his own. He despises Falcone, and he's tried so hard to get his life turned around. He never would have willingly put himself at risk. What did you do? Threaten him with jail?"

"We didn't force him to do it, Cassie. We asked for his help, and he agreed."

She shook her head. "Not just to be a good citizen. Not without some reason."

"You're right." Smith walked over to the window and gazed out for a moment before facing him. "We told him—"

"I told him," Remy interrupted, taking the responsibility. Taking the blame.

Smith shrugged as if it didn't matter. "That his mother needed help. She thought he was the best one to give it."

"His *mother?* Meghan's in New Orleans?"

"She was."

Very slowly Cassie sank down in the chair. All those years, Reid had hoped that his mother would come back. All those years, he had waited for her, and now she had finally come. She had finally needed him, and he had agreed. He had risked *everything*—maybe even death—for a woman who had made his life impossible from the day he was born. He was a better son than Meghan could ever deserve.

"You said she *was* in town. Where is she now?"

"We had to move her yesterday. She said Jimmy was getting suspicious. She was afraid of what he might do if he suspected that she was working with us."

"It never crossed her mind to worry about what he might do to her son, did it? Or yours, either." Bitter anger chilled her voice. "You moved her, but you left Reid there to deal with the consequences. You knew Jimmy was suspicious of her, but you didn't care that he would also, naturally, be suspicious of her son."

"Of course I care. You think I want anything to happen to Reid?" Remy had the grace to look offended. "If we had pulled him out, too, Jimmy would have believed that he was involved. He would have figured that Reid had been part of Meghan's scheme all along—that he took the job so he could help her get away. Falcone would have gotten the truth from him one way or another, and then he would have…" He didn't finish. He didn't need to. "This way it looked as if she ran out on him along with Jimmy. Just like before."

From the window, Smith spoke again. "How do you know about any of this, Cassie?"

Lacing her fingers together, she recounted every detail of Reid's visit—save the kisses. When she was done, Remy exchanged glances with Smith. "I don't suppose anyone has any outstanding warrants on him, do they?"

Smith shook his head. "But Falcone doesn't know that."

He pulled Cassie to her feet, slid his arm around her shoulders and started walking her toward the door. "If you see him again and you have a chance to talk, tell him to sit tight and not to worry if a couple cops come to pick him up."

"What are you—?"

"You don't need to know any more than you already do. Keep this to yourself, Cassie. As long as Falcone is walking around free, *no one* can know that Reid was working for us. If Falcone even suspects such a thing, sometime, somehow, he *will* make him pay."

"But his parents—"

"Are just going to have to trust him. Until Falcone is behind bars or dead, Reid's role in this is going to be your secret. Understand?"

She didn't want to, but she did. It would be hard for Reid, having to start over, having to re-earn the respect and trust he'd lost, and it would surely be even harder knowing that he hadn't done anything wrong. Everyone who'd thought and said the worst of him owed him an apology, but he couldn't collect. He couldn't tell them that he'd been working for the good guys, that to do it, he'd had to appear as one of the bad guys. He would have to keep that knowledge to himself and let the others think what they would.

She said a subdued goodbye, took the elevator to the ground floor and stepped outside onto the sidewalk. For a moment, she simply stood there, oblivious to the people and the traffic passing by, concentrating instead on all the unsettled emotions bouncing around inside her—guilt that she hadn't had enough faith in Reid. Relief that he really hadn't done anything wrong. Fear that he might pay a dear price for it anyway. Contempt for a woman who could risk her only son this way. Frustration because all she could do was worry. She couldn't call him, couldn't be with him, couldn't know that he was safe.

With a heart-heavy sigh, she started toward her car. As she stepped off the curb into the crosswalk, a car glided around the corner and stopped directly in front of her, blocking her way. Before the fact that it was a black limo could register, before she could even think about turning and running, the door swung open and a man coming up from behind took a firm grip on her arm and literally swept her into the car. She would have stumbled if another man inside the car hadn't caught her and lifted her without effort onto the seat, where she found herself face-to-face with Jimmy Falcone.

Reid was in the garage, using a soft cloth to dry the last few spots on the just washed Jag when Vince came out of the house and headed his way. With Meghan gone, he had little to do, but he didn't doubt that Vince or Jimmy would soon correct that. He just hoped Sinclair handled things on his end before it came to that.

Vince came to a stop a few feet away, brushed his jacket back and rested both hands on his hips. He didn't look too happy. And was it just coincidence that his stance made the pistol holstered on his belt easy to see and easier to reach? "The boss wants to see you inside."

Slowly Reid stepped back from the car and reached for his jacket. "What's up?" he asked, sounding less worried than he felt. "Does he have something he wants me to do?"

"He wants to talk."

Shrugging into the jacket, Reid adjusted it, then straightened his tie as he walked toward the house. With Vince only a few feet behind, he had the unpleasant feeling of a prisoner being escorted to his fate. Had Jimmy decided not to believe him regarding Meghan's disappearance? If he had grown suspicious of her, was he equally suspicious of her son? Did he wonder how, only a short while ago, she could have wanted Reid around enough to finagle a job for him and yet, just a few weeks later, she could walk away without giving him a clue?

They went into the house, through the kitchen and down the broad hall to Jimmy's study. The door was closed, which wasn't unusual. According to Meghan, he always kept it closed, whether he was alone relaxing, discussing business with associates or handling problems. Reid's smile was thin. This morning he certainly felt like a problem.

After one rap, Vince opened the door, then prodded Reid to go in. He hadn't moved more than four feet before absolute, pure panic swept over him, cutting off his breath, making his legs go weak. Jimmy was sitting behind his desk, a couple of his men were in the back of the room and sitting in the middle was Cassie.

God help them both.

He started to go to her, but Vince held him back. He had to be satisfied with simply looking, had to assure himself from a distance that she was all right. The color was drained from her face, and she sat with her hands so tightly clasped that she had surely lost feeling in her fingers. He could see the trembles that occasionally shook her, and her dark eyes were frightened, relieved and apologetic. Oh, God, what had she done? "Why is she here?"

"I brought her here," Jimmy replied. "I thought we might all enjoy a chat. So this is your girlfriend."

"She used to be. Until I started working for you."

"Do you know who she is?" Jimmy almost smiled. "Of course you do. The more important question is do you know who her sister is?"

Reid shrugged. "Jolie Kendricks."

"Jolie Wade Kendricks. A reporter—and a damn good one. The nosiest and most persistent woman I've ever met. She caused me more grief than any woman ever should when she was with the *Times-Picayune*. She still pesters me from time to time for that magazine of hers." Falcone gave a dismayed shake of his head before going on. "And do you know who Jolie is married to?"

"The U.S. Attorney who prosecuted you five or six years ago and won."

"The convictions were overturned," Falcone was quick to add. "And do you know—?"

"What is this?" Reid interrupted. "Twenty questions?"

His boss's smile was menacing. "Oh, I have far more than

twenty questions. Out of the blue, your mother takes me up on my offer to come to New Orleans, where she doesn't even get settled in before she implores me to give her son a job so she can get reacquainted with him after all these years apart. I agree, but soon after you come to work for me, Meghan disappears, and you claim to have no idea where she could have gone. So much for maternal angst. The very next day, I find out that your girlfriend is Jolie Wade's younger sister and U.S. Attorney Smith Kendricks's sister-in-law. As you probably know, they're in tight with an FBI agent by the name of Sinclair and with Michael Bennett, who just might be the last honest cop in New Orleans. As you probably also know, Jolie has ties to Nicholas Carlucci, my former legal adviser and confidant, who currently resides in the federal penitentiary in Alabama after trying to send *me* there.''

Reid swallowed hard, hoping to steady his voice. ''Yeah, I know all that. So what's the big deal?''

The smile cooled and hardened a few degrees. ''Maybe I can tell you something you don't know. You know I'm not convinced that you're as ignorant of your mother's plans as you claim. You also know that after the incident with Carlucci, I'm a little more cautious—some might even say paranoid—than usual. That's why I wanted you to move in. That's why Vince went with you this morning to pick up your belongings.'' Jimmy's eyes turned fear-inspiring dark. ''That's why I sent Tony to keep an eye on anyone you spoke to while you were gone. Now, for the part you don't know... Immediately after your visit with Cassie this morning, she made a trip downtown to the same building where the FBI offices are, where Remy Sinclair's office is. Coincidentally Kendricks was there at the same time. Now, who do you think she went to see down there?''

Reid turned to stare at Cassie, all too aware that every bit of the shock he was feeling was apparent on his face. She squirmed uncomfortably under the weight of his gaze, as she damn well should. Didn't she listen to him? Hadn't he made it clear that she was supposed to *call* Sinclair? Hadn't he made her understand that he was in serious trouble, that secrecy was of major importance?

Falcone was waiting for some response from him, but Reid's mind was absolutely blank. He wanted to shake Cassie, to yell at her and chastise her. He wanted to demand to know how she could have put not only his life but also her own in danger. He wanted to do a dozen things, but every one of them would prove to Jimmy that his suspicions were well-founded, and then what kind of trouble would they be in?

The silence in the room grew heavier, alive with tension, distrust and fear. Finally Reid felt compelled to break it before he blurted out a confession, the truth, a lie—anything that might save Cassie's life. He pushed past Vince and covered the distance separating him from Cassie. The fact that she shrank back from him was evidence of the fierceness of the scowl he wore. "You did it, didn't you?"

She swallowed hard, nervously, guiltily, but didn't look away.

"You said if I didn't quit this job, you would go to your brother-in-law and his cop friends. You said you would get them to make my life miserable, and you did it."

Unable to sit still any longer, she got to her feet, her arms folded tightly across her chest. The defiance she was trying to project was almost successful. If he didn't know her so well, he would believe it. He only hoped Jimmy believed it. "Yes, I talked to Smith and Remy, and you're right. As long as you continue to work for him, they're going to make life very difficult for you. It's not hard to do—just a few words from one cop to another, and you won't be able to leave this place without getting harassed every step of the way." Tossing her hair from her face, she shrugged. "It's unethical, probably even illegal—misuse of authority or something—but hey, I'm family. They'll do anything for family." She turned a malicious smile on Falcone. "Especially when it means making life harder for you."

"Damn it, Cassie—"

Before he could say anything else, Jimmy summoned the

men at the back of the room with an upraised hand. "Take her to the sitting room. Have the cook provide her with lunch, and keep her company while she eats."

The look she gave Reid was fearful, but she didn't protest, didn't make the men forcefully remove her. The door closed behind them, leaving Reid in a silent room with Jimmy and Vince. He rubbed his eyes for a moment, then sat down in the chair Cassie had just left. The air still held a faint whiff of her perfume.

"Do you really expect me to believe that the girl loves you so much that she would turn you in to the authorities?"

"Not the authorities. To her brother-in-law and his friends. She's afraid that I'll get into trouble. People who work for you have a tendency to end up dead or in prison."

"So she's trying to save you." Falcone didn't expect an answer. "Why didn't you tell me about her—and her connections—sooner?"

"Why didn't you know? There was a time when you knew every minor detail of a person's life before he came to work for you."

Jimmy gave Vince a narrowed look. "You're right. We should have known."

The silence began building again. Even though his boss seemed to have bought their act, Reid still felt sick inside. He wanted Cassie out of there, wanted her safe and sound on Serenity.

That thought brought him a bitter smile. This estate was one of the most beautiful places in all of Louisiana. No expense had been spared on luxury or security, but Cassie would be a million times safer back home in her little apartment above the shabby bar. Safe on Serenity. Who could ever have imagined it?

"You're going to let her go now." He said it as a statement, though there was no doubt that it was really a question. A plea.

"I don't know. She's a very pretty young woman. She could certainly add beauty to my home."

And, of course, she could be used to control *him*. For her, he would tell Jimmy everything about Meghan, her deal to trade his freedom for her own and his own role in it. For her, he would say anything, do anything. "You can't seriously be considering keeping her here. You made such a point of reminding me who she was. Have you already forgotten? Jolie? Kendricks? Sinclair? Bennett?" He gave a warning shake of his head. "You don't know what trouble is until you start messing with one of their own. They'll destroy you this time, and all the lawyers, threats and bribes in the world won't save you."

Vince spoke for the first time. "He's right, Jimmy. She's not worth the trouble she'll cause. Let me take her back now."

"And what's to stop her from running straight back to Kendricks to tell him that she'd been kidnapped?"

"Me." Reid rose from the chair. His smile was meant to be careless, but it felt feeble. "She got into this because she was worried about me. I can convince her not to say anything to anyone, or I'll suffer the consequences."

Falcone considered it for a moment, then nodded. Before Reid could feel too relieved, though, he added one less than assuring promise. "You certainly will."

Cassie sat in the Mercedes's back seat, hands tightly clasped in her lap, and stared out the window. She felt like such an idiot. She had made a major mistake that could have been— still could be—of potentially fatal proportions. If she had caused Reid any further trouble...

He was sitting across the seat from her, staring out his own window. She couldn't blame him for being angry. He had taken a risk to ask her to do one simple thing for him, and she had blown it. She had gotten herself kidnapped and given Falcone reason to look with even more suspicion at Reid, and she hadn't even gotten a chance to pass on Smith's message. Reid would have to be satisfied with knowing that Remy was aware of his predicament and would do his best to get him out.

As the car left the bridge, she twisted in the seat to face him, reaching out one shaky hand. "I'm sorry."

He looked at her hand a long time before slowly wrapping his fingers around hers and holding on tightly. The gesture warmed her, but it didn't ease the scowl that had settled on his face.

She slid across the seat so she could lower her voice, so Vince in the front seat would at least have to strain to hear. "Come home with me, Reid. Forget Falcone, forget his job and come home." This was his chance. He was away from the estate, away from Jimmy and all his goons. There was only Vince, who was armed, but surely he wouldn't use a gun on a crowded downtown street at lunchtime. Reid could get out of this car and into hers and drive away with her, and there was little Vince could do about it.

His grip grew tighter, but he still didn't look at her. "I don't have a home anymore," he reminded her. "O'Shea threw me out, remember?"

"Because he was angry. Once he realizes that you're back to stay, he'll be happy to have you."

"Yeah, sure, he will. Until the next thing I do that he doesn't approve of."

She didn't respond to that. This wasn't the time or the place to try to convince him of Jamey's complex emotions. Besides, they were nearing the downtown block where Vince intended to drop her off. She didn't have time to waste. "Forget about Jamey and everything else. Come home with *me*. Stay with me. Live with me."

"Live off you? Remember, if I quit this job, I'm out of luck. Jamey sure won't take me back, and the garage probably won't. Who does that leave? Who's going to hire a punk like me?"

Before she could answer, Vince spoke. "Where do you want out?"

She looked around and saw Remy's office building. She told him where her car was parked, then used her free hand to force Reid to look at her. "Please," she whispered. "You

don't have to go back there! Please come with me now. Come
back to Serenity where you belong.''

"I've made my choice, Cassie," he said quietly, with fi-
nality. "I'm sorry it hurts you, but you knew what I was when
you got involved.''

She knew. He was a decent, honorable man who would do
nothing to protect himself until he was certain that she was
safe. He wouldn't take this opportunity to free himself from
Falcone. He wouldn't do anything to further fuel Falcone's
paranoia, even if returning to the estate meant that he was still
in danger.

With a sigh, she stared past him out the side window, not
realizing until a horn sounded behind them that it was her own
car she was looking at. They were double-parked beside it and
holding up noonday traffic. Pulling free of her, Reid opened
the door and slid out, then waited for her to join him on the
street. She did so, pausing intimately close to him. "You know
where to find me.''

Finally he smiled, a crooked little grin that didn't ease the
emotion in his eyes, and he mouthed two words. "I will.''

She touched him one last time, then moved around him to
her own car. By the time she got the door unlocked, he had
already climbed into the front seat of the Mercedes and they
were driving away. She stood and watched until they were lost
in traffic, then climbed into her car, lowered her head and tried
to say a silent prayer, but one word was all she could say.
Please. She trusted God to understand the rest. *Please watch
over him. Please keep him safe. Please bring him home.*

Please.

It wasn't fair how quickly good times passed and how bad
times just dragged on. The time Reid had had with Cassie had
flashed by—a few days that had lasted only minutes—while
these weeks with Meghan and Falcone had literally crawled.
He'd lived a couple of lifetimes since they'd left Cassie on a
downtown street and driven away yesterday afternoon. He sus-

pected he would go through a couple more before Sinclair found some way to get him out.

He'd wanted to go with Cassie yesterday, had wanted it more than even she could imagine. But after Jimmy had announced that he didn't trust him, it would have been sheer folly to get out of the car and refuse to return to the estate. Some of Falcone's men—Vince, Tony, who knew who else—would have shown up on Serenity to reclaim him, and they wouldn't have taken no for an answer.

No, he had to stick with this job until Sinclair somehow came through. The agent knew of his situation, and he would take appropriate measures to get Reid out free and clear, with no disappearing acts, no threats to his life, no future danger. Sinclair had to deliver. Reid was counting on him.

Feeling restless, he paced the length of the garage. It was a gathering place not just for the drivers and Jimmy's full-time mechanic but for everyone who didn't have someplace better to be. There were a half-dozen men there now, playing poker with an afternoon baseball game on the television in the corner. He'd spent a lot of time with the men, but he didn't know any of them. He didn't want to know anyone who carried a gun for a living, neither cop nor crook. He just wanted to be a part-time grease monkey and bartender, with a father who was someday going to have to forgive him, a stepmother who thought he was a better man than he really was and Cassie, who made him a better man.

Someday he was going to marry her and spend the rest of his life with her.

Provided that he got out of this alive.

Activity at the other end of the garage drew Reid's attention that way. The poker game had abruptly ended, and everyone was on his feet, pulling on a suit coat. Vince separated from the others, came straight to Reid and pulled him into the workroom where a wide variety of the best mechanic's tools available was neatly stored on pegboard and shelves. ''Your girlfriend kept her word,'' Vince said, leaving the door open with a clear view of the driveway outside. "The cops just came through the gate. They were asking about you."

Reid hid his relief behind the sullen mask that had always been his protection. "This isn't legal. I haven't done anything wrong."

Vince's look was derisive. "Come on. You're a punk. You've been doing *something* wrong ever since you were a kid."

The car that pulled around back was unmarked, the officers out of uniform. The driver was a stranger, but Reid recognized his partner as Michael Bennett. They parked in the middle of the cobblestone drive and climbed out, both taking long, leisurely looks around before starting toward the garage.

"Can I help you?" Jimmy came out of the house, looking dangerously annoyed. It would have shown more respect for the cops to go to the front, ring the doorbell and be properly escorted to his study, where he would control the conversation and tell them exactly what he wanted them to know. Instead, coming to the back gave the impression that they were going to bypass him and conduct business their way. Disrespect angered Jimmy.

It was Bennett who spoke. "I understand Reid Donovan works for you."

Jimmy shrugged. "A lot of people work for me. What is your interest in Reid?"

"I've got some questions to ask him."

"Questions about what?"

"That's between him, his lawyer and me. You aren't his lawyer, are you, Jimmy?"

Annoyance was steadily giving way to anger. "I think this is harassment, Detective Bennett. I believe it's illegal."

The cop made no effort to pretend innocence. "Harassment? I'm a cop. He's a suspect. Questioning him is my job."

"A suspect in what?"

"Where should we start?" Bennett asked dryly. "The kid's got a rap sheet that rivals yours when you were his age. He's done a little of everything. Of course, you know that, since a lot of his criminal activity was on your behalf.''

Jimmy didn't bother to protest his innocence. ''This is because of that girl, isn't it?''

''What girl?''

''That girlfriend of his. Cassie Wade.''

''She's a sweet kid, isn't she?'' The detective made a great show of looking around again. ''So where is Donovan?''

''Maybe he's not here.''

''Maybe I don't believe you. Maybe I'll get a warrant and some backup and come back to search the place. Maybe a warrant that would let us look everywhere—every building, every room, even your study. No telling what we might uncover.''

Warrant. Bennett had said the magic word that could strike fear in Jimmy's black heart. Even from this distance, Reid could see his sudden uneasiness. He could hear the false bravado in his voice when he responded. ''You're bluffing. Besides, you're out of your jurisdiction. This isn't New Orleans.''

''Then I guess I'd have to bring the FBI back with me. They don't have to worry about things like city limits and jurisdiction,'' Bennett said mildly. ''So it's your choice. You can give him to me, or you can give him to them. What'll it be?''

One minute passed into the next, and no one spoke. No one moved. Reid was starting to believe that Jimmy would call the cop's bluff. He would order Bennett and his partner off his property and tell them to come back with the warrant and someone authorized to execute it over here—local cops, maybe, or parish, state or federal. And while they were gone to get their warrant—*if* they could even get one—what would happen to Reid?

Just as he was about to face the answer to that grim question, Falcone broke his silence. ''Vince, send Donovan out here.''

In the workroom, Vince looked at Reid and shrugged. ''You

ought to hang on to Cassie. You could do worse than a woman who knows how to get things done.''

Reid didn't reply. He simply walked out of the storeroom and through the garage into the sun. Jimmy gave him a derisive look. ''You're more trouble than you're worth, kid. Go home, and don't bother coming back.''

As he reached the car, Bennett faced him over the roof. ''You need to pick up your stuff?''

Reid nodded. At Vince's insistence, he had brought everything he owned with him—one duffel bag filled with jeans and shirts, a few toiletries and a couple of sketch pads. He would happily leave it all behind for the chance to get out more quickly if it weren't for the drawings. Those sketches were the first things he'd ever done right in his life, and people—Cassie, Jamey, Karen—seemed to like them. He wanted to keep them.

Escorted by Vince and Tony, Reid and Bennett went to the small cottage he'd been assigned. While the other three men waited, he changed into his own clothes, then packed everything he'd owned before Meghan and Remy Sinclair had come into his life. As an afterthought, he took a few of the purchases Meghan had made for him: one dark gray suit, a shirt, tie and shoes. If fortune was with him—and he believed it was—he would have use of a suit sometime soon. If not, well, he could give it to someone who needed it.

They returned to the car, where he climbed into the back seat, but he didn't relax, not until the electronic gates were closing behind them and the ornate iron fence was rapidly disappearing from view. Then he breathed a sigh of relief heavy enough to make Bennett turn to look at him. ''The next time anyone asks a favor of you that involves Falcone, do yourself a favor and tell him no.''

''I intend to.'' A mile or two passed in silence before he spoke again. ''Out of curiosity, could you have gotten a warrant?''

Bennett shook his head. ''You haven't done anything of interest to us or any other agency in a long time. But Falcone didn't know that. He suspected, but he didn't know. Considering the interest we always have in *him*, he probably figured it was best not to test us."

Silence settled again until they were on the New Orleans side of the river. Once more Bennett looked back. "Where do you want us to drop you?"

Reid knew exactly where he wanted to go—*home*—but there were a few things he needed to take care of first. He glanced around at the buildings that lined the Central Business District streets, then gestured up ahead. "At the corner."

The cop pulled to the curb, and Bennett extended his hand. "Thanks."

After a brief hesitation, Reid accepted it. "Yeah. Thanks."

For too many years, reasons for celebration on Serenity had been precious few and far between. That had changed with Karen's arrival and her first neighborhood cookout. Since then, they'd had a back-to-school party, Halloween, Thanksgiving and Christmas parties, parties for holidays and birthdays and for no special days at all. This Friday evening's cookout was in honor of spring, Mrs. Gutierrez's seventieth birthday and everyone's desire to get out, have fun and socialize.

Everyone's but Cassie's. She was there because she felt obligated, because as a teacher at the school, she had a responsibility to set a proper example. She was there because she couldn't stand waiting alone one minute more, couldn't stand not knowing about Reid one second more. She was there, helping play hostess, pretending to care about what was going on around her and hoping that no one could see how much she hated being there.

How much she hated Reid *not* being there.

She was fixing a hot dog for Marina Taylor's six-year-old when quiet moved like an encroaching wave across the crowd. Only the children seemed unaffected. They continued to play under the trees or munch contentedly. All the adults were still, though, and looking with great seriousness from her to the street, then back again. Blindly she held out the hot dog, nearly missing the waiting hands, then stepped away from the table. A path opened between her and the lone figure standing on the sidewalk there.

Her throat tightened, and she felt the ticklish urge to both laugh and cry as she crossed the grass. She retained control, though, until she was standing, just as she had yesterday, at the edge of the grass where the old drive had once crossed.

Reid came to stand directly in front of her. He was carrying an army-surplus duffel over one shoulder with a single vinyl suit bag draped over it, and he was wearing familiar faded jeans and a white T-shirt. Just the clothes told her what she needed to know. He was safe, and he was home.

"Is it over?" she asked softly. He nodded, and she blew out her pent-up breath. "I'm so sorry, Reid, for not having faith, for not doing exactly what you—"

"I love you."

The rest of her apology forgotten, she stared at him. She would bet that was the first time in his life he'd ever said those words, and she knew he meant them. She could see it in his eyes and in his faint smile. She couldn't stop herself from smiling, too, as she curled her fingers in his shirt. "I love you." The words were inadequate to express all the emotion bubbling inside her—the relief, the happiness, the need, the desire, the pure, sweet joy. "Oh, God, Reid..."

With his free arm, he pulled her close, tangling his fingers in her hair, brushing kisses over her forehead, her cheek, her jaw. All too soon, though, he released her and glanced toward the crowd in the yard. Cassie didn't need to look to know that his gaze was focused on Jamey, standing at the top of the side steps with Karen at his side, or that Jamey was staring back.

She reached for his hand. "Come and talk to him."

"And tell him what? The truth has to stay our secret, remember?"

"Tell him you've come home to stay. Tell him you've missed him. If you have to, tell him you're sorry. Just talk to him, Reid. He's your father. You're his son. *Talk.*"

He let the bags slide to the ground, then, holding tightly to her hand, he started across the yard. The opening the guests had made for her widened as everyone took a few more steps back, each turning to watch as they passed. This was Reid's test. People in the neighborhood looked up to Jamey. They knew he was honest and decent, knew they could count on him to look out for them. If he accepted Reid, they would, too. If he turned his back on his son, so would they.

At the bottom of the steps, she tugged her hand free. Reid looked at her, seeking encouragement that she offered with a nod, then climbed the next few steps alone. He stopped one step below his father. He greeted Karen first with a smile and a squeeze of her hand, then simply stood there for a moment, staring down at the floor, before, with a deep, shuddering breath, he met his father's gaze. "I quit the job with Falcone."

For a long time, Jamey just looked at him. On the porch, Karen was holding her breath, and down below, Cassie was doing the same. It would be so easy for Jamey to react in a manner that was guaranteed to push Reid even further away. He'd wasted much of the eleven years he'd known his son doing just that. But not this time. Keeping his voice carefully neutral, he said, "So you've come back."

Reid nodded.

"For how long?"

"To stay."

There was another long silence, then Jamey asked, "You need a job and a place to live?"

From behind, Cassie could see the tension that held Reid stiff slowly ease. "I have a place, but I could use the job."

"You can start Monday."

"Thanks." Reid stood there for one awkward moment, then turned. Before he'd gone more than a step or two, the sound of Jamey's voice stopped him.

"I'm glad you're back, Reid. I've missed you."

His gaze meeting hers, Reid almost smiled. That was the closest, she suspected, that Jamey had ever come to expressing affection to his son. Reid looked touched. Slowly turning back, he extended his hand, clasping his father's for a long moment before quietly saying, "I've missed you, too."

Around them conversation started again. What had held the potential for a very bad scene had been defused without so much as a raised voice, and the party could go on. They didn't realize that a miracle of not so minor proportions had just taken place. For the first time in their twenty-six-year relationship, father and son had shared an honest, open exchange without any of the bitterness or distrust that had underlaid even their most unimportant conversations in the past. The neighbors who had witnessed it didn't realize its significance, but Cassie did. Karen did. Jamey and Reid certainly did.

As he came down the steps, Reid slid his arm around Cassie's waist and drew her through the crowd with him. "Where are we going?" she asked, although she knew full well their destination: a two-room apartment with a bed that had been far too lonely these past few weeks. Like her life. Like her heart. A place where they could make up for their past, treasure their present and plan their future. A place where they could express their love all over again.

The bar was quiet, all its regular customers across the street indulging in a livelier celebration than usually took place here. Cassie led the way upstairs, unlocking her apartment door, pausing while Reid took a quick look around at the work she'd finished since he'd left. The half-round table stood against one wall, a battered old bench Karen had donated against the other, and rugs were scattered on the floor. With potpourri on the table and a big basket overflowing with dried flowers on the bench, the hallway was almost perfect. All that was missing was Reid's framed art on the walls. Now that he was back...

His smile when he faced her was gentle. "You've done a lot of work."

"It was something to do while I missed you."

"It almost makes me regret what I have to ask."

"What is that?"

He set his bags down inside the door, claimed her hand and pulled her into the bedroom to the window. He settled her in his embrace, her back to his chest, his hands clasped tightly at her waist. "Remember the day before school started? Karen invited both of us to Sunday dinner, and I wound up down there—" he gestured next door "—on the porch."

She remembered, of course. She remembered every day she had spent with him, whether they'd actually been together or just two people in a crowd. "You were doing a sketch of O'Shea's."

"And you were asking about that house."

"You said that anyone who wanted to buy it should have her head examined."

"Yeah, well, I guess I need *my* head examined, because I bought the place today."

Stunned, Cassie turned in the circle of his arms. Like most of Serenity, the house next door was shabby and in need of work. From the cracked sidewalk out front to the rusted fence with its discarded gate, the piles of rubbish that dotted the yard and its years of neglect, it called for attention, cash, back-breaking labor and love. Lots of love.

"I know it needs work, and you've already done a ton of work making this place livable. I know it's a major expense and a major commitment, but...will you live in it with me? Will you help me fix it, paint it and make a home of it? Will you raise our children in it?" He swallowed hard, looked away, then back again. "Will you marry me, Cassie?"

She looked from him to the house outside. One short month ago, he had been scornful of the idea that anyone would want the place, and now *he* wanted it. Only one short month ago, he had been equally unconvinced that anyone would want *him*. What a difference thirty days made.

Looking back, she wrapped her arms around his neck and gave him her biggest, brightest, happiest smile. "Marriage, babies and a lovely old house. What more could a woman want?"

"One other thing. Actually, two." He moved to the opposite side of the window, taking her with him. "See the tree down by the fence?" The streetlight shone on a small tree, its root ball bundled in burlap. "That's an oak. Once we get it planted, we can get some cuttings from Karen's wisteria to plant around it. You see, there's this legend..."

He repeated her mother's tale in soft words accompanied by soft kisses and softer touches, seducing her with his voice and his hands, sliding her clothes off, sliding his own off. As they moved to the bed, coming together on the thick white comforter, joining, filling, welcoming, loving, he finished the story in a husky murmur.

"And their wish came true. He was transformed into the strongest, tallest oak in the forest, and she became the wisteria vine, clothed in delicate purple blossoms, entwined with her true love for all eternity."

And their wish came true. Oh, yes. Every wish she had ever wished had come true in Reid.

For all eternity.

* * * * *

Take 4 bestselling love stories FREE

Plus get a FREE surprise gift!

Welcome to the Towers!

In January
New York Times bestselling author

NORA ROBERTS

takes us to the fabulous Maine coast mansion
haunted by a generations-old secret and introduces
us to the fascinating family that lives there.

Mechanic Catherine "C.C." Calhoun and hotel magnate
Trenton St. James mix like axle grease and mineral
water—until they kiss. Efficient Amanda Calhoun finds
easygoing Sloan O'Riley insufferable—and irresistible.
And they all must race to solve the mystery
surrounding a priceless hidden emerald necklace.

Catherine and Amanda

THE Calhoun Women

**A special 2-in-1 edition containing
COURTING CATHERINE and A MAN FOR AMANDA.**

Look for the next installment of
THE CALHOUN WOMEN with Lilah and Suzanna's
stories, coming in March 1998.

Available at your favorite retail outlet.

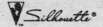

As seen on TV!

Free Gift Offer

With a Free Gift proof-of-purchase from any Silhouette® book, you can receive a beautiful cubic zirconia pendant.

This gorgeous marquise-shaped stone is a genuine cubic zirconia—accented by an 18" gold tone necklace.

(Approximate retail value $19.95)

Send for yours today…

compliments of ▼ *Silhouette*®
™

To receive your free gift, a cubic zirconia pendant, send us one original proof-of-purchase, photocopies not accepted, from the back of any Silhouette Romance™, Silhouette Desire®, Silhouette Special Edition®, Silhouette Intimate Moments® or Silhouette Yours Truly™ title available at your favorite retail outlet, together with the Free Gift Certificate, plus a check or money order for $1.65 U.S./$2.15 CAN. (do not send cash) to cover postage and handling, payable to Silhouette Free Gift Offer. We will send you the specified gift. Allow 6 to 8 weeks for delivery. Offer good until December 31, 1997, or while quantities last. Offer valid in the U.S. and Canada only.

Free Gift Certificate

Name: _____

Address: _____

City: _____ State/Province: _____ Zip/Postal Code: _____

Mail this certificate, one proof-of-purchase and a check or money order for postage and handling to: SILHOUETTE FREE GIFT OFFER 1997. In the U.S.: 3010 Walden Avenue, P.O. Box 9077, Buffalo NY 14269-9077. In Canada: P.O. Box 613, Fort Erie, Ontario L2Z 5X3.

FREE GIFT OFFER   084-KFD
ONE PROOF-OF-PURCHASE
To collect your fabulous FREE GIFT, a cubic zirconia pendant, you must include this original proof-of-purchase for each gift with the properly completed Free Gift Certificate.

084-KFDR

CHRISTINE FLYNN

**Continues the twelve-book
series—36 HOURS—in
December 1997 with
Book Six**

FATHER AND CHILD REUNION

Eve Stuart was back, and Rio Redtree couldn't ignore the fact
that her daughter bore his Native American features. So, Eve
had broken his heart *and* kept him from his child! But this
was no time for grudges, because his little girl and her
mother, the woman he had never stopped—could never stop—
loving, were in danger, and Rio would stop at nothing to
protect *his* family.

For Rio and Eve and *all* the residents of Grand Springs,
Colorado, the storm-induced blackout was just the beginning
of 36 Hours that changed *everything!* You won't want to
miss a single book.

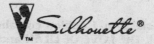

Available at your favorite retail outlet.

Return to the Towers!

In March
New York Times bestselling author

NORA ROBERTS

brings us to the Calhouns' fabulous
Maine coast mansion and reveals the
tragic secrets hidden there for generations.

For all his degrees, Professor Max Quartermain has a
lot to learn about love—and luscious Lilah Calhoun is
just the woman to teach him. Ex-cop Holt Bradford is
as prickly as a thornbush—until Suzanna Calhoun's
special touch makes love blossom in his heart.
And all of them are caught in the race to solve
the generations-old mystery of a priceless
lost necklace…and a timeless love.

Lilah and Suzanna
THE
Calhoun Women

**A special 2-in-1 edition containing
FOR THE LOVE OF LILAH and
SUZANNA'S SURRENDER**

Available at your favorite retail outlet.

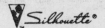

Look us up on-line at: http://www.romance.net   CWVOL2

162

From the bestselling author of *Jury Duty*

Laura Van Wormer

It's New York City's most sought-after address—a prestigious boulevard resplendent with majestic mansions and impressive apartments. But hidden behind the beauty and perfection of this neighborhood, with its wealthy and famous residents, are the often destructive forces of lies and secrets, envy and undeniable temptations.

Step on to...

RIVERSIDE DRIVE

MIRA BOOKS

**Available in January 1998—
where books are sold.**

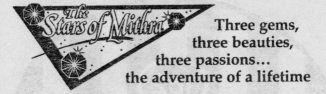